W9-CCN-600

YOU CAN CHECK OUT ANYTIME YOU LIKE . . . *PERMANENTLY.*

Sixty-nine was an unforgettable year for the students at Delphi High School. That was the year the Homecoming celebration got drunkenly—and violently—out of control; when the Homecoming Queen disappeared with the football hero; and when the class bully's body was found floating facedown in the river.

The Queen is now a Hollywood star. Her gridiron hunk is a much-hated coach. And sharp-witted, sharp-tongued Tory Bauer is a hash-slinger at the local cafe with a talent for solving crimes. With the Eagles blaring in the background, the hapless Class of '69 is gathering in Delphi for the first time in over two decades—and Tory is on the case once again. Because history is beginning to repeat itself in bizarre and very deadly ways.

Other Tory Bauer Mysteries by
Kathleen Taylor
from Avon Books

SEX AND SALMONELLA

Avon Books are available at special quantity discounts for bulk purchases for sales promotions, premiums, fund raising or educational use. Special books, or book excerpts, can also be created to fit specific needs.

For details write or telephone the office of the Director of Special Markets, Avon Books, Dept. FP, 1350 Avenue of the Americas, New York, New York 10019, 1-800-238-0658.

THE HOTEL SOUTH DAKOTA

A Tory Bauer Mystery

KATHLEEN TAYLOR

AVON BOOKS NEW YORK

This is a work of fiction. Names, characters, places, and incidents either are the product of the author's imagination or are used fictitiously. Any resemblance to actual events, locales, organizations, or persons, living or dead, is entirely coincidental and beyond the intent of either the author or the publisher.

AVON BOOKS
A division of
The Hearst Corporation
1350 Avenue of the Americas
New York, New York 10019

Copyright © 1997 by Kathleen Taylor
Published by arrangement with the author
Visit our website at **http://AvonBooks.com**
Library of Congress Catalog Card Number: 96-96957
ISBN: 0-380-78356-8

All rights reserved, which includes the right to reproduce this book or portions thereof in any form whatsoever except as provided by the U.S. Copyright Law. For information address Jane Dystel Literary Management, One Union Square West, New York, New York 10003.

First Avon Books Printing: March 1997

AVON TRADEMARK REG. U.S. PAT. OFF. AND IN OTHER COUNTRIES, MARCA REGISTRADA, HECHO EN U.S.A.

Printed in the U.S.A.

RA 10 9 8 7 6 5 4 3 2 1

If you purchased this book without a cover, you should be aware that this book is stolen property. It was reported as "unsold and destroyed" to the publisher, and neither the author nor the publisher has received any payment for this "stripped book."

This is for Kris, Jane, and Mouse,
like me, members of Snohomish High School's
Class of 1970.

Acknowledgments

This book would not have come into being without the patient, unflagging support of the Cheerleading Crew: Jody Weisflock, Lorah Houser Jankord, Dave and Diane Willis, Diane Jankord, Betty Baloun, and the newcomer Shirley McDermott, of the Uncommon Buffalo. I also want to thank Jane Dystel and Carrie Feron for listening to me whine, and prodding me along, and believing that I could do it.

And of course, nothing in my life would ever be accomplished if not for Terry, Curtis, Genevieve, and Matthew.

Prologue

With all due respect, Robert Fulghum got it wrong—kindergarten is not where life's important lessons are learned. Sharing and napping and neatness are all well and good, but the sexless elementary school environment does nothing to prepare you for the hormonal whammy that awaits. With the possible exception of how to handle an IRS audit, everything you really need to know about the world of grown-ups, you learned in high school.

For better or worse, every adult triumph, tragedy, success, failure, friendship, and betrayal echoes an earlier counterpart. One way or another, the life and death issues of adolescence affect your later ability to think, react, and cope.

In 1969, I was a high school sophomore. Vietnam was on the other side of the world, and Woodstock, the first one, might as well have been on the moon. For me, a life and death issue involved finding a date for homecoming. The only thing I had in common with the rest of my generation was the notion that love was all we'd need, and an unshakable confidence in our own immortality.

Unfortunately, we were wrong. On both counts.

Life and death issues are not always comfortably abstract. Then or now.

It took a couple of decades, a few tragedies and betrayals, and a windy afternoon standing along the bank of the James River looking down at a dead body in the water, for me to realize that the past has a long reach.

And that, for some people, high school lasts forever.

1

The Hotel South Dakota

Late August

However nonchalant you might think you are, now, about the collective experience called high school, everything you are, or might have been, has roots in those years.

A good many otherwise intelligent people waste their entire lives trying to reinvent themselves, either in the exact mold of their youth, or into the exact opposite—neither of which can be easily accomplished under the gaze of Those Who Knew Us When.

The disaffected leave, usually at the first opportunity, swearing never to return. But the siren call of Hometown whispers a taunting melody, drawing them back, sometimes to dash them on the rocks of their own dreams.

It's interesting to observe the flailing of those who thought they'd reached escape velocity, only to discover the irresistible pull of Delphi's gravity field.

On the other hand, if you never left, you're not allowed to stand on the sidelines and watch.

"I don't get it," Del said, handing me an open envelope. "What do they want us for?"

We were past the mid-morning rush. Aphrodite's Delphi Cafe was moderately full of locals looking for an excuse not to go back to work between coffee break and lunch. None of us had any meals up, and Rhonda was making the rounds with the coffee refills, so I stood behind the counter, warily eyeing the stack of mail Del had brought over from our trailer.

It was mostly bills anyway, mostly having medical return addresses—radiologists, orthopedists, consultants. There was an ominously thick packet from the hospital in Aberdeen. Though none were addressed to "Tory Bauer, middle-aged, overweight, widowed waitress," the bright red URGENT messages stamped on the outsides of the envelopes were a clear indicator of my status as one of America's working uninsured.

Del's mail, however, consisted of cheery predictions from Publishers' Clearing House, her bimonthly copy of the *Elvis Sightings Newsletter* (motto: "Elvis is alive, and *we've* see him"), and the letter she held out.

The return address listed the "Delphi Float/Reunion Committee," and it was addressed to "Ms. Delphine Bauer" and "Mrs. Tory Atwood Bauer." Inside was an invitation to all members of Delphi High School classes of 1965–1975 to work together to build a float for the town's Seventy-fifth Anniversary Football Homecoming Parade/Game in September, and to help plan our portion of the All School Reunion that would follow. The committee sincerely hoped each and every DHS alumnus would pitch in "for the greater glory of the school" in general, and our decade in particular. To that end, a general meeting was planned for the following evening. The letter was signed by reunion chair Debbie Wetzler Fischbach, wife of the current high school football coach, ex-cheerleader, and member of the 1969 Delphi Homecoming Court.

"Looks to me like they want volunteer labor and donated supplies to enter a float in the homecoming parade," I said, stuffing my unopened bills in a drawer behind the counter.

"I realize that," Del said, exasperated. "I wasn't asking

what they wanted with us. I was asking what they wanted with *us.*"

I fished a knitting needle out of the drawer, turned around and scrunched down a little so as not to disgust the patrons, inserted the pointed end inside the short-arm cast I was now wearing, and scratched vigorously. "Aah," I said quietly.

"Will you please not do that in here?" Aphrodite called from the kitchen where she was smoking a cigarette over the grill. "Makes us look bad."

"I can't help it," I said, grinning. "The cast is hot and it itches. And besides, no one would know I was doing this if you didn't make a special point of announcing it."

"Is Tory scratching inside her cast again?" Rhonda called from the other side of the cafe. "Gross."

"I could go home and do this in private, and let you serve the public without me," I threatened, though of course I didn't mean it. I had already been off work far longer than I could afford. The healing broken arm was the last remnant of some nasty injuries I'd received a shade more than a month ago. I was counting the minutes until the cast could come off, though the resultant unpaid medical bills provided a discomfort that outweighed the deep itch of reknitting bones.

"Never mind, scratch all you like." Rhonda laughed.

"I don't know about that," Ron Adler said, from his regular booth by the window. "The idea of Tory's dead skin flakes floating through the air kinda gives me the willies." Small and neat, with thinning hair and a face that receded sharply from nose to Adam's apple, he blinked furiously, an unconscious tic that accented his every word.

"You be good or I'll come over there and scratch right over your coffee," I warned.

"Watch out, she means it," Del said loudly to Ron, for the benefit of the rest of the cafe crowd, who was, as always, listening in. "An injured, hot, and itchy Tory is a crabby Tory."

"Yeah," I growled in agreement.

"You got that right. In fact, the only time Tory smiles these days is when Stu McKee comes over," Rhonda teased, also for the benefit of the crowd.

This month she was playing Earth Mother, in all-natural fibers, flowing, floor-length skirts, long blond hair braided down her back. A nineteen-year-old vegetarian newbie, aiming for wise and worldly. Last month she was a hippie. Next month, maybe a space alien. We do not try to predict Rhonda Saunders's fashion statements; we go with her flow.

I busied myself by swabbing the countertop, avoiding eye contact with everyone.

"Actually," Rhonda said, flipping her braid over one shoulder, "I think it's nice that Tory cheers Stu up a little. He's been so sad lately."

Del snorted. "He looks pretty chipper for a man whose wife left him . . ." She paused. ". . . for another state."

Minnesota, to be exact.

Renee McKee had returned to her home state last month, and speculation was rampant as to whether South Dakotan Stu would follow his wife, or stay here in Delphi, perhaps to embark on a new relationship. Since Delphi was officially insulted by Renee's desertion, the cafe straw poll overwhelmingly favored the latter.

Rhonda placed a comforting, worldly arm around my shoulders and said to Del, "You be nice. I think it's cute. Stu's wife is gone, and Tory hasn't dated since—"

"—you were in diapers," Del interrupted.

"Since *she* was in diapers." Ron blinked.

"Since *Aphrodite* was in diapers," someone else added. "Right around the turn of the century."

In the kitchen, Aphrodite harrumphed.

"Since Nicky died," Rhonda finished firmly, with a stern glare at the crowd in general. "It's about time she got out again, and if Stu McKee has a crush on her, I say fine and dandy."

"No one has a crush on anyone. And *she*"—if they could refer to me in the third person, so could I—"is far too busy even to think about romance."

Del, who knew I was lying, and Rhonda, who guessed, both smiled.

"Besides," I said, desperate to change the subject, especially since I had spotted Stu ambling across Delphi's dusty main drag, toward the cafe from the Feed and Seed Store he ran with his father, "my dance card is full." I made a quick decision that I knew would divert attention. "I'm going to do what Debbie Wetzler Fischbach asks—I'm going to help plan the big reunion and homecoming parade. That'll keep me more than occupied for the duration."

"What?" Del and Rhonda asked together.

I smiled. Stu came in and sat down. No one else noticed.

"Just what I said. I think it'll be fun—they won't expect me to do any actual 'building,' of course." I waved my cast. "But I can help plan and stuff envelopes and lick stamps."

"But why in the world would you want to?" Rhonda asked, bewildered. She had not been out of high school long enough to work up any nostalgia.

"That's what I want to know," said Del, who had been out long enough, but still had not worked up any nostalgia.

"It'll be interesting to find out what everyone's doing these days," I said over my shoulder as I arranged a paper placemat and silverware in front of Stu. "What can I get you?" I asked him. Nonchalantly.

"Is it too late for the breakfast special?" he asked, tilting a Cargill cap back off his forehead a little, and locking cool green eyes directly on mine with a small smile.

"I think we can talk Aphrodite into whipping up another plate of cholesterol, sodium, and nitrosamines," I said, squashing a return smile. "And how would you like your cholesterol?"

"Over easy," he said, "with extra crispy nitrosamines, and I want real saturated fat on my toast. None of that imitation healthy stuff."

"Gotcha," I said, grinning, until I caught Ron Adler watching us closely. I handed the slip to Aphrodite, who grunted in approval, turned, and ran directly into Del, who had followed me behind the counter.

"What do you mean, it sounds like fun? Debbie Wetzler and that snooty bunch never paid a bit of attention to you, or me, all through high school. And you never joined a committee in your whole life."

"I know," I said, carrying coffee over to Stu. I shrugged again. "I know, but that was more than twenty-five years ago, and it seems like we should all be past worrying about who was popular and who wasn't."

I had announced my intention to join the committee only to change the subject, but I found, to my own surprise, that I really did want to do it.

"I bet Tory was popular, anyway," Rhonda said, being diplomatic.

"Yeah, right," Del huffed, tucking a stray red tendril back behind one ear. She'd fixed her hair in a sort of uplift with a twist on top. It looked good with her tight jeans and artfully unbuttoned plaid shirt. "We *all* were popular."

Del had been popular. With the boys. And sometimes with men. She still was, though that wasn't exactly Rhonda's point.

"Rhonda," I said gently, "even back in the pioneer days, when I was in high school, fat girls were never popular."

"Oh Tory," she said sternly, "of course you were popular, no matter what your size. And I bet you were just as sweet then as you are now." Rhonda *had* been popular—cheerleader, homecoming queen, surrounded always by a crowd of adoring boys. She had no idea what it was like to be the fat girl in a small school.

I sighed. Sweetness has never been one of my ambitions.

"I wasn't sweet and I wasn't popular. In fact, I don't think anyone even noticed me, except for Del," I explained. "And I was far too busy mooning over Nicky Bauer to care."

"And look what that got you." Ron Adler blinked, jumping back into the conversation.

"Hey, that's my dead first cousin you're talking about," Del warned.

"I bet Stu noticed you," Rhonda said slyly, determined to play matchmaker.

"I highly doubt it," I said. Using the cast for balance, I managed a left-handed pickup of the steaming plate of bacon and eggs Aphrodite pushed through the opening between the cafe and the kitchen.

"I was a couple of years ahead of Tory," Stu said to Rhonda as I set the plate in front of him. "In fact, I was in the same class as Debbie Wetzler. But yes, I did notice her. She was smart and funny, even back then."

"It's in the Fat Girl Rule Book," I said, supremely tired of being the main subject of this conversation. "We had to be smart and funny. And sweet. It was supposed to make up for not having any dates."

"You did too date," Ron said. "If I remember correctly, you married Nick before the end of your senior year."

"Yeah, and look what that got me," I reminded him.

"So why in hell do you want to be on that stupid committee?" Del asked.

People were straggling in; the cafe was noisier.

"I'm curious," I said, realizing the truth as I said it. "Some people actually got away from Delphi, and I want to know how it worked out."

"Is living vicariously through others in the Fat Girl Rule Book too?" she asked, grabbing a tray of filled water glasses.

"Of course, it's part of the charter," I said, laughing.

"Well, you won't catch me at that stupid meeting," Del said. "And I bet Ron won't be there either, right?"

"Well." Ron blinked furiously. "Actually, I was thinking of going."

"Me too," said Stu.

"Have they all gone off the deep end?" Del asked the ceiling.

"I wouldn't do it, except Gina's making me," Ron said, wide-eyed.

Ron's wife, Gina, co-chair of the float committee, was a couple years younger than me. She had been in the second tier of popularity—not exactly cheerleader material, but not entirely hopeless either. Her marriage to Ron had always been a puzzlement

Del elbowed me in the ribs and put the tray of glasses down on Ron's table, ignoring the other customers. I slid into his booth with her—we had both heard the same thing.

"You say Gina is *forcing* you to be on the committee?" Del asked innocently, examining her fingernails.

"Yup." Ron squirmed. "That's right exactly. I wouldn't do it otherwise, but you know how it is. Gotta keep the old lady happy."

He gestured emphatically with every word, but did not blink. Even once.

I glanced at Del for confirmation. She nodded surreptitiously.

"Give me a break, Ron," I said harshly, "name me any time you actually did something because it made Gina happy."

Ron swallowed.

"Oh, Tory, you're being too hard on Ron. He's just being a good husband," Del cooed, leaning over the table just a little. That jump started the blinking process again, as well as a slow blush that crept up from Ron's neckline as his eyes darted down the front of Del's blouse. "Right, Ron?"

"Um, yeah, sure." No blinks.

"This is ridiculous," I said. "Whatever your reason for being on the committee, I'm sure it has *nothing* to do with marital obligations."

"Well, I'm curious too," he said, blinking defensively. "Just like you."

"See," Del said to me. "I knew he could explain."

"Bullshit," I said flatly. "Why are you suddenly Volunteer of the Week?"

"Yes, tell us," Del fluttered. "Please."

Ron looked down at his hands, up at the ceiling, vainly

at Stu for help, wide-eyed, and anywhere but at Del and me.

"I can't tell you," he whispered, blinking.

We had him. The good waitress/bad waitress routine works every time.

"Sure you can." Del reached across and ran a light finger from Ron's wrist to his elbow. She was not above using Ron's long-standing unrequited crush to her own advantage.

"You better," I said, "or I'll call Gina myself and ask."

"Oh Jesus, don't do that," Ron said quickly, glancing all around to see if anyone else was listening. "All right, but you gotta promise not to tell anyone. It's supposed to be a surprise."

Del and I nodded, and promised. And lied.

Stu leaned over the back of the booth, intently listening to every word.

Ron swallowed, blinked, and opened his mouth. And closed it again.

"*She's* coming back for the parade, going to ride on our float. No one's gonna know in advance. The whole town is gonna shit," he said in a rush, then sat back, blinking and smiling, enjoying his bombshell.

"She's coming back here? To Delphi?" Del asked, unbelieving.

"After all this time? Are you sure?" I asked.

"How do you know?" Stu, who slid in next to Ron, asked.

"Shhh," Ron whispered. He leaned over and said softly, "A few months ago, Gina and Deb Fischbach got together. They wrote to her agent in Hollywood and he forwarded the letter and she actually wrote back. And she's coming. To Delphi, to be in the parade. On *our* float."

We sat back. Stunned.

We did not have to ask who "she" was. We all knew.

She was J. Ross Nelson, AKA Janelle Ross, 1969 Delphi Homecoming Queen, expatriate South Dakotan, Hollywood actress, honest-to-God famous person. The only one Delphi has ever produced. Her picture regularly showed up in *People* magazine and some of the less sleazy tabloids.

"But she hasn't been here since—" I stopped, thinking back, trying to remember.

"Since 1969," Del finished, squinting in concentration. "Since the night of the homecoming game. The night of that kegger by the river."

"God, you're right," I said, almost overwhelmed by resurfacing memories of my first nonabstract encounter with life and death. "She disappeared after that homecoming party. Didn't even finish her senior year."

"I know which party you mean." Rhonda wrinkled her brow. "Wasn't there some sort of scandal? I wasn't even born then, and I heard about it. So it had to be big."

"You might say that," Del said dryly.

"Didn't some kid die?" Rhonda squinted, trying to remember ancient history.

If Janelle hadn't become J. Ross Nelson, all of the details of that night would have been long, and deservedly, forgotten.

"Drowned, right? That's it, at a kegger by the river." Rhonda beamed like a contestant who'd bet a bundle on Double Jeopardy.

"Yup," Del said shortly.

"Considering it was homecoming and all, at least a couple of you guys musta been there. At that party. When it happened, I mean," Rhonda said to us, dismissing the possibility of kids, even of our elderly generation, skipping a kegger.

I looked at Del, Ron, and finally Stu, who all sat quietly. "Everyone was there, Rhonda. Even me. In fact, that was my first date with Nick."

"And look what that got you." Ron laughed, never one to resist running a joke into the ground.

"Yeah, I should have taken it as an omen."

Rhonda chewed a lip pensively. "Isn't it sorta mysterious, though, that this girl, homecoming queen no less, disappeared the same night from a party where someone actually died?"

"You been watching too much Perry Mason," Ron said.

"Perry who?" Rhonda asked.

Ron ignored her. "There was never anything mysterious about that party. And Miss High and Mighty J. Ross Nelson didn't disappear until later, because I saw her in town the day after."

"But it had to have been terrible for you. I mean being there when a classmate, someone you knew, died," Rhonda persisted. Novice Earth Mothers like their revelations to be dramatic.

"None of us were *at* the river when Butchie Pendergast died. We didn't know that he'd drowned until the next day," I explained finally. "And I don't think anyone realized that Janelle and Doug were gone until school on Monday."

"Doug who?" Rhonda asked.

"Doug Fischbach." Ron blinked.

"Wait a second," Rhonda said, frowning. "The big movie star disappeared with Mr. Fischbach, our football coach?"

"Well, she wasn't a movie star then, and he wasn't a coach," I explained. "They were both just high school kids."

"Our Mr. Fischbach, who happens to be married to Mrs. Fischbach? The Mrs. Fischbach who is in charge of all the homecoming stuff?"

"Yes, that Mrs. Fischbach," Del said. "The one who invited J. Ross Nelson back to Delphi."

"That's going to make your reunion meetings interesting, to say the least," Rhonda said softly.

"No shit," I agreed.

"Gina is gonna announce all of this at the meeting tomorrow night," Ron said seriously. "So you have to act surprised. You and Stu," he said to us. "And even though you aren't going to the meeting, Del, you have to keep it quiet too."

"Sure," Del lied. "But you know, I might just drop in on the meeting after all."

She grinned evilly.

Ron groaned.

Rhonda, obviously meditating on the strangeness of drownings and disappearances, asked, "But why is she coming back? She made a life and a name for herself in the real world. Why would *anyone* want to come back to Delphi?"

I thought for a minute of the reasons I had for joining the reunion committee. I considered the newly resurfacing memories of that after-homecoming party, and realized perhaps J. Ross Nelson understood that Messrs. Felder, Henley, and Frey's observation about Hotel California might also apply to South Dakota: Check out any old time, just don't expect to leave.

2

Unrequited Love's a Bore

One of Delphi's enduring mysteries is Ron Adler's unrequited crush on Del. Not that his having a crush on her is in any way mysterious. Half of the males in Delphi have, at one time or another, had a crush on Del. And Del, with her red hair and ample heaving bosoms and liberal notion of what exactly constitutes a good reason to hop in the sack, encourages adoration. And not from afar either.

Actually Ron's unrequited crush is rare and mysterious for exactly that reason.

The unrequitedness has nothing to do with the fact that Ron is married—Del often treats marital status as a challenge. And a long acquaintance with Gina wouldn't slow her down at all.

"I don't know." Del shrugged when I had asked for an explanation. "I guess he's more valuable dressed. He has the inside track on all kinds of info and an irresistible urge to talk, and runs a fully functional garage to boot."

"But aren't you even a little bit curious? I mean, about what he'd be like, you know, in bed? After all, you've known him forever," I said.

"You've known him forever too, aren't you curious?" Del countered.

I suppressed a small shudder.

"Well, I don't actually find him repulsive," she said thoughtfully, "and the little fart might make up in enthusiasm what he lacks in expertise . . ."

Ron Adler was not one of those men one would automatically assume knew what to do in the lovemaking department, unless blinking counted as a kind of foreplay.

"But he knows his way around a carburetor," Del continued, "and that's more important. Besides, you know what they say about a man's reach exceeding his grasp."

I suppose that wasn't the only reason she kept the acquaintance fully clothed and out of the bedroom. But I understood—I liked Ron, blinks and reach and all.

I even liked Gina, though we had nothing more than the standard prairie "Hi howarya" relationship.

But I felt absolutely no loyalty to them. Or to their secrets. And I had no intention whatsoever of keeping quiet.

Which was why I stood in the main room of the library Neil Pascoe runs from his lovingly restored, three-story Victorian house, waiting while he shepherded several small, noisy children through their book choices. Medium height and slightly more than medium build, Neil seems perfectly content to spend his life restoring old cars and running the library by his own unusual rules.

Since he personally owned all the books, he was lax about due dates and fines and such. Paradoxically, the less he cared about when a book (or videotape, or music CD) was returned, the more punctual borrowers became.

If he was unavailable, books could be signed out on an honor system that, amazingly, everyone honored. The children loved him, their parents trusted him, and almost everyone forgot, almost all the time, just how rich the Iowa Lottery Commission had made him a few years back.

In Neil's library, quiet was not mandated. Today as he stamped books, Neil led a gang of little ones through an enthusiastic, if lyrically inaccurate, rendition of the Beach Boys' "Little Deuce Coupe."

". . . Little loose goose," the kids warbled. "She got the big lips, daddy . . ."

They soared to a rousing finale, each grabbed a handful of Hot Tamales from the crystal bowl on Neil's desk, and they ran screaming, with their books, into the blazing August sunlight.

It wasn't just lyrics they mangled. One day last summer, I heard a group of third-graders beg for "Lucelia" by "Simon and Garfield."

"You know, when Presley was little," I said, of Del's thirteen-year-old son, "he used to turn up Jimi Hendrix full blast and play air guitar to 'scuse me while I kiss this guy."

Neil smiled and aimed a remote at the stereo across the room. The Beach Boys faded into Patsy Cline's "Crazy."

"Ah, that's better," he said, sitting down behind the antique oak desk. He pushed the chair back, propped his Birkenstocks on a pile of papers next to the telephone, and ran his hands through dark hair shot with premature gray.

"Busy day, huh?"

"Apparently everyone in Delphi has developed a sudden yen to read," he said, cleaning his glasses on the edge of his T-shirt. He shooed Elizabeth Bennet, his calico cat, off the desk and grinned.

"Got something for you," I said, arranging myself comfortably in my usual chair, opposite the desk. I could hardly wait to drop Ron's news on Neil.

He sat up. "I have something for you too," he said and disappeared below the desk, rummaging in a box at his feet. He sat up and handed a book to me. "Just came in this morning."

"Juggling for Beginners?" I read the title, puzzled.

"I thought it might help get your coordination back after your cast comes off."

I tapped the cast on the desk ruefully. "I didn't have any coordination before the accident. If I had, this probably wouldn't have happened."

"Well, it'll help get your strength back then," he said, tossing me three soft balls, two of which I missed completely. "These go with the book. Maybe you'll work up an act for the next Phollies."

"Yeah, right," I said doubtfully, trying left-handed tosses of the ball I still had. My first, and hopefully last, experience working up an act for our local talent show, the Delphi Phollies, had ended in disaster, the remnant of which I still wore on my right arm.

"So." He sat up. "You have something for me too?"

"Ah, yes," I said, remembering why I'd ventured across the street in the hot sun to begin with. "You know about the All-School Reunion and the parade float competition for homecoming."

He raised an eyebrow and waited. Of course he knew.

"Right," I said hastily. "Anyway, Debbie Fischbach asked Del and me to be on the planning committee. And I'm going to do it."

"A little out of your usual range of interests, isn't it?"

"I guess I'm curious to know if everyone else's life has been as weird as mine. Besides, they can't work me too hard." I pointed at the cast. "I'm just going along for brainwork and to buy a round of drinks at the meetings."

"And unrepentant nosiness." Neil smiled. "A perfectly good reason. How did Mrs. Fischbach end up running the show?"

"She and Doug have only been back here a year," I said. "I assume she was flattered into it."

That's how it works; when new people move in (even if they're actually former residents who were gone a few years, like the Fischbachs), committee chairmanships are thrust upon them, boards offer vacant seats, and positions of power are generally forced their way, until they are totally exhausted by the sad fact that no matter how hard they work, nothing ever changes in a small community. Then someone new moves to town and the whole process starts over.

"This year it's the Fischbachs' turn to butt heads with Delphi," I said. "Who's planning the festivities for your decade?"

Neil was about ten years younger than me, still in grade school when I graduated.

"No one so far," he said, grabbing a handful of Hot Tamales and then offering the bowl to me. "We're not as efficient and obsessive as you old folks."

"Well, you whippersnappers better get to it, it's going to be exciting," I said, finally warming to the real reason I'd brought up the subject.

"Nah, reunions aren't as much fun as they used to be back when I was just Neil Pascoe, Delphi Weird Guy."

"You mean in the good old days, before you became Neil Pascoe, Millionaire? People don't ask you for money, do they?"

"Not directly, but almost everyone has a little something they'll let me invest in," he said. "Or worse yet, they want to introduce me to their sister, or daughter, or recently divorced cousin."

"Yeah, being Neil Pascoe, Single Millionaire, must be a tough job, all right." I laughed. "You could always tell them you're gay."

He laughed. "Wouldn't matter. They'd happen to know a really nice guy, just coming out of a long-term relationship, who'd be perfect for me."

"So what do you tell them?"

"I tell them," he said, brown eyes calm behind thick glasses, "that I'm waiting."

"Oh," I said, looking down.

We sat in an uncomfortable silence as Patsy finished belting "I Fall to Pieces."

"Anyway, even if you aren't committee-ing, you'll definitely want to go to the reunion," I said finally.

"Of course," Neil said, mouth twitching. "You think I'd miss the great and famous J. Ross Nelson's return to Delphi?"

"Dammit, how'd you find out?" I was severely miffed. "And to think I broke a secrecy oath to run over with the news."

"You forget, Gina Adler comes in almost every day before school." Neil laughed. "She's had that 'I know something' look for a couple of months already. It took me this long to break her."

"Pretty slow," I said smugly over my shoulder as I walked to the pop machine in the next room. "It took Del and me about thirty seconds to make Ron spill the beans. Want one?" I hollered as I punched in a Diet Coke. Pop in Neil's library was still just a dime, which makes me feel slightly guilty. I left a couple of my tip quarters on top of the machine.

"Sure, get me a Barq's," he said, and continued as I handed the can to him, "so what exactly do you know about the wonderful honor about to be bestowed on us?"

"Only that she's coming for the parade, it's supposed to be a surprise, and people are already buzzing. Rhonda has it in her head that there was a connection between the drowning of Butchie Pendergast and Janelle's disappearance back in 1969."

"She's such a romantic," Neil said. "You're a mystery buff—is she on the right track?"

"Nah," I said. "At the time, there were rumors about the two of them, but that was just the kind of wild speculation that circulates through a small school system whenever anything unusual happens. I don't think anyone ever really thought there was a connection between Janelle's disappearance and Butchie's death, though the last time I saw either one, they were together.

"Mostly, we're more interested in the fact that Janelle was invited back to Delphi by the wife of the guy she disappeared *with*. Especially when you remember that Doug and Debbie were high school sweethearts. They were engaged to be engaged when Doug and Janelle ran off."

"That's right." Neil tilted his head, remembering. "We even heard about it in the grade school. She and Doug left town together, and three days later, Doug came back alone, with a big grin and a bunch of dirty stories. And she hasn't been back to Delphi since then, huh?"

"Nope," I said. "But we got her for our float. And we're gonna win the competition. So ha ha."

"And how exactly did that come about?" Neil asked.

"Somehow Gina Adler and Deb Fischbach arranged it."

"Evidently you scandalmongers are wrong—if the old connection between Janelle and Doug bothered his wife, Debbie wouldn't have gone out of her way to arrange for her return."

"You're probably right. It *was* a long time ago," I agreed, grabbing more candy. "We're just lucky Janelle was able to fit us in, between magazine interviews, made-for-TV movies, and appearances on *Dick Clark's Celebrity Bloopers.*"

"Who'd ever expect Delphi to produce real tabloid fodder?" Neil asked the air. J. Ross Nelson's affairs of the heart (and bankbook) were regular headline material, and not just in South Dakota either. "Of course, *I* didn't know her, I was too young, and certainly too insignificant for notice," Neil said, munching Hot Tamales. "How about you?"

"I was a couple of years younger than her, a sophomore when she was a senior, but believe me, I was insignificant too." I strained to remember. "I think Janelle Ross only spoke to me twice. In fact, the first time was in the bathroom at school, the day I met Del."

"Sounds juicy," Neil said. "Tell me more."

3

....

Plug Nickel

I didn't have to explain to Neil that I didn't really meet Del in the downstairs girls' bathroom at school, the year I was a sophomore and Del was a junior.

We've all lived in Delphi our whole lives, and Delphi is far too small for everyone not to know everyone else. That goes double for a school system where each grade has a maximum of thirty kids, and the meager student body is sometimes bussed in from farms and from even smaller communities twenty or more miles away.

So, as lifelong residents, Del and I did know each other before that fateful meeting. But we didn't *know* each other.

And we certainly weren't friends.

I was chunky and clumsy, and early on had picked up the reputation for being smart, which is the kiss of death if you are overweight. Being an only child who preferred reading to sports, and living on a country farm with my mother and dotty grandmother, didn't help.

Not that my fellow classmates were mean, or even disdainful. They, mostly as a group, ignored me completely, unless they needed help conjugating irregular Spanish verbs or a quick synopsis of *Jane Eyre* for a book report.

Del, on the other hand, kept no more than the minimum proficiency required in any subject. Except partying.

Good-looking, and a trifle over–made up, at the age of seventeen, Delphine Bauer was an exotic, dangerous creature—cynical, indifferent to authority, and, rumor had it, not a virgin.

She was fascinating, and more than a little intimidating.

Not that she'd ever deigned to notice me. The library was not one of her usual haunts.

September of 1969 was unusually wet; frequent rains had delayed the corn harvest and disgruntled the farmers. However, the intermittent downpours had not dampened the homecoming fervor that swept Delphi High.

With just one period to go before the assembly where the homecoming king and queen candidates would be announced, interest in the outcome of the schoolwide balloting was rabid. Conversation buzzed excitedly in the hallways as students rushed to the last formal class of the day.

The only sure bets were Janelle Ross and her best friend, Debbie Wetzler, for queen, and football co-captains Dougie Fischbach and Stu McKee for king. The rest of the court was up for grabs, to the intense delight of the rest of the student body.

I'd ducked into the girls' room in the hallway next to the auditorium to repair a run that I could feel slowly snaking its way from thigh to knee, in my last pair of wearable nylons. There were less than three minutes before class.

The door on the far stall, under the open window, was closed, but the institutional green room was empty otherwise. I balanced my books on the edge of a chipped porcelain sink and rooted in my purse for a bottle of clear nail polish, which I shook vigorously. I hiked up my skirt and carefully applied polish to the run's source, just below a garter, and then brushed goop around the far end of the run.

The swinging door burst open, and in piled a confusion of black, gold, and burgundy short pleated skirts, monogrammed V-neck sweaters, tennis shoes, and pom-poms. High-pitched giggles, bubble gum, skinny legs, and perfect hair. The Delphi Football Cheerleaders, all talking at once—rapid, nervous chatter about a party planned after the homecoming game on Friday, the cheers and skits they were working on, and, of course, their assorted boyfriends.

Subjects that had no relevance in my life.

I stood there uncomfortably, polish in hand, not wanting them to think I was eavesdropping. Unfortunately, proximity to any kind of physical ideal renders me even more awkward than usual. I turned and knocked my purse into the sink, spilling the contents, including a paperback copy of *Valley of the Dolls* that I was secretly reading.

Scrambling to shove the book, assorted pencils, hair clippies, and notes to myself back inside, I need not have worried. I might well have been invisible.

I squeezed over as far as I could as they arranged themselves in front of the long mirror over the row of sinks, speedily ratting hair and smoothing bangs and reapplying eyeliner and pale pink lipstick, demanding each others' approval for every change or addition. None of them carried books or purses. They shared a comb and makeup from a communal zipper bag.

"What do you think?" Debbie Wetzler asked, arms high overhead as she reinforced the superstructure and smoothed the surface hair back into a shape indistinguishable from its earlier incarnation.

"Boss," Janelle Ross said absentmindedly, removing an errant lipstick smudge with her little finger. She was the only one who seemed calm. "You too, Lisa, I really love what you're doing with your hair."

"Really?" Lisa Franklin asked worriedly. "You think

so? I mean, it's not weird or anything. Is it?" Blond and petite, still wearing braces, Lisa was, by general consensus, about to be an also-ran.

"Nope, it's perfect. Would I kid you?" Janelle flashed a thousand-watt smile at Lisa, who smiled weakly in return.

"Oops, gotta go," Janelle announced, confident and unconcerned. "No potty breaks once we're on stage, right, troupe?" She grinned and ducked into a stall.

The others giggled halfheartedly and continued making minute changes in their appearance.

I had quietly finished replacing the contents of my purse and was trying to make an unobtrusive exit when Janelle wailed from the stall.

"Oh God. Perfect timing," she said, plainly disgusted. "Damn."

Lipsticks froze mid-stroke, mascara wands hovered as they all turned around, mouths open.

The cheerleaders all looked at each other, waiting for someone to say something. Janelle beat them to it.

"Any chance one of you guys has a plug? My little friend just decided to visit."

Frantically they searched themselves, as though cheerleader skirts had a secret tampon compartment. The makeup bag was also devoid of feminine hygiene supplies.

"How about you . . ." Debbie turned to me, then paused.

"Tory Atwood," Lisa filled in. "She's nobody. A sophomore."

All eyes focused on me expectantly.

"Sorry," I said, feeling stupid. "Fresh out."

"Well, are you sure?" Debbie asked sarcastically.

"Yes, I'm sure," I said, having just been thoroughly reacquainted with the entire contents of my purse. Their collective insecurity surprised me—I had always thought the inner life of a cheerleader ran as smoothly as the outer. It had not occurred to me that they could be ambushed by their periods, like ordinary mortals.

"I have a nickel though," I said. "You know, for the

machine." I pointed to the ubiquitous Kotex dispenser on the far wall. Most girls never ventured forth without a couple of emergency nickels in their purses. Just in case.

"What do you think, Janelle?" Debbie asked loudly, not taking her eyes off me. I guess they needed to decide if my nickel was worthy.

"Yes, yes, anything, just hurry up. We're gonna be late," Janelle said through the door.

I fished a nickel out and handed it to Debbie, who twisted the handle and lobbed the small gray box over the stall door.

"Thanks, I owe you one," Janelle said when she came out, smiling and smoothing her skirt down, front and back. "Come on, let's go see what they're doing in the auditorium."

She smiled, and it took me a moment to realize that the most popular girl in the school was inviting me to go along with her. The others cast sidewise glances at each other, surprised and not especially pleased.

"Let's go," Janelle said again. "You just saved my dignity, if not my life."

"God, Janelle, you must be kidding," Lisa said in a theatrical whisper. "She's only a sophomore."

Janelle cocked her head at me, silky brown hair swept long over one shoulder, and smiled.

Just then a toilet flushed and the door to the far stall opened, and Delphine Bauer stepped out.

All conversation stopped as Del calmly inspected her own hair, which was long, red, parted in the middle, and held back by a small ribbon tied in a skinny bow on top. She then reached into her purse.

I thought she was going to hand a tampon to Janelle.

Instead, she brought out a small silver lighter and a pack of cigarettes. We all stood openmouthed as she flicked the lid open, thumbed the strike wheel, lit one, and took a long drag.

Expressions of naked distaste passed over several faces as Del blew smoke out of the corner of her mouth.

"Well, are you coming?" Janelle asked me, not smiling now.

The bell rang, echoing down nearly empty hallways. I was officially tardy for English. A first.

"We better go," Debbie insisted. "It's late."

"Yeah," Lisa chimed in, "and it stinks in here."

Ordinarily, I would have jumped at the chance to hang out with the School Cool, but Debbie and Lisa's snottiness made me want to defend Del. Not that she needed my help.

I looked to Janelle for a indication of her attitude.

She was carefully neutral.

"Tory can't," Del said in an exaggerated drawl. "She's already promised to help me write a paper on who's buried in Grant's Tomb. Sorry."

"Well?" Debbie asked me, impatient and impolite. Ignoring Del.

Janelle raised a quizzical eyebrow.

I glanced at Del, who was now leaning against the sink, still smoking. She dropped a long slow wink that the others couldn't see.

Then, for some reason I still cannot fathom, I said to the most popular girl in Delphi, "You go ahead, I'll catch up a little later."

Janelle shrugged. I was aware that the invitation would, in all probability, never again be extended. "Suit yourself."

Then she, and the others, left.

I paused for a moment, contemplating the choice I'd made. Not the only one that day with far-reaching consequences.

"Wow," Neil said, enthralled. "Del and J. Ross Nelson, both at the same time."

"Hey," I said, "wait till you hear the rest."

4

Sweet Delphi

I did not begin my sophomore year at Delphi High with any sort of major life-change expectations. I don't suppose I had any sort of expectations at all, outside of a vague happily-ever-after scenario in the back of my brain.

"So you chose Delphine Bauer over Janelle Ross in the girls' can," Neil said. "Interesting move."

"Actually," I explained, "I was just being pragmatic."

Neil raised an eyebrow and waited. On the stereo, Sam Cooke didn't know what a slide rule was for.

"Well, even if the once and future queen was not setting me up for some especially nasty cheerleader prank," I said through a mouthful of Hot Tamales, "her power wasn't absolute—she could invite me along, but she couldn't make me fit in. I didn't want to trail after them like some stray they'd decided to be kind to."

"So you decided to trail after the school bad girl instead?"

"Del just pulled me along in her wake," I said, settling back in the chair to explain. "An hour after that, my fate was sealed anyway."

I remembered looking down at my feet, unsure what to say next.

"You don't want to hang out with that group of snobs anyway," Del had said, lobbing a cigarette butt into the toilet, where it landed with a hiss. "They don't think anyone matters but their own little crowd." There was bitterness in her voice.

"I don't even know them," I said, shrugging. "They're cheerleaders."

Explanation enough.

Del leaned back on the sink and crossed her arms under an already ample bosom. "So what do you do?"

"Gotta start with the hard questions, huh?" I smiled ruefully. Del answered with a small grin. "I don't do anything—I come to school, I go home, I help my mom out on the farm. I read." It sounded pitiful, even to me.

"I suppose you're one of those smart ones, always waving your hand, got all the answers."

"I try not to be," I said. "School just comes easy for me. It's not like I work at it or anything. Sometimes the answers are just, you know, there when I need them."

Del narrowed her eyes, and then evidently decided not to hold that against me. She lit another cigarette.

I nervously glanced over my shoulder at the door. Expecting an angry teacher to burst in and haul us both off to the principal's office.

"Relax," she said around the cigarette. "No one comes in here during last period. It's sort of my hangout."

"Well, I really should get going," I said, wondering if my clothes would absorb any smoke smell. "The bell rang a long time ago." I picked up my books.

"It's a short period anyway, I thought I'd ditch," Del said, watching my face for a reaction.

"You mean just leave? Before the day is over? Now?"

"That's what the word *ditch* means," Del said patiently. "What, haven't you done it before?"

"It wouldn't do me any good to ditch." I avoided her question. "I live on a farm. I ride the bus. There wouldn't be any point."

"You lead one hell of an exciting life, girlie," Del said, patting my shoulder. "I suppose you're a virgin too."

Delphine Bauer was probably the only girl who I knew, for sure, wasn't a virgin. I had a few suspicions about some other girls, especially those in long-term relationships. But I knew only one sure hit—Del, who didn't seem to care if everyone knew what she did.

I shrugged. *Valley of the Dolls* notwithstanding, literature was no substitute for experience. I knew I couldn't fake it with an expert.

"So are you at least going with anyone? Seeing a guy?"

"Not at the moment," I said primly. Not at any moment. And not because I didn't want to. So far, no one had shown the slightest interest in me.

"Well, watch out for Nick, then. He sniffs out you're still a virgin, and you'll be a goner."

I knew who she was talking about. Nick Bauer, Del's cute cousin. His reputation for partying and getting into trouble was almost as bad as Del's.

"I am not that easy," I said archly.

The bell rang, the halls filled with the noise of students on their way to the assembly.

"Sweetheart, we're all that easy," Del said, picking up her books and slinging her purse over one shoulder. "Come on, let's go see some hearts get broken."

She pushed through the door, and with nearly no hesitation at all, I followed her into the hallway.

Almost immediately I heard my name being called.

"Tory, Tory, wait up." I turned to find my eighth-grade cousin, Junior, running to catch up with me.

"Hurry," I said to Del. "Pretend we don't see her."

But it was too late.

"Tory, can I sit with you at the assembly?" Junior panted, pulling up her knee socks and then rearranging the knit headband that held back her dark shoulder-length flip.

"Sorry, we sit in the upperclass section. No kiddies allowed," Del said, underestimating Junior's tenacity.

"But Tory's not an upperclassman," Junior pointed out.

"Ah, but she's an upper lower classman," Del said, "and sometimes we make a special dispensation for them. On the other hand, we *never* let junior high kids sit with us. Wouldn't be dignified."

Junior, who generally made my life miserable in and out of school, wasn't about to give up that easily.

"What are you sitting with *her* for, anyway?" she asked me. "Does Aunt Fernice know you're hanging out with—" She stopped and wrinkled her nose. "Is that cigarette smoke?"

"Of course not," I said hastily.

"I wanna sit next to you, or I'm going to tell," Junior said firmly.

"No," I said.

"Go away," Del said.

"You better let me," Junior said, louder this time.

"Is there a problem here, ladies? Aren't you supposed to be seated by now, Miss Engebretson?" asked Mr. Kincaid, the new chorus director and junior high geography teacher. He was impossibly young, impossibly handsome, and far too much like a real person to be a teacher. Half the girls in school had crushes on him.

Including, evidently, Junior.

"Oh, Mr. Kincaid," she simpered, "can I sit in the high school section with these guys? It's all right, Tory is my cousin, and she invited me."

Junior flashed a phony grin our direction, knowing we wouldn't contradict her.

"No, you better go find the rest of your classmates. Hurry now before all the seats are taken," he said to Junior, whose face fell.

"But—" she said, whining.

"No buts," he said sternly, smoothing blond hair back from his forehead.

Junior opened her mouth and closed it again, glared at me, and flounced off.

"Thanks," I said to Mr. Kincaid. "She's kind of a pest."

"Well, some rules are best observed." He smiled conspiratorially. "Now, isn't there someplace you're supposed to be, too?"

"Yes sir," Del said politely, guiding me by the elbow into the auditorium.

That had been my first real contact with Mr. Kincaid. His other duties, senior class adviser and yearbook adviser, were completely out of my sphere. Much to my disappointment.

"Wow, he's cool," I whispered as we climbed up the bleacher stairs.

"No kidding," Del said. "I'd take junior high geography if they'd let me."

"Del, up here," I heard someone say.

"This way," she said to me over her shoulder, picking her way into the middle of a bleacher row near the top, gingerly stepping over piles of books and purses that had been placed on the floor. I followed.

The noise level in the crowded auditorium grew steadily. The pep band was seated in a semicircle onstage below, tuning up. Janelle and Debbie and the rest of the senior cheerleaders were sitting on the edge of the stage, legs idly swinging in the air. They weren't talking to one another. Janelle looked happy and calm, and Debbie was trying hard to fake it. Lisa was nervous and near tears.

The football team, wearing burgundy home jerseys and blue jeans, was seated in chairs onstage too, beneath the gold Delphi banner appliquéd with profiles of Apollo, our unofficial mascot. Dimly, I could make out number 69, Dougie Fischbach, and number 10, Stu McKee, sitting in the back row center. Dougie was a typical high school star jock, ignoring those who weren't part of his particular crowd. Stu, while still a jock, seemed somehow nicer.

Sitting next to Stu was Butchie Pendergast, destined to be another Dougie Fischbach—big and tough and mean enough to make the varsity team as a sophomore. His presence was already felt, both in and out of uniform. And like Dougie, he was a bully and a whiner. He especially enjoyed making life miserable for those he considered beneath him. Including me. I hated him. And so did everyone else, except for the in crowd, coaches, and the hometown cheering section—people who never looked beyond performance on the field.

Principal Voltzman stepped out onstage, shushed the crowd, and led us in a droning rendition of the Pledge of Allegiance. I caught sight of Junior in the kiddie section. She was peering intently into the upper stands. Looking for me, I suppose, preparing to report everything to her mother. And mine.

I became aware of some whispering beside me. Though going through the proper motions, Del was actually carrying on an animated discussion with the guy standing next to her.

Then the band director led an up-tempo version of the school song, a seriously goofy poem set to music and written before the word *breast* was known to generate giggles among adolescent boys. The favorite line was: "Within her breast, she holds the past, sweet Delphi is its name." It was inevitable that local parlance for copping a feel came to be known as "searching for sweet Delphi."

There were snickers on the other side of Del. I stole a peek around her and saw Ronnie Adler, who gazed at Del longingly through rapidly blinking eyes. On his other side stood a good-looking boy with very dark curly hair and lively brown eyes, who was not much taller than me.

"Tory, do you know my cousin Nicky Bauer?" Del whispered, by way of an introduction. "This is Tory Atwood; I caught her smoking in the girls' can."

"I know Tory Atwood," Nicky said. "Everyone knows Tory Atwood. Don't you know Tory Atwood?" he asked Ronnie, who blinked in reply.

"Shhh," Del whispered, "we're getting to the good part."

Student body president Gerald Messner approached the microphone and cleared his throat. An anticipatory hush fell over the crowd.

"Good afternoon," Gerald intoned, and then winced at the high feedback whine.

"It's interference from your braces," one of the football players called. Probably Butchie.

Everyone laughed.

"Funny, funny," Gerald responded, then cleared his throat again and drew a folded sheet of paper from his pocket. "I have here a list of the 1969 Delphi High School homecoming royalty candidates. From these ten outstanding seniors, it will be our job as a student body to select our honored queen and king. It is an awesome responsibility, one we should all take seriously."

Gerald paused, while a few students hissed and hooted.

"I'd like those whose names are read to come to center stage, please." Gerald theatrically opened the paper and slowly announced the list of names.

Reactions were immediate and noisy—applause and gasps. I didn't catch most of the names called, though I certainly heard Janelle Ross and Debbie Wetzler, as well as Dougie Fischbach and Stu McKee.

Obviously miserable, Lisa Franklin, whose name was not among the chosen, tried to keep up appearances. She shot a venomous glance at the triumphant Janelle before leaving the stage with as much dignity as she could muster.

"That's all I need to see," Del said. "Let's get out of here."

"But the assembly isn't over yet; we haven't been dismissed," I said.

"So what? No one will notice—it's chaos in here."

Del was right. Everyone seemed to be wandering around—congratulating the winners or commiserating with the rest. A glowing Janelle talked animatedly with Stu McKee on stage, while Debbie got an overly enthusiastic hug from Dougie, her longtime steady. They stood together at the pinnacle of high school popularity.

Lisa Franklin leaned against the doorway, furtively wiping tears away. Mr. Kincaid, who had been snapping photos for the annual, pulled a hankie out of his back pocket and handed it to her.

No one paid any attention to the upper bleachers except Junior, who gazed at me with a hard expression.

"Okay, let's go," I said recklessly. "I'd rather wait for the bus outside than stand around in here." I figured if I could cut class, I could also cut the rest of the assembly.

"Bus, who said anything about a bus?" Nick Bauer asked, deliberately placing himself between Del and me, to my absolute astonishment. He stood so close, our arms touched. An electric tingle ran through me.

"I ride the bus," I said idiotically, unable to look directly at him.

"There's no need to ride a stupid bus. We'll take you home. Right, group?" he asked the others. Ronnie merely nodded, but Del grinned knowingly.

"Told you so," she mouthed.

I could feel a blush creeping up from my neckline.

My mother and I had never discussed circumstances in which I might accept rides from Delphi's wild crowd. Junior would waste no time making sure she heard about it.

"Well, ah," I said, trying to decide if the risk was worth the distinct possibility of even more excitement, when Nicky Bauer reached out and placed a finger under my chin and lifted my face up.

With a practiced twist he flipped his hair out of his eyes, which sparkled with an irresistible glee. He smiled and I could not help returning the grin.

"Let's go. We'll pick up a Coke or something," he said, winking. "You can sit up front with me."

"And from that moment, my future was written in stone," I finished.

"Well, yeah," Neil said, "at least until a couple of years ago."

As if I needed reminding. Maybe it was time to chisel in a new inscription.

5

Rhonda in the Nineties

REUNION COMMITTEE MEETING DAY

I don't know how the tradition of homecoming started, but it no longer has much to do with football. The actual game is incidental to the festivities these days. In fact, except for providing the uniforms and players, homecoming has little to do with the school at all. It is now more or less an excuse for the town to celebrate itself.

Local merchants and committees have found numerous ways to poke their civic and commercial noses into what was, essentially, an excuse for a few kids to dress up in fancy clothes and for the rest to goof off.

And like Christmas, homecoming is no longer just a one-day blowout—it has expanded not only into homecoming week, but an entire preparation season. Most years, we got by with a flurry of activities a couple of weeks before the big game. But this year's seventy-fifth annual homecoming celebration required something more formal and tedious from Delphi residents.

It demanded at least a month of studious preparation, multiple meetings, volunteer conscription, donated supplies, and effort bordering on real creativity to live up to our self-imposed expectations.

Even though the celebration was going to be held in mid-September, not exactly prime tourist season, the response from alumni had been amazing. Over two hundred former students of good old DHS were planning to return for the final weekend of activities, among which would be a banquet, the All-School Reunion, and the parade, and if you weren't doing anything early Friday evening, there was that little matter of a football game against archrivals Hitchcock-Tulare.

Someone had even suggested a mini-competition for the Queen of Queens, an exercise in which one ex-homecoming queen would be crowned to reign over any other ex-HQs who could be persuaded to compete.

"Forget it," Rhonda growled when approached with the idea. "If I'd known it was gonna follow me the rest of my life, I'd have declined."

Like most of Delphi, I happened to witness Rhonda's coronation last year. She had seemed, at the time, to be just as delighted with winning as every other tiaraed victor.

"You can't tell me that you didn't enjoy parading around in a crown and velvet cape for the adoring masses," I said to her as I carried plates of lukewarm Hot Turkey Combos to a booth of bus passengers. I was getting good at balancing plates on my cast.

We were unexpectedly busy because a half-full Jackrabbit bus had pulled in just before dinner rush, ostensibly to check on a pneumatic problem. But since Del had disappeared into the bus, I figured the problematic pneumatic system belonged to the driver.

"The crown gave me a headache, and the cape weighed a ton and smelled awful," Rhonda complained. "Believe me, it wasn't as much fun as it looked."

"Poor baby," Del said, back inside again, a bit disheveled but radiant. "Must have been tough being the most popular girl in school." She idly trailed a finger along the bus driver's collar as he contemplated the menu and nervously twisted the gold band on his left hand.

"That's just what I mean. You get the most votes in some dorky school election, and all of a sudden people treat you like you went out and campaigned for it or something."

Obviously, Rhonda was far too serious a person to have enjoyed the shallow pleasure of receiving an award in front of a large, cheering audience. Or far too young to admit it.

"Well, back in the old days, girls actually wanted to be elected homecoming queen. I'd have killed for it myself," I said, a little surprised by that bit of public honesty. "And I certainly remember some real electioneering by several of the candidates." I pinned another order to the carousel above the divider between the cafe and the kitchen.

"Me too," Del said, with a pot of coffee in her hand. "In fact, I think that's the one and only time Debbie Wetzler was ever nice to me." Del grinned. It would probably not please Debbie to know that her defeat still provided intense satisfaction to Del.

"Well, I sure didn't," Rhonda said.

I believed her. Rhonda was one of those congenitally perky types who could be truly happy for a best friend's win, even if it meant her own loss.

The bus passengers were slowly making their way out, to the exaggerated relief of disgruntled locals, who were not used to waiting for booths in their own cafe.

"Maybe we should have a contest for ex-homecoming kings," I said. "They could give a prize to the one who has the most hair and can burp the loudest."

"Yeah, with a trophy for anyone who can snap his old letterman's jacket." Del laughed.

"Sounds fine to me," said Stu McKee, who, like most middle-aged guys, was a little thicker around the middle and a little thinner on top than he used to be. On the other hand, he still looked pretty good, even if his jacket didn't fit perfectly anymore. He'd been waiting patiently at the counter for an empty booth and listening to our conversation. "I could sit in the stands and watch."

"That's right," Del said with a mock bow. "I'd forgotten you didn't actually win the crown."

The general expectation had been that Stu and Janelle would reign over the 1969 festivities. When Doug had been named king, Debbie Wetzler (the future Mrs. Fischbach) had been forced to pair up with Stu for the ceremonies.

"Were you going out with Janelle at the time?" I asked Stu. I had no specific memories of them being together, but I missed a lot in those days.

"Janelle didn't date," Stu said firmly. "She chewed guys up and spit them out."

"If she liked you, you had it made." Ron blinked. Ron could still have fit into his high school letterman's jacket, if he'd earned one to begin with. He slid into the booth opposite Stu rather than sit alone at the counter. "But if she didn't, watch out."

The cafe was quiet enough now for us to be able to finish a sentence or two without being interrupted by empty cups and dropped silverware and ringing cash registers.

"Janelle thought I was going to win, and she thought she was going to win," Stu said ruefully. "Janelle Ross never did anything without carefully weighing the percentages."

"That just proves she wasn't infallible," Del hooted.

"What was the percentage in disappearing with Mr. Fischbach after that kegger?" Rhonda asked. "And then not coming back three days later when he did?" Rhonda had spent the last day boning up on the details of that long-ago party. She now knew more about it than we, who had been there, could remember.

"For one thing, we're still hashing it over, more than twenty-five years later," I said. "Talk about your grand exits."

"And for another, she ditched Delphi pretty well permanently," Del said, tucking her shirt in a little more firmly, for Ron's benefit. "That's something the rest of us never quite did."

"But she's coming back." Ron blinked.

"There's only one way to leave Delphi permanently," I said.

"Even that doesn't work," Rhonda chirped. "I mean, look at that poor boy who drowned. He's been dead forever, and people are still talking."

"As far as I can tell," Del said, pouring herself a cup of coffee as she slid in next to Ron, who blinked in appreciation, "you're the only one who's talking about Butchie Pendergast."

"And you're not talking about the person," I continued. "You're just trying to turn the whole situation into an intrigue."

"And believe me," Stu finished, "Butchie Pendergast was never a 'poor boy.'"

Rhonda leaned over the back of the booth. "So tell me about him. Who's homecoming escort was he?"

"He wasn't anyone's," I explained. "Butchie was in my grade. He just hung out with the older jocks."

"Like you?" she asked Stu.

"Not me." Stu shook his head. "I thought he was a jerk. He was Doug's friend."

"What'd he do that was so awful?"

"Believe me," Del said, getting up again. More customers were coming in. "You don't wanna know."

Rhonda trailed behind her. "Even if he was a creep, didn't it throw the whole school for a loop when he died? These days, they bring in grief counselors when something like that happens. The long-term afteraffects can be horrible."

I shrugged, working my way behind the counter again, swabbing tables and picking up empty plates. "It *was* awful. It's always a shock when someone your age dies. Especially when you're a kid yourself. But underneath, though we didn't admit it out loud, we were a little relieved that he was gone."

Rhonda was shocked. "You can't possibly mean that."

She looked at Ron, Del, and Stu. They nodded.

"I don't suppose anyone actually wished him dead," Stu said softly. "But once he was, no one missed him."

"You guys are awful," Rhonda said, reading the confirmation in our faces. "He probably suffered from low self-esteem, or attention deficit disorder, or something like that." She was sorely disappointed in all of us. "Maybe he was hyperactive."

"He could have been a middle child," Del added wickedly. "Or maybe he forgot his inner child."

"If Butchie Pendergast suffered from anything, it was a surplus of self-esteem," I said gently. "He beat me up in the third grade. He constantly terrorized his own younger brothers and sisters."

"He didn't just pick on the younger ones." Ron blinked mournfully, speaking from experience. "He bullied anyone who was smaller than him."

"He broke a guy's finger once, just for back-talking," Stu said.

"What about the rest of his family?" Rhonda asked. "They must have been devastated."

"Butchie's dad was a drinker with a heavy fist. His mom was always 'falling down stairs' and breaking bones. The rest of the kids tried to fade into the woodwork—living with Pendergast Junior and Senior had to have been hell. His dad drank himself to death less than a year after Butchie died, and the rest of the family packed up and moved away shortly thereafter."

"Wasn't there some kind of help for him? For all of them?" Rhonda, who came of age in the nineties, asked. "Where were the social service people? The counselors?"

"No such thing, back then," I said. "Maybe with help, he would have grown up to be an upstanding citizen, but we'll never know. As it was, he got drunk and went for a swim late at night in high water, and drowned. It was a stupid thing to do and a stupid way to die."

"I can't help thinking that this kid's death had something to do with whatsername going away," Rhonda said stubbornly. "Didn't *anyone* think so at the time?"

"No, we all thought she was knocked up." Ron blinked.

Rhonda threw a sharp glare that withered Ron's smirk.

"Actually that was the rumor," Del explained. "You might not realize it, but in those days, a pregnant girl was immediately expelled from school."

"You mean they'd kick her out?" Rhonda was aghast. To her, this was worse than our ambivalence about Butchie. "That's terrible. They couldn't do that now."

"You got that right." Ron chuckled. "Otherwise, there'd be no girls in school at all."

We all glared at Ron that time. He blushed and apologized halfheartedly.

Rhonda mulled the injustice. "So, was she pregnant? Was there a baby?"

"A lot of people thought so, but Del and I knew otherwise," I said.

I repeated the story of Janelle Ross bumming nickels for the Kotex machine only days before she disappeared.

"You guys are so lucky. Everyone in my class is ordinary and boring," Rhonda said. "*Your* reunion is going to be interesting, anyway."

"Yes, it will be fucking fascinating," Del said. "That's why we're all going to the meeting tonight."

"I can't wait until everyone finds out that J. Ross Nelson is actually coming." Ron blinked.

"As if they don't all know already," Del said. "Nothing that juicy stays quiet around here."

"Well, um, maybe," said Ron, who'd been the first to spoil his wife's surprise.

"Some of us intend to work for the greater glory of Delphi," I said primly. "I expect it will be a dull and ordinary meeting."

"Speaking of which . . ." Stu turned to me, lightly placing a warm hand on my elbow, just above the cast. "Do you need a ride tonight?"

He locked his astonishing green eyes with mine, smiling.

All words deserted me. Renee had been gone a fairly decent interval, and we'd discussed going public. Evidently, Stu had decided on his own that now was the proper time.

"Well, ah, it's only two blocks from the trailer to the bar," I said finally. "I don't suppose I need a ride."

Conversation in the cafe stopped. Everyone strained to listen.

"Yes." Stu smiled, even wider. "But would you *like* a ride? I'll be specific—would you care to go to the reunion meeting with me?"

For months, I'd yearned to be seen in public with Stu McKee—to end the hiding and sneaking. To stop looking over my shoulder, to stop worrying we might be recognized at out-of-town motels.

"Sure," I mumbled, unable to meet Stu's eyes. I had the distinct feeling that stepping into Delphi's full scrutiny would be every bit as uncomfortable as hiding from it.

Ron was already up, ready to pay his ticket. The quicker to get back to his garage and spread the word.

"See you tonight," Stu said to me softly, at the till. "Smile, this is supposed to be the fun part," he whispered, then leaned over and planted a soft kiss on my forehead, and left before I could say anything.

"Ha!" Rhonda hooted triumphantly, doing a little rope sandal victory shuffle. "I knew it, I knew it, I *knew* it. Didn't I tell you?" she asked me. "Did I not tell her?" she demanded of Del, who was somber.

"Yup, you predicted it all right," Del said. "The interesting thing will be to predict what's gonna happen now."

"What do you mean?" Rhonda asked, confused. "Tory and Stu are gonna be the cutest couple in Delphi, and everyone's gonna be happy for them. Right?"

All evidence to the contrary, Rhonda thought she lived in a land of happily-ever-afters, where married men divorced their wives to marry middle-aged waitresses.

"If you say so," Del said to her, patting my shoulder.

In the kitchen, Aphrodite saluted me with her cigarette.

I winced at the notion of being half of Delphi's cutest couple, though that was not the most interesting thing about these recent developments.

The most interesting thing was that, for a brief and inexplicable instant, I'd nearly told Stu no.

6

Second First Date

The last few months of sneaky afternoon sex notwithstanding, I was about to go on my first date since high school.

My real first date was for the fateful homecoming party of 1969, the one everyone was suddenly remembering in varying degrees of detail. In fact, that kegger by the James River was, technically, the only date I had with Nick. At least it was the only one where he actually asked me to go somewhere specific with him.

After that, we just wound up together. I fell so immediately and terminally in love with Nick that I followed him around, generally making myself available between his many amorous adventures. We accidentally became a couple, and when we got married, it wasn't because Nicky got down on bended knee to ask.

"Well, I guess we better do it then," was his romantic reaction to my announcement of an impending arrival. By the time we realized it was a false alarm, it was too late for either of us to back out. Not that I would have. Nick Bauer was my obsession, and I willingly traded any sense of peace and security I might have had, just for the opportunity to be with him.

Not that Nicky was a bad guy. He was amiable and funny, gentle, and irresistible—and pathologically unable to resist those who found him so.

Our life together consisted mainly of his grand ideas and my grand heartbreaks, interspersed with some genuinely good times. I would likely have been content to continue on that path forever, if Nick hadn't died in a stupid car accident.

Since then, my life had consisted of work and books and afternoons at the library with Neil. Until Stuart McKee moved back to Delphi, and into my bed. A transition that took so little effort that I never did sit down and figure out just how I ended up having an affair with a married man. Or why.

Now that Stu's wife had left him, we were free to take the affair to the next logical step—official dating. Which, for some reason, filled me with a dread I hadn't felt when we were trying to keep the whole thing secret.

I had not the slightest clue as to how to conduct a real relationship with an adult male. Nick was not mature enough to qualify as grown-up, and however pleasant, sex with Stu did not qualify as a relationship.

This was new territory and I was terrified.

Truly, I didn't know anything about Stu that didn't involve the insertion of one body part into another. I felt as though I was on a blind date, except that I already knew what he looked like. Naked.

"So." I turned to him brightly. "What's your favorite color?"

"Huh?" he asked. He'd parked his pickup at the bar, two blocks up from the trailer, and walked over to collect me.

"Never mind," I mumbled. "Just making conversation."

"You're nervous, aren't you?" he asked, amused.

"I can't figure out why you're not," I said, though his breezy self-confidence was one of the things that attracted me to Stu to begin with. That and his gorgeous green eyes.

He was out of uniform—wearing none of the logo-covered promotional giveaways that are standard dress for a Feed and Seed Store owner. In faded denims and a short-sleeved white cotton shirt, he was a poster boy for the Middle-aged Midwestern Male—slight paunch, strands of gray in his receding sandy-brown hair, handsome and weathered, with a wide grin.

"Buck up, kid." He laughed. "No one's going to bite." He swept into a low bow. "Shall we?"

"We could just stay here instead," I said. "Presley's out for the night, and Del is already at the meeting. We'd have the whole trailer to ourselves."

"As tempting as that offer is, we'd still have to go outside eventually. It might as well be now. Besides, the committee is expecting us, and they'll only talk more if we don't show up."

We walked from the trailer along Delphi's main drag. The evening was breezy and cool, on the cusp of another wet and dreary fall. Rain was forecast. Stu waved and smiled at the drivers who passed us on the way. Every one of them stared openmouthed when they realized who he was with.

"You're enjoying this, aren't you?" I asked, surprised. "I mean, you know what kind of reaction this is going to get around here."

"It's good to stir things up a little," he said, placing a warm hand on the back of my neck as we walked, so as to remove all spectator doubt that we were actually together. "And anyway, we're not going to be nearly as interesting to everyone tonight as Deb Fischbach's bombshell."

I hoped he was right.

We were at the door to Jackson's. I could hear laughter, and Garth Brooks on the jukebox inside. I inhaled, gathering my courage.

"It's gonna be fine," Stu whispered in my ear, standing aside for me to go in first.

I stepped into a dark, smoky world, and paused to let my eyes adjust. For a weeknight, there were quite a few people in the bar. Small tables were pushed together, and groups sat, busily scribbling and talking, while pitchers of beer sweated beside them.

I spotted Del toward the back, at the far end of a long table. There were five or six people sitting on either side, all yakking animatedly. Del saw me, raised an eyebrow, and lit another cigarette.

"Tory, Tory, come over here a sec." I turned to see Rhonda waving madly from a table filled with mostly underage drinkers.

"Pitcher of beer all right with you? I'll get one and meet you at the table," Stu said, gesturing toward Del and the others. "You better see what Rhonda wants before she explodes."

Rhonda couldn't wait until I made my way to her table. She met me halfway, wearing a long denim jumper over a gauzy shirt. Her hair was braided and wrapped up around her head like a Swedish grandma's.

"I been waiting for you two to get here," she whispered conspiratorially. And a little slurrily. Evidently vegetarian earth mothering didn't preclude the underage imbibing of an occasional pitcher or two of Bud. "I just wanted to tell you again that you and Stu are so cute together. And I am sure it'll all work out fine."

"What do you mean?"

"Well, I got to thinking about Stu and the fact that he's still married and all," she said seriously. "Don't get me wrong. I like him a lot, and he's a really great guy. But a lotta times relationships like this don't work out—what with there being a wife already."

And a son, I silently added.

Rhonda continued, "But it's not like you were seeing each other *before* his wife left. I'm sure you know what you're doing." She nodded to herself. "It'll be great. For both of you."

She hung an arm around my neck and gave me a swift hug. She had a lot more confidence than I did—I wasn't at all sure that I knew what I was doing. But I certainly did not want to discuss timing, or ramifications, with a tipsy Rhonda, so I changed the subject.

"What are you doing here?"

She brightened. "Well, I called a buncha classmates, and we decided that we couldn't let you old farts walk off with all the homecoming prizes. So we're here having a meeting too. It's more fun than I thought it'd be." She walked me to her table, reached for her beer mug.

"I thought you weren't interested in reliving your high school glories," I teased.

"I'm not," she said seriously, "but since most of us college kids make it back to good ol' Delphi for home-coming, we decided that a little reunion would be nice. Besides," she said, waving at someone behind me, "we got a secret weapon that's gonna blow all of you out of the water."

"Oh? And what might that be?" Not that I particularly cared about winning, but it would take a pretty major surprise to eclipse the return of J. Ross Nelson.

"We're not telling," Rhonda said smugly to me, and then said to someone over my shoulder, "and you better not either."

"Mum's the word," Neil Pascoe said, grinning. "Cross my heart and hope to die."

"I thought you were skipping the whole reunion thing," I said to Neil. "And how come you're conspiring with Rhonda's bunch anyway? Aren't you a little old for this crowd?"

"We decided to consolidate," he said, wiping his glasses on a napkin. "Lots of the younger ones are off at college and the rest have moved away—we figured we could work together on some sort of float and party."

"And you're the secret weapon Rhonda's going to use to beat the crap outta us, huh?" I laughed.

"Something like that."

"Well, you'll have to keep me informed," I whispered.

"Nope." Neil grinned. "I took a vow of secrecy."

"Oh, so that's the way it's gonna be," I said. "In that case, I'd best get back to my own meeting. It's all very secret and hush-hush too, you know." I turned to go.

"I understand congratulations are in order," Neil said quietly, not meeting my eyes.

I looked over at our table in the back. Stu was watching us with a solemn expression.

"I guess so," I faltered. I had wondered how long it would be before someone told Neil about the date.

"Well, good luck," Neil said quietly, shrugging. "See you later."

With solemn eyes and a parting smile, he turned to Rhonda, who greeted him again effusively, and patted the chair next to her.

I hesitated for just a second, but there was nothing I could do. For better or worse, I had made my decision. I sighed and headed back to Stu.

"Tory, how nice of you to come," Debbie Fischbach said. She smiled cordially, though the smile did not reach her eyes. Her hair was blonder than it had been in her teens, and she'd retained most of her figure, even after three sons. She was bundled up against the chill of the evening in a long-sleeved sweater and high-necked shirt. Her face was lined and looked tired.

I had seen Deb occasionally in the cafe since they'd moved back to Delphi, but we did not travel in the same social circles.

"Tory, I'm so glad you made it," plump and pretty Gina Adler said, with genuine enthusiasm. She had placed herself firmly between Ron and Del, and in a well-choreographed dance, leaned forward or back with Ron, effectively blocking his view. I thought the Adler marriage might have been a little like mine and Nick's—Gina outgunned by Ron's restless longings.

"We really need your input here," Gina said, and Ron nodded, blinking.

"There's an extra chair here for you," my cousin Junior Deibert said, sipping ice water. No alcohol for Junior. She was past her morning sickness phase and was probably the most energetic pregnant woman in Delphi. Except for a noticeable bustline increase and a glow about her, her status was still pretty much invisible, though the news had been broadcast long ago.

"You probably need both chairs yourself." Ron blinked at Junior. "You're sitting for two, you know."

"Or three," I said.

"Or four." Del smirked.

Junior's last pregnancy had produced triplets. Her smile in Ron's direction resembled Debbie's—all surface and no emotion. She didn't even bother looking at Del.

"Thanks, but . . ." I said, words trailing off. Junior evidently hadn't seen me come in with Stu, or if she had, she'd attached no significance to it.

"Tory's sitting here," Stu interrupted, smiling. He patted the chair next to him.

I was grateful for the relative darkness, since I could feel a blush creeping up from my neckline as I sat next to Stu and bravely faced the others at the table.

Stu casually draped an arm around my shoulders and raised an eyebrow in a signal that was part command, part plea, to play along.

I manufactured a grin and placed a deliberate hand on Stu's thigh, letting the body language experts translate that any way they wished.

The reaction was immediate and varied. Several at the table, especially those who knew Ron Adler well, grinned. Del just lit another cigarette and poured herself more beer. Junior's jaw dropped, and Debbie Fischbach's eyes widened in surprise.

Behind us, the conversation in the bar actually stopped, and I could hear chairs scraping, and feel necks craning in our direction. Tammy Wynette twanged "D-I-V-O-R-C-E" plaintively from the jukebox. And then, like the Red Sea rushing back together, noise filled the room again.

At the table, conversations hastily began. Stu leaned over and whispered, warm breath in my ear, "That wasn't so awful, now. Was it?"

I shot a small smile in his direction, gave his thigh a squeeze, then sat forward and leaned my elbows on the table.

"Well, well, well, isn't this sweet?" a voice from behind Stu asked.

We all turned.

"Not missing the absent wife much, are we, Stuie?" Doug Fischbach, glass in hand, asked loudly. He'd been talking to a group of teachers sitting at a table a short distance from ours.

Shortish and solidly built, a former football tackle and present high school coach, Doug had not aged as well as his wife. He'd gained at least thirty pounds and had a large round bald spot on the back of his head, which he tried to camouflage by having the rest of his graying hair dyed and permed. His face was meaty and his eyes were squinted and small. His nose and cheeks were traced with tiny red veins, and he was already, and obviously, drunk.

"Use it or lose it, Stu old boy." Doug laughed. "And with the Minnesota Ice Queen, I bet you didn't use it very goddamn often, right?"

I didn't meet anyone's gaze directly, but out of the corner of my eye, I saw Debbie's lips tighten. She reached into a canvas bag on the floor beside her and drew out a sheaf of papers. "We should probably get started," she said with a small, pale smile, ignoring her husband. "We have a lot of work to do tonight."

"Yup, that's right. You betcha." Doug saluted. "The slave driver has spoken, it's time to get to work." He leaned over to me as he made his way around the table and said quietly in my ear, "You want a *really* good time, you just give me a call. I always could fuck old Stuie right into the ground."

Struggling to keep my face even, I scooted closer to Stu, whose warm hand tightened reassuringly on my shoulder. Debbie saw the move and shot an inscrutable look in my direction, then shuffled her papers.

"Since we all know each other, we'll dispense with the normal meeting format and just get started," she said briskly.

"Some of us know each other pretty damn well, I bet," Doug said to Junior, whose withering look would have mortally wounded a sober man.

"How long's your old lady been gone now?" He leaned over and shouted down the length of the table. "Two, three days?"

Stu tensed beside me. I had been so worried about how everyone was going to treat me on this first public appearance that I had forgotten that Stu might get some flak too.

He just tilted his head and stared back at Doug, who had the grace to snort and lower his gaze. Stu's arm stayed in place, around my shoulder.

We began talking all at once, to cover up the awkward pause.

". . . I had an idea for the float . . ."

". . . beer and hot dogs, and probably some chips and stuff for snacks . . ."

". . . what do you think? Fifteen bucks a head sound about . . ."

". . . chicken wire, paper napkins and spray paint . . ."

". . . I got a trailer we can use . . ."

". . . get together for our own little party after the game on Friday . . ."

". . . yeah, but where?"

"At the river of course. The Mighty Jim," Doug said. "Where we had all of our parties. Where else?"

Conversation at the table stopped again. Someone with taste, probably Neil, had punched James Taylor's "Don't Let Me Be Lonely Tonight" on the jukebox, but his sweet voice, for once, did not calm and soothe.

Doug tilted his chair back, enjoying the shocked silence. "What are you all looking at me for? Don't you think the great J. Ross Nelson might enjoy revisiting the scene of her old crimes?"

"Doug, I don't think that's a very good idea," his wife said quietly.

We all stared intently at Doug, wondering what he was up to. No one even blinked when he mentioned Janelle's name.

So much for surprises.

"It's a great fucking idea and you know it," he said fiercely to her. And then to the rest of us, "Whatsa matter, you afraid of ghosts or something?"

"No one's afraid of anything, asshole," Del said firmly.

Doug's fist clenched and he started to stand up, but Ron Adler put a hand on his shoulder, not to hold Doug down, which would have been impossible, but to remind him where he was and who he was threatening.

Across the table, Debbie blanched, but said nothing.

Doug nodded. "All right, we'll just ask Her Royal Highness where she wants to go. I bet her answer will surprise you."

"That's a good idea," Gina said, trying to smooth things over. "We'll ask Janelle. Maybe she *would* like to tour all the old haunts," she ended weakly.

"I'll ask her," Doug declared. "After all, *I'm* the reason she's coming back to Delphi."

He sat back in his chair again and grinned triumphantly, waiting for someone to question or contradict him.

None of us did, though I could see that we all shared the same thought—whether or not Doug was responsible for her coming back, we all thought he was the reason Janelle Ross left Delphi in the first place.

7

Lies of Omission

There being little else to do in the way of fully dressed, coed recreation in eastern South Dakota, meetings are as much a social gathering as an occasion to work toward a shared goal. We take notes and make plans and delegate duties the same as they do in big cities like Fargo or Sioux Falls. And most of the time, we accomplish whatever it was we set out to do.

But the really important stuff has to be dealt with first. Important issues like the weather, whose crops were doing well, and whose kids weren't. And most fascinating: who was going out with whom. The same stuff we hashed over at the cafe, only with an agenda.

I had hoped that the advent of J. Ross Nelson would sufficiently engage everyone's attention, but I underestimated my fellow committee members. As excited as they all were, that tidbit was already old news to most of the people sitting around the long table at Jackson's. Stu and I had hoped to blend into the committee without being noticed, but Dougie Fischbach's needling about the absent Renee only emphasized our "togetherness."

Probably hoping to muffle her obnoxious husband, Deb Fischbach plowed right into the heart of the meeting. Unfortunately, that did little to stop the curious glances shot our way, though everyone did his polite best to ignore Doug and all of his pointed comments to Stu and bragging about Janelle.

"They're not all coming to the reunion," Deb said, "but we've had almost seventy responses to the survey sheet, from our decade alone. The central committee will collate copies from each of the decades into a master book, which can also be ordered, or checked out from Mr. Pascoe's library here in town."

Del and I had each dutifully filled out our info sheets, noting the milestones of our lives as requested, one hundred words or less per milestone. In my case, it wasn't too difficult: I got married, and Nick died. Del's life had been much more colorful, but far less suited to a G-rated questionnaire.

"Each individual committee is responsible for organizing its own data," Deb continued, "so we need someone to type these up, make copies, and assemble them into a booklet. We also need someone to mail booklets to those who won't attend the reunion. Any volunteers?"

We all looked down at the table, or sipped our drinks, waiting for someone, anyone, to step forward.

"I can type them into the computer at church," Junior finally said, to everyone's relief. "Clay won't care if we do it after his office hours." As the Lutheran minister's wife, Junior had no compunction about exploiting the perks of the position. "But I'll need an assistant."

No one said anything. She turned and smiled at me. "Tory can help with the paperwork."

At her end of the table, Del laughed.

Deb raised an eyebrow. "That okay with you, Tory?"

Junior's take-charge personality has always set my teeth on edge, and I would have enjoyed foiling an attempt to co-opt me into being her gofer, but I realized that my cast would restrict any physical labor I could perform for the committee. And the stack of bills in the drawer at the cafe would severely limit any financial contribution I could make.

I suspected Junior's willingness to overlook our past animosity had a lot to do with her curiosity about Stu and me, and as little as I relished the opportunity to work with her on anything, helping to put the 1965–1975 booklet together would give me a chance to do what really interested me: snoop into everyone else's lives.

Deb, Junior, and Del all watched me expectantly.

"Yeah, sure." I sighed, figuring I'd regret the decision, ignoring Junior's smile. She loved getting her own way. "Let me see 'em."

Deb handed the pile of papers down the table and Junior moved next to me.

The rest of the meeting continued as we sifted though the stack, reading random entries.

"This is interesting," I said to the whole table. "Guess which teacher made the biggest impression on the student body?"

"Mr. Kincaid," all the women said in unison.

The men raised their eyebrows.

"I never did see what was so wonderful about Mr. Kincaid," Stu said.

"He was so understanding," I said, and I wasn't even in any of his classes.

"He was so young," Del said.

"And soooo cute," crooned Junior.

"Yeah, the girls liked him, all right," Doug said nastily.

We ignored him.

"He's still pretty cute," Gina, who was a teacher's aide, said. Ron frowned.

"And nice," I added. Hugh Kincaid was an early morning cafe regular.

"And young," Del added. "He's only about five years older than me. He was just out of college when he started teaching at Delphi."

Doug snorted. "What a loser. His whole career wasted in Delphi."

"What does that make you?" Del asked pointedly. "You're back in Delphi too."

"I'm here because the fucking school board begged me to do something with that mess you call a football team."

"And with your obvious leadership qualities, I'm sure you'll do a sterling job," Junior said in her sweetest, most sarcastic voice.

Doug decided he wasn't up to sparring with Junior, which proved the man hadn't pickled all of his brain cells. He turned away, and the rest hurriedly got back to their meeting.

Junior focused on me again.

"Can you type with that thing?" She pointed at my arm, surreptitiously checking out Stu's arm draped across the back of my chair.

"Junior, I couldn't type even before this."

"Well, you can read the stuff to me as I type then," she said, as bossy now as she had been in junior high. "We'll have to work out some sort of cover design too. What do you know about art?"

"Not a thing. I don't even know what I like," I said, pouring the last of the beer into my glass.

"I'll get us another pitcher," Stu said, standing up. He flashed a small, private smile at me. He was making a break for it.

"Here, let me pay," I said, reaching for my purse, wishing I could escape Junior as easily.

"Nah, I'll get it. You keep working." He laughed.

"Get me one while you're at it, Stuie old boy," Doug said. "Lord and water, cloudy."

"Anyone else?" Stu asked. "It's my turn to buy a round anyway."

No one in Delphi ever turned down a free drink, so Stu ambled up to the bar to place the rather large order.

Junior watched Stu's back, and when he was safely out of earshot, she leaned closer and asked, "So how long has this been going on?"

"How long has what been going on?" I asked innocently.

When the affair was being kept carefully under wraps, my only lies were ones of omission—I simply didn't mention to anyone that I was having frequent, enjoyable sex with Stuart McKee.

"You know very well what I mean," she said, exasperated. "How long have you been seeing Stu?"

"I've seen Stu in the cafe almost every day since he moved back to Delphi," I said truthfully.

"What does your mother think about you dating a married man?" Junior asked, trying another tack.

"He's separated," I said, making a small distinction. "And this is our first time out. I don't think you could call it 'dating' yet. Besides, Mother gave up, long ago, trying to influence my romantic decisions."

"Well, after Nick Bauer, who could blame her?" Junior asked the air. Then she turned her thousand-watt smile on Stu, who arrived back at the table with a full pitcher of beer and a tray-carrying waitress in tow. "Would you like to help Tory and me collate reunion book pages?" she asked him.

The notion of sitting in the Lutheran church office with Junior as Stu ran the stapler made me shudder.

"I'm not very good at that kind of stuff," he said diplomatically. "I'll be more useful working on the float and donating giveaways for the parade."

"If you feel that way, then I wouldn't dream of pressuring you," Junior lied.

Stu nodded politely, and then said to me, "Excuse me for a minute, I see someone I have to talk to."

"At least he's getting you out of that trailer," Junior said, watching Stu's back with narrowed eyes. "You've been hibernating ever since Nick died."

"Yes," I said. "It's Stu's good deed for the year. It qualifies him for the Widow Assistance Badge."

"And Tory's eligible for the Horny Abandoned Husband Badge." Doug laughed. He had exceptionally acute hearing for a drunk man.

And a loud voice.

Everyone at our table heard him, and from the set of Stu's shoulders, so did those at the surrounding tables.

"I'll be right back," Deb said suddenly, standing up. "Excuse me." She turned abruptly and walked stiffly toward the bathroom. She had been drinking gin-and-tonics through most of the meeting, but was not, as far as I could tell, affected by the alcohol.

Her husband watched her walk away, eyes flat and lips set. Then Doug stood and stretched, a phony smile pasted on his face.

"Gotta drain the lizard," he announced. "You all be good now." He patted me on the shoulder as he walked around the table and followed his wife.

We sat frozen until both Fischbachs were out of sight, and then, as if on signal, huddled and all started talking at once.

"What's he mean, *he's* the reason she's coming back . . ."

". . . not true, Deb and I both wrote the invitation letter . . ."

". . . that's right, I saw it . . ." Blink, blink.

". . . more likely, he's why she left . . ."

". . . always thought that myself . . ."

"It was that party you know, that started it."

"Or ended it, you mean."

"What party?" That was Junior, playing innocent.

"The party after the homecoming game in 1969," Del said, purposely blowing smoke in Junior's pregnant face. "The one where Deb caught Doug and Janelle Ross doing it in the backseat of Butchie Pendergast's car."

"After which Doug and Janelle disappeared together for three days . . ."

"Well, at least Doug disappeared for three days. Janelle never came back," Ron said, blinking.

"You're a little young for your memory to be going, Junior," I said.

"I remember that Doug was gone for a while," Junior said, "but no one told me anything about sex in cars."

She looked so sincere, I would have believed her, except that I knew better.

"Don't give me any of that shit," Del said. "You were there."

"I was where?"

"At the party when all of that happened," I said.

"No, uh-uh." She shook her head fiercely. "I was just a kid, I didn't go to drinking parties."

"Of course you did," Del said.

"Don't you remember?" Gina Adler asked.

Del raised an eyebrow at me. I shrugged. Junior goes for psychobabble in a big way—maybe she was practicing denial.

"I'm trying to remember what exactly happened after that," someone said.

Among other firsts, that particular evening also included my introduction to alcohol. Though I definitely remembered Junior being there, and I can still replay everything that happened between Nick and me, some of the peripheral events of the evening, and their order, were a little fuzzy.

"Wasn't there a fight?"

"There's always a fight."

"Doug hit Stu," Gina said quietly.

"That's right," I said, remembering. Everyone nodded.

I peeked over my shoulder to see if either Fischbach was back in the bar proper. I spotted Doug across at the far wall, gesturing and talking loudly with a group of teachers.

Stu was sitting with a couple of farmers, drinking another beer and laughing. We lowered our voices.

"Deb was crying and Stu was comforting her, and Doug was jealous." Ron blinked.

"Well," Gina said, "Stu wouldn't have had to comfort Debbie if Doug hadn't been, you know, in the car with Janelle."

"That's right," Del said loudly. "I'm sure Aphrodite can order bulk supplies through the restaurant." She picked up a pen. "The best deal would be for a gross of hot dogs, but that's too many for just our group, don't you think?"

"We aren't gonna need any more than six dozen all told." Ron blinked.

He'd seen Deb emerge unsteadily from the bathroom too.

"She can get baked beans and potato chips and stuff too," I said.

By the time Deb got to the table, we had actually worked out how much food to order.

The rest of the meeting's business was wrapped up speedily. Stu offered to provide caps and pencils and such to toss from the float during the parade. Ron said he'd find a clunker car to tow the float.

"Well, that's about it," Deb said, standing up. "How about we meet two weeks from tonight and compare notes. We should make good progress by then." She gathered her books and looked around for Doug.

"You ready to go?" Stu whispered quietly in my ear.

"More than ready," I said. I'd had enough of smoke and tension and snoopy relatives.

"Good, just give me a minute to pay the tab," Stu said. "and then we can blow this joint."

At the bar, Doug was loudly ordering another round for the teachers. He said something to Stu, who said something quietly to him in reply.

"What's with Junior?" Del asked from behind me. "Does she actually expect us to believe she doesn't remember being at that party?"

"Well, she *was* pretty drunk."

That had been an evening of firsts for Junior too.

"So was everyone else, but none of us have trouble remembering being there. Besides, she didn't *arrive* drunk."

"I know." I shrugged. "But Junior doesn't usually lie. You know how awful that night was for her, she probably doesn't *want* to remember."

"Maybe minister's wives have to convince themselves they never did anything wrong. Or stupid," Del said.

"Well, in Junior's case that wouldn't be hard. She was always such a goody-goody, except for that party, she never did anything she wasn't supposed to."

"Yeah but if she really doesn't remember being there, she doesn't remember how you saved her," Del said darkly. "And she sure as hell doesn't appreciate it."

That was okay by me. I had always assumed that Junior was too embarrassed to bring the subject up.

I was about to tell Del that, when angry voices from behind, and the sound of breaking glass, interrupted us.

Conversation in the bar stopped. We all turned, open-mouthed, to see a furious Doug Fischbach swing a roundhouse punch that connected solidly with Stu's left eye.

Stu dropped like a rock.

8

Loonatics

If the kitchen is the heart of the home, then the McKee heart is definitely loony. At least one of them anyway. It didn't take much guesswork to figure out who had decided to cover every available surface with our neighboring state's bird: loon dishtowels, framed loon prints, loon wallpaper borders, loon candles, carved loons sitting on artfully distressed wooden corner shelves.

The plaid burgundy and forest-green color scheme was aggressively Minnesota Rustic. The few pieces not loon-encrusted were obviously ancient, or made from rough wood and punched tin. Stu now sat at the kitchen table, a piece so purposefully shabby that it must have cost a fortune in a Minneapolis furniture store.

After restraining and calming Doug, both Neil and Ron had offered to drive Stu home from Jackson's. Instead, I brought him home in his own pickup, and intended to walk back to the trailer as soon as he was settled (and I had a chance to peek furtively at the rest of Renee's design scheme).

I'd finally located the refrigerator, nestled inside a large wooden cupboard, successfully camouflaged from the twentieth century. "Here." I handed Stu a loon dishrag wrapped around a couple of ice cubes. "Hold this on your eye. It'll keep the swelling down."

Stu's left eye was swollen almost closed, a bruise just starting to tinge the outer edges purple. "I feel like such an idiot," he said, gingerly touching his face with the ice pack.

"Why?" I asked. "You didn't start the fight."

"I didn't finish it either," he said ruefully. "I can't believe that son of a bitch dropped me with a single punch."

"You weren't expecting it. Reasonable grownups don't settle their differences with their fists." I inspected the rest of his face for damage. "I think you're more upset that you didn't get a chance to swing back at him than you are about being hit."

"I suppose you're right. It wasn't exactly the evening I'd pictured for us. Pretty pitiful first date."

I pulled out a chair and sat at the table, smoothed the hair out of his eyes, and shrugged. "I like playing Florence Nightingale."

He slumped back and closed his other eye. We sat in silence a minute or so. Stu had been too upset, or embarrassed, to talk during the ride to his house. I watched him a moment, then asked the question that had been on my mind for the past hour.

"What set Doug off in the first place?"

He sat motionless. "You know how Doug is."

"He doesn't seem to have changed much from high school," I said. Doug had been a hothead and a bully then too. "So, he just suddenly decided to poke you one in the snotbox, huh?"

"Something like that," Stu said quietly.

I supposed Doug had been saying more unpleasant things about Renee. And me. I am a pacifist by nature, but if I'd had to listen to him much longer, I'd have taken a swing at him myself.

Stu didn't seem to want to elaborate.

"You think the superintendent will come down on him for this?" I asked. "Everyone's gonna hear about it."

"Yeah, I know. But he's got the football team winning for the first time in a decade. They'll just be relieved that my eye didn't hurt his hand."

"I heard he's rough on the kids too, yelling and shoving and things like that," I said, repeating some cafe gossip. "Especially Cameron."

Cameron Fischbach was Doug and Debbie's oldest son, due to start his senior year in high school. He was the team's star tackle.

"Every coach is rough on every kid, Tory," Stu said, smiling, opening his functional eye again. "And it's especially hard to be the coach's son. But believe me, none of 'em care as long as they win."

"If you say so," I said doubtfully. I've never been a coach worshipper, and could not imagine why anyone would risk public humiliation and abuse for the greater glory of a team. "Well, I'm just glad that Presley is still in junior high. I bet Doug self-destructs before he makes it to high school."

"We can only hope," Stu said. "My face can't take many more meetings with Doug Fischbach."

I sat back in the chair, looked up, and noticed, for the first time, that the loon on the corner shelf above the table was really a telephone. A coiled cord snaked out from under its tail, and a small red light flashed on and off in the base.

"I think you have a call," I said to Stu. "Your bird is blinking."

He craned his head up and squinted at the phone. "Damn answering machines are more trouble than they're worth." Without standing, he reached overhead and punched a button.

I heard the soft whirring of the tape rewinding and the click as it prepared to play.

"Hi Dad," a small voice said. "Mommy said I could call you, but you're not home. I got to go swimming today and we're gonna go buy school clothes tomorrow. I really love it here—there's lots to do. Mom says to tell you to call if you get home early. Love you."

It was Stu's five-year-old son, Walton—who was also living in Minnesota with Stu's wife. I'd only met him once, and managed to forget his existence most of the time.

Without looking at me, Stu said, "I suppose I better call them back. It's not that late."

"That's okay, I gotta go anyway." I slung my purse over my shoulder. "I have to work tomorrow morning." I turned to leave.

"Don't go," Stu said softly. "Please, this'll just take a minute. Go check out the stereo in the living room—there's a surprise for you."

He grinned carefully, an adorable middle-aged man with the beginnings of a terrific shiner.

I sighed. I truly hadn't planned to spend the night with Stu. A first like that deserved some sort of ceremony—champagne and peignoirs. I didn't even have a toothbrush with me.

"Del will worry if I don't come home," I said, though Del would in all probability not even notice. I eyed him critically. "You don't look like you're up to any extracurricular activity."

"I'm not," he said ruefully, "but sometimes it's just nice to snuggle."

"You sound like Ann Landers," I said, considering the logistics. I'd have to get up at least an hour earlier than usual and sneak back to the trailer to shower and change for work, where the hot topic was certain to be the fracas between Doug and Stu.

"Please," he said again softly, giving me an irresistible puppy-dog look.

"Okay," I said. "Make your phone call."

He grinned like a small boy. "Good. Check out the stereo first. The bathroom and bedroom are just down the hallway. I'll be there quick as I can."

The living room was decorated in Early Lake Cabin, with dark wood paneling and sturdy tweed upholstered furniture. I had to search a little to find the stereo, which was inside a large oak wardrobe. On top was an assortment of James Taylor cassettes still in their store wrappers.

I was touched almost to the point of tears. There was no overlap in our musical tastes—Stu actually liked country; I loved James Taylor and assumed everyone felt the same way.

In the kitchen, I could hear Stu's soft voice, making easy conversation with his son. Not wanting to eavesdrop, especially if he was going to talk to Renee, I unwrapped and plugged *Gorilla* into the slot, then wandered down the dark hallway in search of the master bedroom to the strains of "Mexico."

In contrast to the other rooms, the bedroom was distinctly feminine—white on white everything—from the bedspread to the lampshades to the scattered area rugs on the oak plank floor. This was the kind of bedroom I would choose, if I had unlimited resources and any skill at combining accessories. Renee's good taste here made me hate the room on sight.

Since Nicky's death, I had forced myself to be unsurprised by waking up alone, to be resigned to the fact that there wasn't another warm body in bed next to me, to sleep without the gentle rhythm of someone else's breathing, someone else's legs to press cold toes against.

Unfortunately, I had schooled myself too thoroughly to forget the lesson quickly. Especially in this room, where the undiluted essence of Renee was too strong.

After his phone call, Stu came in, undressed, apologized for "pooping out," kissed me softly, and fell immediately asleep. The cold pack, which he'd been holding on his eye, had slipped and was slowly melting on the sheet between us. I was wide awake.

I snuggled closer to Stu, enjoying the presence of another body in the same bed, even if it was this particular bed. Carefully, listening for a change in his breathing, I slipped a leg over his, and an arm around his middle.

"Night honey," Stu exhaled with another snore.

The sight of Dougie throwing a punch at Stu had triggered my fuzzy memory. I lay next to Stu, trying to sort it out.

We were at the river, of course, in the dark after the 1969 homecoming game. A small bonfire had almost burned out, though it threw sparks into the night air with every breeze. Couples were everywhere, scattered on blankets, talking, laughing, drinking, making out, and maybe even doing a little more than that.

Someone had plugged an eight-track tape of Tommy James and the Shondells into a car stereo, and "Crystal Blue Persuasion" echoed into the darkness over the rushing river sounds.

"Here," Nicky'd said, handing me a Coke bottle, "see what you think of this."

"Thanks." I took a sip; it had a sweet, kind of cherry taste. "What is it?"

We had spread a blanket by some bushes. Nick was sitting next to me, his arm settled around my shoulders. I was having a wonderful time being at an actual party with Nick Bauer. Even more, I was enjoying being seen at a party with Nick Bauer.

"Sloe gin and Coke." He grinned. "You can't get drunk on it, it's too sweet." He took a swig directly from a half-pint.

"Okay," I said, and chugged as much as I could without choking. I knew that sloe gin was alcohol, and I also knew that no matter what it tasted like, if it was alcohol, it would get me drunk.

I just didn't care.

With his sparkling brown eyes, curly dark hair, and infectious smile, Nick Bauer was the cutest boy I'd ever seen. And if he wanted me to get drunk with him, that was fine by me.

"Gimme some more," I said, handing the empty bottle back to Nicky, who grinned widely.

"Sure thing," he said, standing up. "Let me get another Coke from the car."

Del, wearing snug jeans and a poor-boy sweater pulled tight over her hips, sat down on the blanket next to me and watched Nick's retreating back.

"Go slow on that stuff, it'll sneak up on you," she warned, fiddling with the yarn bows tied around her pigtails. "And so will Nicky, if you don't watch out."

"Good," I said. "That's what I'm hoping for."

"Tough talk for a virgin," she said, peering at my face. "Are you sure you know what you're doing?"

"Nope," I said, "but I intend to find out." My mother had dutifully impressed on me that all boys wanted "one thing only," but so far no boy had wanted anything from me. If handsome Nick Bauer did, I was determined to grab him before he changed his mind. Besides, I wanted to know if Jacqueline Susann had her facts straight.

"Suit yourself." She shrugged, standing again. An older, out-of-town boy had stepped from the bushes and was obviously waiting for Del to join him. "Be careful, kid."

"Sure," I said.

"What did she want?" Nicky asked, handing me another full bottle and watching Del walk away.

"Nothing much," I said. "She was just trying to talk me out of sleeping with you."

The sloe gin had obviously hit me.

"I see," he said, looking at the bonfire. "And did it work?"

"Nope."

He laughed out loud and turned to me, face close to mine, and said, "You know, I really like you. We're gonna be great together."

"I sincerely hope so," I said, a little dizzy, and not just from the liquor.

Then he kissed me, a wonderful first kiss, the kind that First Kiss Dreams are made of.

I was leaning into the kiss, when a shout and a cry on the other side of the bonfire interrupted us.

Damn, I thought, though I would never have said that out loud. Not in 1969 anyway.

Nick pulled away. Damn again.

A crowd had gathered around an old two-door Impala, cheering and hooting.

"What's going on?" I asked, irritated by the interruption just when things were getting interesting.

"I don't know," he said over his shoulder. "I'm gonna check it out. I'll be right back."

As far as I could tell, the crowd had discovered a couple in the backseat of a car. That probably wouldn't have caused an uproar by itself, if there hadn't been a blond girl crying and shouting, beating hysterically on the hood.

Trying to get a better view, I stood up just in time to see Stu McKee, in a burgundy and black letterman's jacket, pull the weeping Debbie Wetzler off the car and into his arms, where she collapsed, sobbing.

The car door swung open and Doug Fischbach emerged, zipping his jeans. Even from a distance, I could see the nasty look on his face. He stormed around to the front of the car and shouted something unintelligible to Debbie, who buried her face further in Stu's shoulder.

Doug grabbed Debbie's arm and roughly pulled her away. Stu tried to interfere, and through the crowd, I saw Doug take a swing at Stu.

Nick ran back to the blanket. "Come on, you gotta see this." He pulled me up.

"Who was in the car with Dougie?" I asked, panting to keep up.

"That's the good part." He grinned.

From the other side of the car, the door opened and the backseat folded forward. Janelle Ross, hair and clothes disheveled, emerged.

I was flabbergasted.

"But Doug and Debbie have been going together for ages," I protested. The literary world of Jacqueline Susann had not prepared me for real-life infidelities.

"Yeah." Nick grinned salaciously. "But that's not the best part."

We worked our way to the front of the crowd, though the fight appeared to be over already. Stu was sitting in the dirt, and Doug and Debbie were shouting at each other. Janelle leaned against the car and watched the scene impassively.

"The best part," Nick continued, "was what Doug said to Stu just before he hit him."

"And what was that?" I'd asked.

"Tory?" a sleepy voice said.

The bonfire and the river and 1969 faded away. I remembered I was in bed with Stu McKee, in his loon-filled house.

"Sorry," I whispered. "Did I wake you?" I must have been talking out loud.

"Sorta," he said. "I was wondering if you were going to do anything about that . . ."

"Do anything about what?" I asked, confused.

"That," he said, pointedly. "Or should I just roll over and go back to sleep?"

I realized, with equal parts humor and horror, that as I'd been reminiscing about Nick and Stu and that kegger, I had unconsciously slipped my hand inside the waistband of Stu's shorts.

And woke him up.

"Sorry about that." I laughed softly. "Didn't realize what I was doing."

"That's okay," he said. "I was starting to enjoy it."

"I thought you were too tired for extracurriculars."

"I must have been wrong," he said. "I do believe we could give it a shot."

So we rolled together, a pair of loonies in a pure white bedroom, finding warmth and comfort in each other.

9

Hot Topics

THE NEXT DAY

I can remember the first time I saw J. Ross Nelson on the big screen. The uproar after her disappearance with Doug Fischbach was intense and predictable. His reappearance in the middle of the week following homecoming, accompanied by a smirk, but not by the 1969 homecoming queen, overshadowed schoolyard interest in the drowning of Butchie Pendergast. Wild stories surfaced everywhere.

Some thought Janelle had just run away. Others favored a kidnapping theory. One kid swore he'd seen her hitchhiking. He said she got into a semi-rig with Oregon license plates.

Occasionally a Midwest girl disappeared from school for a four- or five-month period, only to reappear as though nothing had happened—in those days, unmarried teenagers rarely kept their babies. But Del and I, and the rest of the cheerleaders, knew that was not the case.

Speculation reached its wildest point when a vocal segment of the student body became convinced that Janelle had actually drowned along with Butchie. The school administration tackled the problem in typical 1969 fashion.

Mr. Voltzman addressed the school over the loudspeaker. "It has come to my attention," he'd droned, "that a few irresponsible students have been spreading rumors around our school and in town. I am deeply disappointed in those gossiping students."

He went on to say that Mr. and Mrs. Ross had given him permission to announce that Janelle had transferred to another high school for personal reasons. He ended the announcement with a specific threat to suspend any students caught spreading stories to the contrary.

I don't suppose it was so much the threat as the fact that in Delphi there is always some new scandal to focus the attention, but interest in the whereabouts of Janelle Ross eventually died down.

I had forgotten her entirely when, a few years later, at the drive-in in Redfield, a familiar tenor of voice, and a certain tilt of head, caused me to put aside my tub of buttered popcorn and pay attention to the movie.

"Nick," I'd said, elbowing him in the ribs, "look at that girl."

"I am." He grinned.

"No, not her, the one with her blouse on, toward the back of the room."

"Which one?"

"The one who's making out with the frat guy, over on the couch. He's trying to put his hand up her shirt."

"Just searching for sweet Delphi." Nick laughed, making a grab for me.

"Yeah, her," I said. "Doesn't she look familiar to you?"

"Who cares?" he said. "I never look above the chin."

"Well, check out her face for a minute. Quick before she gets killed."

It was one of those schlock horror movies where only the virgin survived to make the sequel.

Nicky shrugged. "She sorta looks familiar."

"Sorta," I said emphatically. "Doesn't she look exactly like Janelle Ross?"

"Well. Now that you mention it . . ."

"That *is* Janelle Ross," I said, amazed.

I had been convinced, Nick less so. Her character was dismembered a couple of scenes later, so the last we saw of her that night was her severed head resting on a shelf in an open refrigerator, next to a bowl of potato salad.

There were no VCRs in those days, and the projectionist flatly refused to rewind the closing credits, so I was never able to prove that Janelle was in that movie. Of course, no one believed me, and after a while Nick joined the opposition, declaring that he'd never thought it was Janelle, anyway.

Vindication came a few months later. An article appeared in the Aberdeen paper heralding the advent of a new Hollywood star—a former South Dakotan (Delphi was not mentioned) whose on-screen name was J. Ross Nelson.

"I forget," Rhonda said, wolfing down one of the soyburgers she had badgered Aphrodite into putting on the menu. "Where did the 'Nelson' part come from?"

"She probably made it up." Ron blinked.

"I think Nelson was Janelle's husband's last name," I said, squinting to remember old magazine profiles. "She's divorced now, but he was her agent or manager or something like that, when she first started acting."

I had expected the mess between Doug and Stu to be the main discussion topic in the cafe. And it had caused some excited speculation and conjecture. I'd had to endure ribbing, and a couple of salacious blinks from Ron, but for the most part, attention focused on the reemergence of J. Ross Nelson. Though her appearance was supposed to be a parade surprise, word got out immediately, and conversation buzzed excitedly with the news.

"I hear that Crystal at the store is going to order in all of her movies so we can rent them." Ron blinked. "There's a couple I can't wait to see."

There had been a civic lifting of the nose about

Janelle's career—she didn't acknowledge Delphi, and Delphi was happy to return the favor. Of course, we secretly kept track of her all along. Now that she was coming home, there was a public and avid interest in her oeuvre.

"It's kinda exciting to see someone you knew, up on the silver screen," Ron continued.

"You just want to see someone you knew *naked* on the silver screen," Del said scornfully.

Though there was a certain amount of nudity (most of it Janelle's) in every movie she made, and her roles were, at least at first, mostly horizontal, the movies themselves weren't porn. There were monster flicks, a few slasher movies, a couple of weepers, and a solid list of B action/adventures and made-for-TV movies. Janelle had built up a creditable resume of Other Woman, Best Friend, Trusty Secretary, and Murdered Rape Victim roles.

And in recent years, she had started to get some good notices in movies of a slightly higher caliber. Her voice had matured into a pleasant throatiness, and her looks and figure had survived the ensuing decades.

"She's pretty buff for an old chick," Rhonda said.

"Best body money can buy," Del said.

"No, she must have done it all naturally," Rhonda insisted. "She has one of those nutrition and exercise tapes out."

"Sure." Ron blinked. "Boobs of Steel."

"Boobs of Silicone, you mean," Del said.

"You think she's been enhanced?" I asked.

"Give me a break, Tory," Del said, sitting next to Ron in his booth. "We're all the same age—do we look like her?"

"I *never* looked like her," I said. "And they can do wonders with lighting and makeup."

"Well, good lighting isn't going to make her chest larger than it was in high school."

Aphrodite set out a roasted chicken and mashed potato special on the counter for me to pick up.

"So, is all this as fascinating to you teachers as it is to the rest of us?" I asked Hugh Kincaid as I set his dinner in front of him. "Or are you above the fray?"

"Of course we're fascinated." He laughed. "We're human, aren't we?"

Though he was older, his blond hair was faded, and, like the rest of us, he was a bit heavier, the years had been kind to Mr. Kincaid, who was still the cutest teacher in the school. He sometimes slipped away to the cafe for lunch, rather than to his little house across from the school.

The place was nearly empty, except for regulars, who were perfectly capable of getting their own coffee refills if Del and Rhonda were too busy discussing body implants to notice empty cups. I sat in the booth opposite Hugh.

"The general consensus has teachers being some sort of cross between Superman and space alien," I said. "No one thinks you're really human."

"Oh, we're human all right," he said. "Human enough to be glad we have to supervise that damn parade so we can see our very own movie star in person. We're just as curious as everyone else about what she's been doing."

"I always thought you guys knew," I said, leaning back. "I figured that the teachers and administration had the whole scoop and just refused to pass the juicy stuff along to the students."

"Nope," he said, neatly buttering a bun. He pointed at me with his knife. "Well, I take that back. I can't speak for the administration. If any of the teachers knew what really happened, they sure didn't tell me."

"I always thought that Mr. Voltzman knew more than he let on," I said. "He seemed to have slightly more than the usual principal's interest in her."

"That's why they spell it P-A-L, you know." Hugh laughed.

"You think there was something going on between them?" This was a delicious bit of speculation—something that had never occurred to me before.

Hugh was slightly horrified. "No," he said, "no, no, no. That's not what I meant at all. The year that Janelle disappeared was only my second year of teaching, and I still had all of my ideals intact. It came as a great shock to me to discover just how much interest the teachers and the administration showed in the personal lives of the students.

"You kids would go about messing up your own lives, going steady, breaking up, getting pregnant, cheating on each other, and never realize that we teachers knew almost as much about the intimate details as you did."

"I don't know why the school should be any different than the rest of Delphi," I said. "We're all interested in everyone else's intimate details. Besides, it would probably surprise you to know how much the students know about the teachers' lives too."

It could not have been easy being the cutest teacher in school for more than a quarter of a century. For years, Hugh Kincaid's every social move was watched—we were thrilled when he finally became engaged to a teacher from another school district, we despaired over the incredibly long engagement, and we mourned the speedy demise of the eventual marriage. These days, Mr. Kincaid was either the most discreet, or the loneliest, guy in town. Opinion was evenly divided.

"Well, it takes some of the focus off me when the nicest widowed waitress in town is seen in public with a recently separated businessman." He grinned. "So how does Casa McKee look?"

"Like L.L. Bean exploded," I said, grinning. "I shouldn't be surprised that someone told you already."

"This *is* Delphi after all," he said. "But I didn't have to be told. I saw you two together last night."

"You were there?" I asked. "At the bar?"

"Yup, sitting in the back. We got the full scoop from our inebriated football coach."

"Jesus," I said, blowing my bangs off my forehead. "He's lucky Stu doesn't bring charges against him."

"There were plenty of witnesses who saw Doug take the first, and only, swing," Hugh said. "And several of us who heard what he said to Stu just beforehand."

"Oh?" I asked, curious. Stu hadn't wanted to talk about

Doug at all, either last night or early this morning, in bed. Or later at the cafe when he came in for breakfast and faced the full community interrogation with a spectacular shiner.

"What did Doug say?"

"It was baffling, really," Hugh said, remembering. "I missed the first part of the conversation, but I did hear Doug's last comment before he decked Stu. It was not the sort of question one would expect to precede an altercation. He said, with an expletive or two deleted, 'You never change, do you?' "

10

Saving Junior

I don't know if there were other computers that Junior could have used to enter and collate the reunion information sheets, but dragging me into her husband's office at the Lutheran church served an even deeper purpose than committee work.

Junior's proselytizing soul was in continual unrest over my steadfast disinterest in being Saved. She had slowly learned that I would not listen to any sort of preaching, so just getting me on church property constituted a victory for her.

Settled in her hometown, in a marriage that seemed to be both happy and stable, Junior turned her considerable energy toward taming the world and making it conform to her view of Right and Proper. Junior's undivided attention could be both intense and uncomfortable.

She had not entirely given up on me.

I stood at a long table that was strategically placed under a large mural made of little glass pieces mortared into an asymmetrical cross, sorting out reunion sheets according to year of graduation. Certain that Lutheran conversion rays were being beamed on me from all directions, I reflected on the fact that Junior almost always got her way.

Named Juanita Doreen II, a burden imposed by my Aunt Juanita Doreen the First, Junior saddled her oldest daughter, young Juanita Doreen III, in the same fashion. Thankfully, in my family, there was room for only one Juanita, so eight-year-old Tres and her mother made do with lifelong nicknames.

Junior sat at the computer, a bewildering array of beige boxes that beeped and whirred alarmingly. She squinted at the screen, clicking keys, muttering to herself a little.

"Tory, come here and tell me what you think," she commanded, her eyes not leaving the screen. "Do you like this font?"

I walked behind the desk, careful to keep Junior and her fetus between me and any stray computer radiation, and peered at the monitor.

"Sure," I said. "What's a font?"

She turned and looked up at me. "You *are* joking, aren't you?"

"Junior, how would I know anything about computers?" I asked. "It's not as though the trailer, or the cafe, is crawling with them."

"You know what I say to that," she said primly.

Yeah, I knew. Her spiel had three main points: Go back to school, do something with your life, and (most important) get away from Del.

"I can't afford any major life changes right now," I said.

"Aren't you getting any help with that?" She pointed at my cast.

"Not enough," I said. I'm going to be paying off that particular adventure the rest of my life."

"You know," she said, "we could do a fund-raiser for you."

The thought of having to smile bravely through a Tory Bauer Bake Sale or a Tory Bauer Benefit Dance was numbing.

"No thanks," I said. The price for accepting that kind of assistance would be far too high. In exchange for financial aid, I'd be at the beck and call of every civic function, board, and committee. "I appreciate the thought, but I'd rather not owe anything to Delphi."

"I wasn't talking about the city," Junior said tartly. "I was talking about the church. We're supposed to be in the charity business."

"It'd be just a tad hypocritical of me to accept money from a church I have no intention of joining," I replied wearily.

"There's such a thing as being too independent," she said, turning back to the computer. "Everyone needs help sometime."

Unfortunately, Junior's notion of help always involved her being in control. But now that we'd had the obligatory lecture, we could actually get down to work.

"I thought we'd use a Wizard to design a form and enter the information into a database which will sort the entries out alphabetically, according to year, and insert the data into the word processing program. We'll format one person per page with justified double columns, frame and insert any scanned BMP graphic files we have, and print out the pages individually. Of course, we'll have to set up a header and reformat the pagination system to fit the master book, but we can do that later. And we'll probably have to meet again to enter any late arrivals into the database. How's that sound?"

"Great," I said, mystified. "All I have to do is read the stuff out loud as you type, right?"

"Yes. You *can* manage that, can't you?"

"I'll give it the Delphi High try," I said, quoting an old cheer.

We established a routine quickly, and worked our way through the stacks faster than I had expected. Junior was a remarkably fast and accurate typist.

"The computer has a spellchecker," she explained, sighing, when I complimented her on her typing. "It fixes the typos for me automatically."

I pretended to know that and continued on. Only an hour into the ordeal and we were up to 1969 already.

"Maiden name Franklin, first name Lisa, current married name Hauck-Robertson," I droned, before realizing whose info sheet I was reading. "Whoa, that's Lisa Franklin. Her last name is Hauck-Robertson? What'd she do, marry a hyphen?"

"I wouldn't know," Junior said. "Come on, I have to get home and cook supper soon. We don't have time for idle speculation."

"You're no fun at all," I mumbled. I raised the sheet again, and read off Lisa Franklin Hauck-Robertson's professional stats. "She's coming to the reunion," I said, unable to resist another digression. "And like almost every other female from 1968 on, she remembers Mr. Kincaid fondly. 'Really helped me through some thorny adolescent perturbations' she says. And that's an exact quote. I've never met anyone who used the word *perturbation* in a sentence before. Remind me to avoid Lisa completely."

"Tory, can we please get on with it?"

"Yeah, yeah, yeah. McKee, Stuart," I read, then stopped short. He'd listed Renee as his wife. I reminded myself that she *was* still his wife, though I was irrationally grumpy about having to say her name out loud.

For once, Junior resisted the urge to comment. She typed steadily as I read. "Messner, Gerald, married for the fourth time, wife Monique, occupation, 'owner of a small software firm in Northwest Washington that develops antivirus programs and security protocols for networked systems,'" I read. "Must be a good market for security protocols these days, he has a second home in France. What do you want to bet that Monique is under twenty-five and never wears a bra?"

Junior didn't answer.

We continued on, Junior doggedly typing through my digressions. She had no comment about anyone's fondness for Mr. Kincaid. She had no interest in the triumphs and tragedies that I found so fascinating. She didn't care where anyone lived or how many kids they had.

She was intensely serious about getting the job done, and that was starting to irritate me.

"Maiden name Ross, first name Janelle, married name

Nelson, occupation, vampire, hobby, sucking the blood of innocent children after sundown," I said.

Junior typed every word into the computer.

"Okay, that's it," I said, setting the rest of the pages down. "What is the matter with you? You're not paying any attention at all. Reread that last entry."

Angrily, she deleted a couple of lines. "I suppose you think that was funny," she said.

"Well, actually, yes," I said. "But that's not the point. You're typing away like we're curing cancer. Lighten up a little."

"I have a lot on my mind," she said, facing the screen again, hands in her lap.

"About the baby? Or babies?" I added hopefully. We were all dying to know.

"No, everything there is fine," she said softly. She was quiet a moment, and then said, "It's this reunion thing. It's got everyone remembering that homecoming party again."

"That's understandable—Janelle is coming back to town and the party was the last time anyone saw her. Is it bringing up some old bad memories for you?"

"No, that's the problem," she said, facing me. "It isn't bringing up any memories at all. That whole night is a total blank. I've been trying for days, and I can't conjure up a single image from it."

"Really? Nothing at all?"

"Not a thing," she said. "Too many people have told me I was there to doubt it, but I'm too embarrassed to ask any of them what happened. You were there, did you see me?"

"Uh, yeah," I said. "I took you home. Actually Del, Nick, and I took you home. To my house. We had to; your mother would have killed me first, and then you."

"I'm going to be sorry I asked this." Junior moaned. "But will you tell me what I did that was so bad that I evidently blocked it out of my memory completely?"

"I don't think *you* did anything—you were just a junior high kid at a high school party. Unfortunately, you ran into Butchie Pendergast."

Junior leaned back in the office chair, closed her eyes, and waited for me to tell her the story.

A widely grinning Nick, who threw no punches of his own but enjoyed everyone else's, had been telling me the "best part" about Dougie Fischbach popping Stu McKee, when I heard a familiar giggle behind a clump of Russian olive trees.

Debbie Wetzler held a rag to Stu McKee's bleeding nose. Janelle impassively rearranged her hair and clothing, while Lisa Franklin chattered in her ear. Watching the scene from the dim outskirts, Del stood leaning back against her date. His arms circled her waist and he nuzzled her neck.

Nick's arm was around my shoulders, he leaned close and said, "Shall we get back to what we were doing before we were so rudely interrupted?"

Unfortunately I heard the giggle again, over the strains of "You've Made Me So Very Happy" from the Blood, Sweat and Tears eight-track cassette that was playing.

"In a minute," I said to Nicky. "There's something I need to do first."

"Sure. Go behind a bush anywhere. I won't peek." He grinned.

"I'll be right back," I said, not bothering to correct his mistaken impression, and ducked around the trees to find exactly what I was afraid I'd find—thirteen-year-old, eighth-grade Junior and her best friend Gina Eisenbiesz, wearing jeans, flowered blouses, and windbreakers, sitting cross-legged on the ground. They passed a bottle of Coke back and forth, laughing their fool heads off.

"God, Junior," I said, disgusted. "What are *you* doing here?"

"Let's see." She leaned against Gina's shoulder and pretended to think. "Looks like we're just sitting here on the ground. What are you doing here?" She handed the bottle back to Gina, who took a long drink.

"Give me that," I said sternly. "What are you drinking?"

"No," Junior said, trying to stand up, but not making it on the first try, mostly because she had a bottle in one hand and the other clutched protectively over her heart. "We're juss havin' a little pop. An' you can't have any. Go get your own. Shoo! Go away." She sat back down with a plop. Both girls collapsed in giggles.

"Jesus Christ, Junior," I said, "you're drunk!"

"I am not," she said slowly, this time getting all the way to her feet. "And you aren't supposed to take the Lord's name in vain. It's blasphemy."

I wasn't about to be lectured by a drunken eighth-grader. By then, Gina had also struggled unsteadily upright. They both stood there, trying their hardest to look innocent and sober.

They managed the innocent part.

"How did you get here anyway?" I demanded.

"With Lila," Gina explained. "But she told us to stay out of sight and not get into any trouble."

"And your mother *let* your sister bring you to a party?" I asked, flabbergasted.

"No, no, no . . ." Gina said.

"See, it's like this," Junior interrupted, shaking her finger at the air. "I'm supposed to be staying overnight with Gina at her house. An' *she's* supposed to be staying overnight at mine. That way both of our mothers think—"

"I get it already," I interrupted. "But how did you talk Lila into bringing you here?"

Lila Eisenbiesz was not in Del's league, but she was still plenty wild, and I did not imagine she'd saddled herself with a pair of children willingly.

"We said we'd tell Mom she was going to a drinking party if she didn't let us come too," Gina added seriously.

"And who gave you the booze?"

"What booze?" Junior asked, wide-eyed.

"We can't tell," Gina said at the same time. "We promised."

"Hey in there, are you all right?" Nick hollered from the other side of the bush.

"Yeah, come over here. I got a little problem."

"Who are the groovy chicks?" Nick asked with a grin.

"These are not 'groovy chicks,'" I said. "These are junior high kids and one of 'em is my cousin. They shouldn't be here."

"They do seem to be a little drunkish," he said, laughing.

Gina and Junior stood together, swaying gently in the evening breeze.

"Yes, I know," I said. "Will you do me a favor? You know Lila Eisenbiesz? The other one is her sister. Lila's around somewhere, will you find her and bring her back here? She has to take these two home before they get in real trouble. It's not safe."

"You're right, some of the guys here can be real jerks," Nick said. "Sure I know Lila—just sit tight and I'll be right back."

I glared at Junior and Gina, who giggled in response, and settled in to wait for Nicky's return. Maybe the evening wouldn't be a total waste—maybe Lila would take these two brats home and smuggle them into bed without anyone finding out about it.

I hummed along to Marvin Gaye in serious make-out mode. Behind another set of bushes, I could hear the unmistakable sound of someone throwing up. Others were laughing and talking.

The music changed again, this time to "In-A-Gadda-Da-Vida." The extended version. By the time the song ended, it finally occurred to me that it was taking Nicky an awfully long time to get back.

I peeked around the bushes but could not see Nick. I decided to go look for him.

"You two," I said as sternly as I could, "stay here. Don't move. I'll be right back."

"Yeah, Tory, sure," Junior swore, hand solemnly over her heart.

"I mean it," I said over my shoulder.

"Hokay," they said.

Someone had added a couple of logs to the bonfire, which blazed brightly. Trying not to disturb anyone, I searched for Nicky but could not find him. Quite a few kids had gone home already.

Finally, on a blanket off to the side, I spotted Del, who emphatically did not appreciate the interruption.

"What the hell do you want?" she asked angrily, sitting up and pulling her sweater down.

"Do you know where Lila Eisenbiesz might be?" I asked, profoundly embarrassed. I explained the situation to her.

"Lila, huh?" she said. She rubbed her forehead for a second, then turned to the boy, who also was not pleased with the interruption. "Hold tight, honey, I'll be right back."

He grumbled, but Del got up and helped me search.

A José Feliciano album warbled from the car stereo into the night. By the end of the third song, we still had not located Nicky. I figured we'd better check on the juvenile delinquents.

"Are you two about ready to go?" I asked, rounding the tree clump.

No one was there.

"Shit," I said, probably the first time I'd ever sworn out loud.

"Forget about Nick," Del said, "it's more important to find those kids. They're drunk and you know what the river is like this year."

Suddenly I was scared. Junior was a pain in the butt, but I did not want to go to her funeral. We searched frantically, getting closer and closer to the water.

"Over here," I heard Del say. "I hear something."

We were near the bank of the James now. Heavy fall rains had swollen the usually placid, meandering creek into something dark and dangerous. Especially for flatland kids who knew nothing about currents.

I pushed ahead of Del onto the grassy bank by the oxbow and stopped dead in my tracks.

"Hey Doug," Butchie Pendergast yelled over his shoulder without looking around, "smell my finger. It's full of eighth-grader."

Butchie was naked, his clothes in a pile away from the

creek bank. He was bent over a small form that was on hands and knees, retching. He turned around, grinning evilly, holding a hand out to us.

He grinned even wider when he saw we weren't Doug. Unashamed, he stood up and faced us. Explicit as she was, Jacqueline Susann had left red, ugly, and bobbing out of her descriptions.

It was my first erection sighting. Gina's first too, from the glassy-eyed look on her slack-jawed face.

She was sitting a little way from Butchie and the vomiting Junior. An empty lime vodka bottle lay on the grass next to Gina. Both girls were nude.

"Wanna join the party, girls?" Butchie asked. "I got enough to go around."

"You creep!" Del shouted. "These are just kids—and they're drunk. They don't know what they're doing."

"Yeah," he said, "but you do. Come on, let's give them a demonstration."

"Not if you were the last man on earth," Del spat.

"Yeah, well, you and your fat friend don't interest me anyway." He was unsteady on his feet. I realized that he was drunk too.

While Del was arguing with the horrible Butchie, I was trying to stuff a limp Junior into her clothes. She and Gina were drunk to the point of passing out. Thanks to Butchie, I'm sure.

I finally found my voice. "You should go to jail for this."

"What for?" taunted Butchie, who had pulled his jeans on again. "I didn't do anything to them. Your precious virgins are safe. We were just going skinny-dipping—no law against that."

I didn't know if there was a law against skinny-dipping or not, but I knew he was right. Butchie was a football star—I was a nobody and Del was the school bad girl. Both Gina and Junior were too drunk to give an accurate account of the evening. No one would believe us.

Furious, I rushed at Butchie, who was a good six inches taller and fifty pounds heavier than me, intending to defend the honor of a cousin I didn't even like.

Del intercepted me, which was a good thing, I guess. Butchie just laughed.

"What's going on here?" a voice behind us asked.

We turned to see Janelle Ross stepping delicately onto the creek bank.

"Butch, are you being an ass again?" she asked, tilting her head.

"Nope." He grinned. "The fat girl wants to go a round or two with me. It should be fun."

"You don't want to fight with Tory." Janelle surveyed the scene. "And you don't want to play around with any little girls."

I was amazed she remembered my name.

"Well, I still wanna go swimming." He pouted. "Wanna go with me?"

"We'll see," she said to him. To me she said, "Get the little ones out of here. I'll take care of Butchie."

I inhaled deeply. "And that was the last time I spoke to Janelle Ross."

"Jesus Christ," Junior said in her office chair, taking the Lord's name in vain. "No wonder I didn't want to remember that."

"You and Gina spent the rest of the night in our bathroom, puking. Mother and I cleaned up after you."

"And you never told my mother," Junior said to herself. Then to me she said, "And neither you nor Del ever said a word about it to me. Ever."

I let Junior contemplate that.

"How did we get home?" Junior asked, finally.

"Del and I found Nick, and he drove us," I said tersely. "Somewhere along the way, we picked up Ron Adler, and Gina spent the whole drive leaning on his shoulder, calling him her hero. I guess she thought he rescued her."

I didn't mention that we'd found Nick in Lila Eisenbiesz's car. With Lila. An occurrence that was to happen at regular intervals throughout our marriage.

As I said to Ron in the cafe, I should have taken that night as an omen.

11

Long Live the King

MID-SEPTEMBER, HOMECOMING WEEK

I suppose there are historians who would swear that the celebration of homecoming is firmly rooted in the fine American tradition of high school competitive sports. But I think there is something more ancient and elemental going on, something that would be familiar to the Druids or Celts.

Each autumn, after harvest season, pre-Christian societies would throw themselves one last bash before the onslaught of winter. Feasts were prepared, games were played, and the village's most beautiful virgin and handsomest young man were named the harvest queen and king. Following a week of revelry and ritual, the comely young couple, fed, pampered, and worshipped, were led to an altar and promptly sacrificed, both in thanks for the previous season's bounty and in hopes of a good year to follow.

While we don't grind the bones of the chosen and sprinkle them on our fields for good luck anymore (and not just because virginity is in short supply), the similarities between the ancient rituals and our modern American celebrations are striking.

Both are a signal of the final passing of summer. Both honor the young, strong, and beautiful. And both require the entire community to bear witness, to mark in our minds and hearts another rite of passage.

"Do I hafta go?" Del whined.

"Of course, Mom," Presley said around a mouthful of cheeseburger, eating his supper as he walked through the cool evening air. "It's like required or something."

We were on our way from the cafe to the school to watch the naming of the homecoming royalty. Though I'd planned to wait for Stu, he had been held up. So I went ahead with Del, Rhonda, and Presley, who, I assumed, honored us with his presence only because he hadn't seen Rhonda for a couple of weeks.

"The strength of any community lies in its support structure," Rhonda said, "and an outward show of that support, such as tonight's coronation ceremony, is important to the tribe as a whole."

Rhonda was back in Delphi for the evening, from Aberdeen where she'd recently begun college classes. I suspected she was taking intro to sociology along with her required freshman courses.

"The group dynamic demands a certain degree of participation and sacrifice from each member," she said, expertly rebraiding her hair as she walked. "As a citizen, it's your duty to contribute." She was walking in front of us, with Presley.

"Is that what they teach in college these days?" Del asked me. "Communism?"

"Yeah," I said. "From each according to his nostalgia for high school, to each according to the number of votes he gets."

"You can laugh," Rhonda said over her shoulder, "but you know I'm right. It's important to support your community."

"Hey, you don't have to preach to me," I said. "I intend to applaud dutifully at every appropriate moment. With both hands." I pointed to my shrunken, but healed and cast-free, right arm.

"Don't let her fool you," Del said. "Tory's only going because she has a date."

"She'd go anyway," Presley said, pushing the rest of his burger into an already full mouth. "Tory always goes to these things."

"I know, she's a real pillar of the community," Del said, carefully eyeing her son. "Why are you so gung ho?"

"Coach Fischbach's orders." Presley, who had recently turned thirteen, shrugged. "I guess he wants to keep an eye on us or something. Being's we're on curfew and all."

Too small and wiry to be much use as a tackle or guard, Pres had tried out for the junior high football team as a kicker, and had surprised everyone with his strength and accuracy. He came home from practice bruised, exhausted, and elated by the romance of playing football.

"I thought Doug was the high school coach," I said to Presley.

"He is. But since we practice on the same field as the varsity, Coach Fischbach oversees our workouts too. He wants to make sure we aren't ruined by last year's fag coaching."

"Presley!" Rhonda and I said together, disgusted.

"Sorry." He laughed, raising his hands in self-defense. "I'm only quoting."

"Well, you should tell your coach that such derogatory terms are absolutely inappropriate from a leadership figure," Rhonda said, hands on hips.

"Oh yeah, I could do that all right," Pres said, "if I didn't mind blowing my nose out of my ear."

"He better not hit you," Del said, bridling. Though it was a little slow to surface, her maternal instinct was alive and thriving.

"He doesn't pay any attention to me at all, except to call me a pansy kicker," Pres said. "But he knocked Cameron right off his feet this afternoon. For missing a pass."

"He smacked his own kid, in front of everyone?" I was shocked.

"Well, I didn't see it, but I sure heard him yelling and screaming. And Cameron was on the ground the whole time, until Coach told him to hit the showers."

"I'm so glad we invited such a charming man back into our midst," I said.

"The team is 4 and 0. Whatever he's doing, it must be the right thing." Pres shrugged.

I tried to explain to Presley that, Vince Lombardi notwithstanding, winning was *not* the only thing. Unfortunately, it was me against the entire athletic mindset—a losing battle right from the start. Or it would have been, if he'd heard me at all. But at the stairs to the school he took off, with a backhand wave, to join friends.

"Come home right after the ceremony," Del hollered after him. "You have homework to do. Remember your curfew." She watched her son disappear into the school. "I guess we should be glad he deigned to walk with us at all," Del said.

"It's just his age," Rhonda said wisely. "Don't take it personally. He'll have to leave home before he realizes how important all this stuff is."

I elbowed Del in the ribs. "Wasn't it just a while ago that Rhonda here couldn't understand what the reunion fuss was all about?"

"Amazing what a couple weeks at a university can do for you," Del agreed.

"You know what they say," Rhonda said, ignoring our teasing. "Home is the place where they gotta let you in if you want to go there." She wrinkled her forehead in concentration. "Or something like that, anyway."

"Are you taking intro to lit this semester too?" I asked.

"Yeah, how'd you know?"

"Lucky guess." I laughed, but Rhonda had spotted a couple of friends waving frantically from across the auditorium, and was already making her way over to them.

The noise level was high, with school kids calling and laughing and goofing off in the lower section, adults finding their seats in the upper bleachers, and the band tuning up on stage behind the heavy burgundy matinee curtains.

"Where do you want to sit?" Del asked.

"Up there somewhere, I suppose," I said, surveying the bleachers, waving at acquaintances, searching for enough room for three.

"When is Prince Charming due to arrive, anyway?" Del asked as we worked our way up the steps.

"Pretty quick," I said. "He had some stuff to finish first, and then he'll be right over."

"Hmm," Del said noncommittally, picking her way delicately to an empty space in the middle of a row in what used to be the junior section, right behind Ron and Gina Adler.

Del was being uncharacteristically diplomatic. Stu had been outwardly cheerful, though distracted, lately. Something was on his mind, and I was afraid to ask what. Considering the amount of time he spent on phone calls to and from Minnesota, it wasn't hard to guess. I tried not to think about it.

"Hi, Tory," Gina twisted around and said, ignoring Del completely. "God, this brings back memories, doesn't it?"

"Sure does." Her husband blinked. And then he blinked some more when Del reached down and patted him on the shoulder.

Gina glared at him, and then asked me, "Where's Stu?"

I was amazed how quickly Delphi had adjusted to the notion of Stu and me as a couple. I was equally amazed at how soon the notion changed from "couple" to "joined at the hip."

"She's meeting him here," Del said, though Gina hadn't been talking to her.

"There he is now," Ron said, pointing down at the railing between the upper and lower bleachers just as the house lights dimmed and the curtain rose onstage.

"You know, for some reason, I have been thinking about the year Stu ran for homecoming king," Gina said quietly to me as we all stood for the "Star Spangled

Banner" as performed by the combined Delphi High School Band and Chorus.

"That's because Janelle is coming back, and we've all been reminded of that year," I whispered. But it wasn't just that. Stu's acknowledged relationship with me put him in Delphi's public eye. And in Delphi, when you're being talked about, your entire history is up for grabs.

People were remembering me. They were remembering Nicky. They were remembering Stu and Janelle. And Doug. And Butchie Pendergast.

For the zillionth time in the past twenty-five-plus years, Hugh Kincaid skillfully led the chorus through the rest of the National Anthem as Stu made his way into our row and stood next to me.

"Sorry I'm late," he said in my ear as the band swung into a subdued version of the school song—the one they played for serious occasions.

"No problem," I said. "What's up?"

We sat again. "Nothing serious. Walton was having a problem in school, and Renee wanted me to talk to him about it, that's all."

"Oh," I said as the current principal stepped to the microphone and opened the evening's ceremonies.

I could not, in good conscience, fault Stu for being a good father, or for being available to his small son by phone. But I marveled at how often these familial mini-crises occurred at the exact moment Stu was expected elsewhere.

"Have you noticed," Gina whispered to me over her shoulder, as the principal droned on, "that it doesn't matter what year, or which kids are running—the ceremony is always exactly the same? That's what makes it so special."

"That's also what makes it so boring," Del whispered back.

And allowing for differences in hairstyle and gown length, both Del and Gina were right. The coronation itself, the congratulatory squeals of the losing girls, the tears of the winner, and the manly squashing of the king's triumphant grin were each year interchangeable. And each year identically predictable.

"We're going to proceed a little differently this year," the principal said, surprising everyone. "I'd like to call Coach Fischbach to the stage if I may."

Doug had been leaning against the door jamb, arms crossed and scowling, scanning the lower bleachers for errant football players. He scowled even more when he realized that he was expected to join the principal onstage.

"Let's have a round of applause for the first coach in twenty-five years to lead the Delphi football team to a winning season," the principal said as Doug mounted the side stairs to the stage.

The crowd rose to its feet in a spontaneous ovation. No one seemed to care about Doug's personality failings—his drinking, his temper, his fondness for certain sexual epithets. They only wanted to salvage Delphi's battered athletic honor with a winning season.

Doug faced the cheering crowd with a hard smile, performed a small bow, and turned to leave the stage.

"Not so fast, Coach Fischbach." The principal grinned. "Though we appreciate what you've done for our town and team, we'd like to ask one more favor, if we may."

The crowd quieted, and Doug stood on stage, not smiling. I saw Debbie Fischbach, down in the first row of the upper bleachers. Even from my vantage, I could see the tension in her shoulders as she watched her husband onstage.

The principal signaled to his right, and from behind the curtain, Hugh Kincaid wheeled out a cart bearing two tall velvet and gold crowns, two tasseled velvet capes, and a bouquet of roses. Smiling, he wheeled the cart past the principal and stopped next to Doug, who remained stone-faced in front of a semicircle of formally dressed young royalty candidates.

"I would like to ask Coach Fischbach to do the honor of crowning our new homecoming court," the principal announced with a wide smile.

Doug stood frozen, obviously surprised, and not

pleased. In the audience, whispering grew as the crowd excitedly discussed the change in routine. Hugh handed one crown and one cape to a reluctant Doug.

"I present to you Delphi's new homecoming king," the principal said grandly, pausing for effect. "Cameron Fischbach."

The crowd erupted in wild applause, delighted that a former homecoming king and current winning football coach was about to crown his own son as the new homecoming king.

Unfortunately, the father and son in question were neither amused nor delighted. Doug awkwardly fastened the cape around Cameron's shoulders and placed the tall crown on his head. Years of drinking had hardened and aged Doug's features into a caricature of his former self, a fact made obvious as he stood next to his young, handsome, unsmiling son. I wondered if anyone, except Debbie Fischbach, noticed that they did not look at, or say anything to, each other.

Ignoring his father, Cameron faced the audience, smiled, and stepped forward to applause as the principal theatrically announced the name of the new homecoming queen.

"Her Majesty, Sandra Saunders."

The whole left side of the bleachers burst into enthusiastic applause as Rhonda's large family congratulated themselves, and each other, on the coronation of the Saunderses' youngest girl.

"They're all here," Gina said excitedly, ticking off the many Saunders sisters. "Glenda, Linda, and Brenda are back home, and Chanda brought her new baby."

"Where's Rhonda?" I asked, trying to spot her in the crowd.

"Over there," Del said, pointing mischievously.

I followed Del's finger, prepared to flash an all-right signal in her direction. But my hand froze at my side as Rhonda threw her arms around the neck of a slightly surprised Neil Pascoe and planted a decidedly unplatonic kiss on his lips, and then turned to me and waved in excitement.

12

I See London, I See France

LATER THAT WEEK

For some reason, six months of heat and humidity creates a kind of amnesia in us. We forget that hot and sweaty is always followed by cold and damp, which is followed by just plain cold.

Unless of course, the farmers want a stretch of a specific kind of weather to keep them out of bankruptcy. Then we can count on September providing just the opposite.

If the fields need a cold snap to finish the soybeans, we get a heat wave. If the corn is dry enough to start combining, we get a three-day downpour. If crops need a couple more dry, frost-free weeks, we can absolutely count on three feet of snow to liven our existence. And no matter how the field work is progressing, we want good weather during homecoming week.

As usual, September was having the last laugh.

"Jesus Christ," Ron Adler exclaimed at the cafe door, rubbing his shoulders and shaking his wet hair. "Can you believe this shit?"

"Been pouring all day," Del said over her shoulder as

she carried plates of meatloaf, mashed potatoes, and green beans to a table full of old farts.

"We got fifty hundredths in less than fifteen minutes," one of them said.

"Over to my place we had an inch and twenty-five before ten last night," said another.

"This ain't nothin' but a drizzle," the first one said, mouth full. "Back in '49, we had us some real rain. Makes this look dry."

"Wasn't either '49. The year you're thinkin' of is '52."

"Hey Tory," Del teased, "what year did it rain so much that Aphrodite got mildew on her cigarettes?

"That would have been '72," I said, pulling a date out of the air. "She got so mad she actually said a whole sentence."

Standing over the grill, Aphrodite growled.

"You're wrong," said an old fart seriously. "It was '69. The same year that kid drowned in the river. Remember how high the water was that fall?"

"Damn near that high now," said another.

"It will be if it doesn't quit raining." Ron blinked.

"Better warn the kids not to be having any parties by the river this year, unless they want to lose another one."

"I doubt the kids would listen," I said.

"Mine sure as hell wouldn't. It was after midnight before he got in last night. Maybe he went for a swim. He left wet clothes all over the living room." Del sighed.

"What was he doing out so late?" I asked. "And on a school night?"

"I don't know. But if he shows his face in here, we're gonna find out," Del said, as the door opened and half a dozen out-of-towners all came in laughing and shaking like wet dogs.

For some reason, heavy rains bring out the wanderlust in South Dakotans. Farmers pop in because they can't do any field work, and it's too early for a beer. And the sightseers, marveling at standing water in the roadside ditches, figure they might as well eat out as at home.

Add to that the fact that kids who wouldn't set foot in the cafe during the summer make it a point to sneak away from school for a hamburger and fries, and you have some idea what a rainy day noon hour is like. The cafe was full, and Del and I were having a hard time keeping up with the crowd by ourselves.

"I miss Rhonda," Del said, trying to juggle several plates at once.

I frowned, remembering that Rhonda had kissed Neil. And then wondered why in the hell that memory made me frown. I missed Rhonda too.

"Selfish of her to get a higher education and leave us to handle the starving masses alone," I said.

"Want some help?" asked an out-of-towner sitting at a table by herself. "I can take plates around. I have experience."

"Thanks," Del said to her, surprised, "but we can handle it."

Del raised an eyebrow at me—this was a new one, customers offering to help the waitresses.

The door slammed open again and Presley stomped in, soaked to the skin.

"Don't you even have the sense to put on a jacket?" Del asked, exasperated as Pres sat at the counter. "You're going to catch a cold."

"Jeez, Mom," Pres said, looking around furtively, to see if anyone overheard his mother. "I can take care of myself." He looked to me for support, "Right, Tory?"

"Sorry. I'm with your mom on this one," I said. "You want me on your side, you gotta get in before midnight on a school night."

"Oh ho, out raising hell, huh kid?" Ron asked.

"No," Pres said hastily. "We were just riding around."

"Who's 'we'?" Del asked sweetly.

"Just some guys," he said vaguely.

"And what were you and 'some guys' doing out so late?" Del continued.

"Nothin', just riding around."

"I didn't think any of your bunch could drive yet," I said severely. Fourteen-year-olds can get driver's licenses in South Dakota. Fortunately, neither Presley nor his friends was fourteen.

"I wasn't with them," he mumbled.

"Bet I can guess what he was doing." Ron blinked. Pres shot him a sharp look.

"Me too," I said. "How about you, Mom?"

"I have a pretty good idea," Del said. "Hope you had a good time because you're grounded the rest of the week."

"Mom, come on," Pres whined. "It's not that big a deal. Everyone does it. They did it when you were in school too."

"He's got a point, you know," Ron said.

"You stay out of it," Del said to Ron. "And you"—she pointed at Pres—"should know better."

"Ah, what's the big deal. So I rode around with a couple of football players and we pantsed a few guys. So what?"

You might think that all of our small-town ceremonies and rituals are charming, but you'd be wrong. In among the coronations and parades and cheering and camaraderie lies another tradition that is not so heartwarming.

"You helped kidnap and transport boys out into the country, in the pouring rain, forcibly removed their pants, and made them walk back to town in the dark, in their underwear," I said to the ceiling. "What could be wrong with that?"

"Oh come on, Tory." Ron blinked. "*Kidnap* is a little strong, isn't it?"

"Did any of the boys volunteer to get in the car with you?" I asked Presley.

"Well, no."

"Sounds like the definition of *kidnap* to me," I said.

"You remember what it's like," Pres appealed to Ron. "It's all in fun, no one gets hurt."

"Well . . ." Blink.

"Well, nothing," Del interrupted. "Fraternities get kicked out of colleges for less than that. And what were you doing with high schoolers anyway?"

"They like me." Pres smiled. "And they're cool guys. I just rode with them."

During homecoming week, the bigger boys would take the underclassmen a couple of miles out into the country, remove their pants, and leave them to walk back to town in their underwear, or worse. Butchie Pendergast and Doug Fischbach used to take the underwear as well. And shoes and socks.

Or they did, until one very irate mother complained to the principal, who then had no choice but to threaten anyone caught pantsing with suspension. After that, the poor kid got to keep his pants, and the bloody nose Butchie gave him, along with a warning about whining to Mommy.

With that exception, no one's actually been hurt, though the potential always seemed enormous to me. And, for the most part, the boys (both the pantsers and the pantsees) seemed to get a charge out of the whole thing. Which I found disturbing.

"Doesn't anyone think all this is a little weird?" I asked.

"What do you mean?" Ron asked darkly.

"Well," I proceeded carefully. It was one thing to trash a tradition; it was another to suggest what I was about to suggest. "Don't you think psychologists would be a little intrigued by an institutionalized ritual involving the removal of male clothing by other males?"

They all caught my drift and vehemently denied the supposition.

"Jesus Christ, Tory, of course not." Blink, blink.

"Don't be ridiculous," Del said, irritated. "It's just stupid kids being stupid kids."

"That's what I was trying to say." Pres grinned. "Thanks, Tory." He grabbed his hamburger and ducked out the door into the rain before anyone could say anything else.

"Yeah, thanks Tory," Del said, disgusted. "Thanks for distracting the conversation so the little shit could escape."

"I wasn't trying to distract anyone," I said, eating one of Presley's leftover French fries. "I meant what I said."

"You can't really think there's anything . . ." Ron swallowed. Most midwestern men cannot bring themselves to say the "H" word in general conversation. ". . . strange about pantsing, do you?"

"Yes, I think it's definitely a latent homosexuality kind of thing," I said. "Rhonda's taking psychology too. I'm sure she'll agree."

My opinion offended them both so much that they had no choice but to ignore me completely. The cafe had emptied again. Del slid in with Ron, lit a cigarette, and puffed furiously. They talked quietly, heads together. Neither looked in my direction.

I sorted through the tickets in my pocket, checking them against the few remaining customers.

"Was everything okay?" I asked the woman who had offered assistance to Del earlier.

"It was great," she said, smoothing damp brown hair back off her forehead. "It's been a long time since I ate in a place like this."

"Wish I could say that," I said, laughing. "But it wouldn't matter even if it had been years. A century from now, this place would still be the same."

"You're right, Tory," she said, tilting her head, a small smile playing on her lips.

Waitresses make lousy eyewitnesses. We rarely notice relevant details about anyone but locals, but something in this woman's voice made me look at her. I mean, really look at her, for the first time.

She grinned widely, locking lively brown eyes with mine. "Delphi never changes."

13

The Once and Future Queen

I've never been a fan of the novels of Danielle Steele or Judith Krantz—the thin, rich, beautiful problems of thin, rich, beautiful people don't interest me much unless their last names happen to be Kennedy or Windsor (though in the latter case, neither thin nor beautiful has much to do with the matter).

If you were to go by the printed page, you might easily come to the conclusion that fully 98 percent of the human race is drop-dead gorgeous. And further, that physical beauty is a common occurrence rather than a rare and lucky coinciding of good genes and cultural perception.

Maybe in California, where bikini-clad nymphets roller-blade past steroidal hulks, such exotic creatures intermix freely with lesser mortals. But here in South Dakota, where the heads are bald, the eyes wrinkled, and the hips large, beautiful people are rare indeed. We corn-fed, beer-drinking, shit-kicking midwesterners tend to think all those pretty faces are mostly a product of smoke and mirrors. Industrial Light and Make-Up.

At least we do until we come face to face with the real thing.

I stared, openmouthed, at the woman who had been sitting alone at a back table for the past hour, eating her meatloaf and mashed potatoes, unnoticed.

"Welcome home, uh . . ." I paused. How did one address a Hollywood actress? Miss Nelson? J.? I racked my brain for what I'd called her in high school, only to realize that during our two encounters, I'd never called her anything. "Janelle."

I had a sudden panic. Had we talked about her as she sat in the cafe?

"I wondered if you'd recognize me," J. Ross Nelson said. "I didn't exactly dress for the occasion."

With shoulder-length fine brown hair pulled back into a simple ponytail, and wearing a faded and frayed sweatshirt and jeans, she looked like an ordinary, if attractive, woman, going about her ordinary, everyday errands. No one you'd give a second glance to, until she looked up.

Then you saw the uncommonly fine bone structure; perfectly shaped, intelligent eyes; and clear luminous skin that glowed with good health—the kind of artlessly natural look that can only be achieved by the expert application of very expensive cosmetics.

"I don't think anyone expected you to show up until parade day," I said nervously. I'd never talked to a real live movie star before. "And they'll be expecting . . . well . . . you know."

"A grand entrance," Janelle said, smiling. "I know. There's time enough for that sort of nonsense. I thought I'd sneak in today and take a peek at the joint. Walk around. You know, indulge in a little hometown nostalgia."

"Nasty weather for a walking tour of your childhood," I said, looking out the window at the continuing downpour.

I laid her ticket on the table beside the empty plate. I was suddenly self-conscious, exceedingly aware of my mousy hair, unglamorous life, and bulging thighs. Feeling like an intruder on her incognito visit, I turned to leave.

"I thought I'd hang out here awhile and wait for the rain to let up," Janelle said. "Things are pretty quiet now, can you sit and talk for a bit?"

For the second time in my life, I was astonished to realize that Janelle Ross was including me in her plans. I shot a look over my shoulder at Del and Ron, who were still engrossed in conversation. The cafe had cleared out entirely, and there was no reason, this time, to decline the invitation.

Janelle caught my look and leaned over the table and said quietly, "That's Delphine Bauer, isn't it? And Ronnie Adler, right? No mistaking those blinks. I remember them both. Are they married to each other? Is that nice-looking boy who was in here a while ago their son?"

I chuckled, trying to imagine Del and Ron's reaction to those questions. "Yes, yes, no, and emphatically no," I said. "The boy is Del's son, but she never married. Ron Adler is married to Gina Eisenbiesz, one of the people organizing the reunion. They have two kids about junior high age. Gina was a couple of years younger than me—you might not remember her."

I doubted Janelle would connect the memory of a very young, naked, inebriated Gina by the river with the briskly efficient reunion coordinator.

Janelle sat back in her chair, grinning. "I knew this would be a good place to start—if you want the inside scoop, go to the local diner. Waitresses know everything."

I tried to remember if any of her published bios had mentioned being a waitress, or if she had only played one on TV.

"Who else is still here?" she asked.

"Well, Mr. Kincaid," I said, wondering if she'd remember any of her teachers.

"No! After all this time? Is he still handsome? Is he married? Divorced? Available?"

You can take the girl out of Delphi, but you can't take Delphi out of the girl. For a person used to hanging out with the glitterati, Ms. J. Ross Nelson was avidly interested in the minute details of everyone's lives. Just like the rest of us.

As we talked, I gradually forgot that she was famous. I even forgot that she had been the prettiest and most intimidating girl in my high school, a former cheerleader, ex-homecoming queen, and definitely not my good friend. We were just a couple of women of the same general age and background, rehashing old acquaintances.

"There was a guy in school," Janelle said, "kind of short, kind of wild, dark-haired and really cute. I can't remember his name, but I think he was related to Delphine. Is he still around? I'd love to see him again."

He would have loved seeing you too, I thought. "You mean Nicky Bauer," I said quietly.

"Yeah, that's him." She paused, seeing my expression. "What, is he in jail? Fat and bald? A jerk?"

"No, a little less exciting than that," I said. "He's dead."

"That's too bad," Janelle said with genuine regret. "Do you know any of the details?"

"Unfortunately," I said, sighing, "I know all of the details. I was married to him at the time."

"Oh, Tory, I'm so sorry. What happened?"

"He was in a one-car roll-over. He and his passenger were both killed."

"Passenger?"

"Yeah, a college cheerleader," I said. I figured I might as well tell her; she'd hear it from someone else anyway.

"Like that, was it?" she said sympathetically. "It's probably not much of a consolation, but my ex-husband had roving body parts too, though I wasn't lucky enough for the creep to die on me. Benny's still around, haunting me wherever I go."

It was an indication of my own prejudices that I was genuinely surprised that beautiful women's husbands might be unfaithful. I guess I thought that being pretty, popular, and successful provided insulation against life's nastier surprises.

After a quiet moment, Janelle continued, with a commiserating smile, "So, who else is around?"

"Well, you probably know that Debbie Wetzler and

Doug Fischbach are married to each other, and living in Delphi again," I said. I was reluctant to remind her of old bad memories, but since Doug and Debbie both claimed to be responsible for bringing Janelle back, I figured the names themselves wouldn't come as a shock.

"Can you give me directions to their house? I want to look them up before I go back to Aberdeen tonight. I have a room up there," she explained nonchalantly.

I told her how to get to the Fischbachs, wondering if I should warn her about Doug's attitude and behavior. But Doug had always been a loudmouthed braggart and a bully. Now he was just an older, drunk, loudmouthed braggart. None of which would be a surprise to Janelle if her memory was in working condition.

"Their oldest son was just named this year's homecoming king," I said. "The principal had Doug crown him."

"How touching," Janelle said. "Is the kid like Doug?"

"He seems okay," I said neutrally. Presley thought the sun rose and set on Cameron Fischbach's shoulders. And though Presley's sense of adventure occasionally got him into trouble, his people sense was usually on target. I was willing to accept his assessment of Cameron.

Janelle sat quietly for a minute, looking out the window. "The rain's letting up. I think I'm ready to venture on." She gathered her things together.

I stood, making the standard farewells, though I wasn't just being polite. I'd enjoyed our chat. Discovering the real J. Ross Nelson had been a pleasure.

I walked her to the till, glancing into the kitchen on the way. Aphrodite, who missed nothing, placed a hand over her heart and bowed slightly in Janelle's direction.

While I rang up the ticket, Janelle said in a soft voice, sorting through her wallet, "Oh yes, there's one more person I'd like to see. Maybe you can help."

The careless, offhand tone of her voice did not fool me.

"Do you remember Stuart McKee? Handsome football player. He was a senior in my class. Nice guy," she said, not looking up. "Is he still around?"

My good feeling was replaced by a sinking sensation. If

famous, beautiful, rich, and thin J. Ross Nelson was interested in Stu, what chance did I have?

"Sure," I said. Careless, offhand. "He works with his dad in the Feed and Seed Store, right across the street." I pointed for her benefit.

She beamed a genuine smile at me. "Thanks. It was great talking to you. See you at the football game, and at the reunion on Saturday."

I watched her tiptoe gingerly around the puddles on Delphi's wet and muddy main drag. As she walked, she shook her hair back, straightened her shoulders, and slung the strap of a canvas bag over one shoulder.

"You were sure yakking it up," Del said, as Janelle picked her way across the street. "Who was that?"

Del was observant, but not as observant as Aphrodite.

I thought about telling her. And then I considered calling half a dozen others. I could probably work up a good-size crowd within fifteen minutes. But autograph hounds and picture snappers would only delay the inevitable.

"Just someone who used to be from around here," I said as Janelle disappeared into the store.

14

Deb's Bombshell

I would have preferred to spend a quiet evening, home alone. I could have listened to some music (James Taylor, of course), folded a basket of clothes, reread *The Murder of Roger Ackroyd,* or gotten falling-down drunk. All to avoid reflecting on the new wrinkle in my own personal horizon—the one involving interest expressed by a Hollywood actress in my married boyfriend.

Obviously, the problem wasn't the movie star, who just happened to be an old acquaintance of the aforementioned fellow. The problem was the guy himself.

Or more specifically, his marriage.

As far as the rest of Delphi was concerned, Stu was the victim, and his search for comfort and solace was perfectly justified. Only Del and Neil knew that was not exactly the case.

Del and Neil and Stu. And me. We all knew the timing of the affair wasn't exactly blameless, a fact I tried to forget. I assumed the relationship was solid, though a nagging voice in the back of my head would periodically remind me that a man who ignored his own vows was not likely to pay strict attention to my assumptions.

Or as Del, who has done ample research on the subject, would say, "A man who cheats on his wife will sure as hell fuck around on his girlfriend."

The pragmatic side of my brain knew that Del was probably right. The rest didn't even want to think about it. Given my druthers, I would have done anything, including cleaning bathrooms at the cafe, to avoid the subject of Stuart McKee and J. Ross Nelson.

Unfortunately, with homecoming on Friday, and the All-School Reunion the day after, committee meetings were frantic and mandatory. The bar was buzzing, the lights were low, and the smoke and noise levels were high, as assorted groups gathered around to finish projects in time for the parade and party.

"I heard she was in town today," Gina Adler said, handing a sheaf of paper to me.

She had to speak loudly to be heard over the jukebox whining about an achy-breaky heart.

I picked up a small stack of pages from the pile in front of me and handed the bundle down the table to Junior, who added her own section. I hummed along with the music. I despised that particular singer, and song, but at least it drowned out some of the conversation.

At our table, everyone had some kind of grudge against at least one other person. Gina and Del were not exactly friends. Del and Junior were outright enemies. Generally, Junior drove me batshit. In a genuine emergency, we would have forgotten our differences entirely. In this case, we back-burnered grievances and worked together, almost pleasantly.

"Has the sighting been confirmed by any reliable sources?" Junior asked Gina. She placed a computer-generated cover design on top and handed her stack to Del, who had been pressed into service to run the stapler.

We were collating our portion of the reunion book. Junior had decided to wait until the last minute to staple the booklets together in order to include any information sheets that straggled in after the deadline.

"Well, Ronnie said that Willard Hausvik saw her walking past the school," Gina said, picking up more papers and starting the process over again. "He said she was all by herself, but she peeked in the windows, and then went inside."

Junior snorted. She counted neither Ron Adler nor Willard Hausvik as a reliable source.

"Well if she was around today, I sure as hell didn't see her," Del said.

I hummed some more. Del narrowed her eyes at me. She knows what I think of Billy Ray Cyrus.

"You're talking about *her,* aren't you?" Rhonda asked over Del's shoulder, monitoring our progress and eavesdropping. She seemed to spend more time in Delphi than at college these days. "Mom saw her too, driving all over town in a fancy car. Wearing some sort of designer outfit and drinking Perrier. Do you suppose they get to keep the clothes they wear in movies? I bet she has a closet full of Gucci dresses."

"I think Gucci only makes purses and shoes," Gina said, frowning. "And scarves."

"Whatever." Rhonda shrugged, heading back to her own table and committee, carrying a full pitcher of beer. "Mom said she was being real snooty, not talking to anyone."

"She seemed very nice in her letters," Gina said firmly. "She said she was looking forward to coming back to Delphi and couldn't wait for the reunion. That doesn't sound snooty to me."

I stayed out of the conversation, concentrating on picking up the right number of pages for each booklet. Reluctant to discuss the ramifications of Janelle's request for Stu's location, I hadn't told anyone, not even Neil, that I had actually talked to her.

"So," Junior said, straightening up with the heel of her hand pressed into the small of her back. She was showing now, quite a bit in fact, fueling rumors of another multiple birth. "How's Stu today? Where is he, anyway?"

"Tory's not his social secretary, you know," Del said,

pounding on the stapler. Putting aside little differences did not preclude sarcastic needling.

"He's working on the float tonight," I said hastily, not wanting to listen to Del and Junior bicker about Stu, whom I'd expected to meet after the float work was done. He'd phoned the bar thirty minutes earlier with an excuse about being tired, and would I mind if he went straight home instead.

Yesterday, I would have wondered if he was going to spend another couple of hours on the phone with Renee. Now a long chat with the estranged wife seemed preferable to a reunion with J. Ross Nelson.

"What do you think, Tory?" Gina asked.

"Huh?" I looked up to find the entire table watching me. "Sorry, I was listening to the music." I hummed a couple more bars.

"Gina asked what you think will happen when Doug Fischbach and Janelle get back together," Junior snapped.

"So what do you think?" Gina repeated. "About Doug and Janelle? And Debbie, since she's not here right now?"

"Yeah," Del said, looking around, "where did madam chairman and hubby dear go, anyway? I expected her to stick around, giving orders and lording over everyone."

"They went to check out the float builders," Gina said, still efficiently stacking booklet pages as she talked. Though Gina was a co-chair of the committee, she seemed to be the one doing the real work. "Said she'd be back soon. To keep us on track."

Del mumbled something rude.

I turned Gina's question back to her, an efficient way to avoid answering it myself. "What do you think? You and Debbie wrote all the letters together. How did she feel about inviting Janelle back here?"

"To be honest, I couldn't tell," Gina said, frowning. "I mean, she seemed fine about it. We both thought it would turn the reunion into something special. But Doug was always around, reminding us to write to her, and for some reason, Debbie does whatever Doug tells her to do."

"Well, if he whacks his kid around during football practice, who knows what he does to his wife," I said darkly.

"I don't know that she seemed afraid of him," Gina said thoughtfully. "And if she was upset about all that stuff from the past, she never let on."

Junior was quiet. Unless the idle gossip originates with her, she has no interest in it. We continued assembling booklets and refilling our drinks. I'd started out with Diet Coke and then switched to Tom Collinses. I was on my third, studiously forgetting anything about boyfriends or movie stars. Lee Greenwood was even starting to sound good.

"Behold, the grand entrance," Del said under her breath as Debbie Fischbach stepped into the bar alone, shaking her umbrella outside the door.

Debbie, swathed neck to ankle in a glitzy sweatsuit unsuited to any activity that involved actual sweat, nodded in our direction. She stopped at the bar, bought herself a drink, and then paused momentarily at almost every table. Each time her greeting was followed by excited chatter and surreptitious looks our way.

"Something's going on," Gina said, watching Debbie work the room. "She's making a point of talking to everyone in the bar."

Debbie schmoozed her way around to Rhonda and her crew. Neil had come in earlier, waved at me, and then sat next to Rhonda. As Debbie talked, he shot an odd look my way.

"Are they talking about us?" Gina asked.

"I hardly think we'd make an interesting topic of conversation for the whole bar," Junior said, frowning.

"Unless Debbie got hold of an ultrasound and is busy announcing that you're having quints, I'd have to agree," Del said wickedly.

Junior ignored her.

"They're still doing it," Gina said uneasily. "I don't think I like this."

I didn't like it either. At each of the tables on Debbie's journey, heads had turned, all right. But they weren't just looking in our direction. They were looking at me specifically.

I considered making a break for the bathroom, but it was too late. Debbie had finally arrived at our table.

"Hello ladies, you're progressing nicely," she said, pretending to inspect the pile of finished reunion booklets. She smiled brightly, but her eyes had a flat glitter and her cheeks a high color.

From a distance, Debbie looked young and perky. Up close, the lines showed under heavy makeup. I did not mistake her smile for the genuine article.

Del, in a preemptive strike, said, "Well, Deb, how about we cut right through the crap and you tell us why you're wearing that shit-eating grin."

"Certainly," Debbie said, taking time to sip.

I felt the whole bar watching us.

"As you know, I've been with our hardworking float builders for the past hour," Debbie said, looking at everyone but me.

"And were they progressing well too?" Junior asked sarcastically. Pregnant women are not noted for their patience.

Neither are waitresses.

"For chrissake, just spit it out," Del said.

"Oh all right," Debbie said, "since you're so impatient." She sipped again, and then smiled. "Janelle Ross is here in Delphi," she said with a flourish.

"Tell us something we don't already know," Del said. "People have been talking about that all night."

"Yes, I had forgotten how quickly stories spread in a small town," Debbie said, patting me on the shoulder. "And who could blame our Tory for telling everyone that she spent an hour chatting in the cafe with Delphi's most famous native?"

I would have defended myself against Debbie's smarmy accusation, but was stopped by Del's stony face. If she had been irritated with me this afternoon for disparaging our hometown traditions, she was really going to be pissed that I had deliberately withheld such juicy news. Silently, I pleaded with Del to let it go for the moment.

"Since we all know that Tory here has been favored by the royal presence," Del lied, with a smile every bit as phony as Debbie's, "why do you think we'll be surprised by your big news?"

"Oh heavens." Debbie laughed. "The fact that Janelle *was* here is old news. But I venture to guess that none of you know that she's *still* here. Or that she's spent the whole evening working on our float. Or that we've all had a wonderful time getting reacquainted."

For a woman who had ample, if ancient, reason to resent and distrust J. Ross Nelson, Debbie was certainly relishing her return.

"Well that's just peachy keen," Del said sweetly. "I bet she and Doug have lots of catching up to do."

Del's frontal attack caught everyone off-guard. We all held our breaths—even Junior, who theoretically did not remember exactly what Janelle and Doug had to talk about.

"Yes indeed." Debbie smiled even more widely. "So much so that we talked Janelle into spending tonight in Delphi, instead of returning to her motel room in Aberdeen." She finished her drink in a gulp and signaled the bar.

"So you have a movie star bunking in your spare bedroom, how nice for you," said Junior tersely. We were all tired of Debbie's attitude.

"Actually . . ." Debbie grinned, and this time there was no strain. She was genuinely enjoying herself. "We don't have a spare room."

Striving mightily to keep a neutral look frozen on my face, I waited. Everyone who was listening in, which was everyone in the bar, waited. On the jukebox, Jimmy Buffett wondered where to go when "de volcano blow." I wondered the same thing.

Debbie continued, smoothing damp blond hair out of her eyes. "Our kids are in bed and it's far too late for a crowd to converge on my house on a school night." She shook her head sadly. "So we're all going over to Stuart McKee's for drinks. No kids there to disturb," she said brightly. "And since Stu is all alone in that big house, he's generously offered to put Janelle up for the night."

She looked directly at me. "Isn't that wonderful?"

15

Safety First

FRIDAY

Where is it written that every marching band in America must play "Louie, Louie"? Administrators have evidently forgotten that the lyrics were considered so mysteriously obscene that the government held hearings to determine exactly how dirty the song really was. Now it's deemed suitable for high school instrumental adaptation, along with tunes like "Lucy in the Sky with Diamonds" (we all know what *that* meant), and "Light My Fire," which was condemned as a drug song, instead of the perfectly satisfactory sex song that it is.

Of course, the administrators are now approximately my age, and maybe they've retained a little of their sense of humor. It seems likely, since I distinctly remember having an earnest conversation with Delphi's current band leader, when we were both in the sixth grade, on the symbolic "cloud" Mick Jagger wanted us to get off of, the intro to which I could just make out as the band rounded the corner down by our trailer.

Ordinarily a distance of three blocks would not muffle

the band's enthusiastic rendition of anything from their sixties' catalog, but the crowd that gathered for the homecoming parade was unusually dense and loud and generously seeded with yakking out-of-towners carrying handheld video cameras. The three local TV stations had staked out strategic corners and were waiting for the main attraction.

Word had leaked, of course, that J. Ross Nelson intended to grace her hometown, and the regional populace, eager for a first-hand glimpse, had turned out accordingly. We locals had the decency to pretend to be interested in the parade itself, though it was so far identical to the homecoming parade held in Delphi, and every other small South Dakota town, every single year. Left to our own devices, we might have ignored it ourselves, but we had our dignity to uphold. Therefore, we applauded and cheered and shamed the rest of the crowd into reacting in a similar manner.

"At least the rain stopped," mumbled Del, standing on tiptoe, trying to see over the people standing in front of the cafe.

In the hierarchy of small-town parades, single adults were relegated to the back of the crowd—the curb was reserved for the elderly, young parents, small children armed with plastic ice cream buckets, and a few exuberant junior high kids, willing to race the little ones for tossed candy.

Though the clouds hung low and gray, and the wind gusted as always, there were patches of blue sky and the sun was starting to peek through, taking the damp chill off the air.

We had already waved pennants at twenty minutes of single-file pickups and antique tractors festooned with twisted burgundy and black crepe-paper garlands and tempera-painted, butcher-paper banners predicting that the Delphi Oracles would "Declare Homecoming Independence Over the Hitchcock-Tulare Patriots." With one-armed tosses, businessmen, committee members, residents of old-folks homes, and assorted religious and political groups flung handfuls of wrapped candy and pennies to wildly excited toddlers who darted into the street to add the booty to their already heavy buckets.

Every once in a while, a compassionate soul with a good arm would purposely toss a few goodies to the adults in the back. As Stu rode past with his father in the Feed and Seed Store truck, he spotted me, waved, and threw a couple of mini peanut butter cups in my direction.

"Some kind of peace offering, huh?" Del asked as she unwrapped a candy and ate it. Del was catcher on the Delphi women's softball team.

"Nothing to offer 'peace' for," I said as a group of 4-H'ers in Western garb pranced by on feisty horses, followed by a kid wheeling a garbage can, broom, and dustpan.

"Oh?" Del asked innocently, one eyebrow raised. "Last I heard, Prince Charming had invited the Fairy Princess to spend the night in the abandoned castle."

An antique fire engine trolled past, sirens wailing. Volunteer firemen tossed fire safety brochures into the crowd, which most of the kids left lying on the damp roadway.

"That's what Debbie wants everyone to believe," I said pointedly. "Stu said it was more like everyone invited themselves over to his house, and Doug was the one who suggested *she* stay there."

"Why would Doug want Janelle to spend the night with Stu?" Del asked, grinning as the entire Delphi first-grade class, all thirty of them, straggled past, each child costumed in a mother's version of the state of Hawaii. There were tiny hula dancers and small boys carrying homemade cardboard surfboards and pineapples. One especially creative outfit consisted of blue tights and construction paper maps of the islands pinned to strategic, if not geographically correct, locations.

"You got me." I shrugged.

On my other side, pregnant Junior shepherded her three-year-old triplets into the street and back repeatedly, yet still had time to eavesdrop. "Your naiveté astounds me, Tory."

Preceded by the toga-clad Flag Corps girls, the marching band, in heavy, gold-trimmed burgundy and black wool uniforms, tootled past, attempting, and failing, to do justice to "Land of 10,000 Dances." Kids of assorted heights and girths sweated under oversize feathered helmets and struggled to keep waist-length capes flipped properly over their shoulders as the wind blew hair into their eyes.

"Presley confirms Stu's version," I said, when we could hear again.

"What would Presley know about it?" Del and Junior asked together.

"He showed up there, last night, to ask Ron Adler something about the junior high float construction," I said, repeating what Pres had told me. "He even brought home an autographed eight-by-ten glossy of Janelle." I'd found it placed prominently on the kitchen table when I got up. "Presley," Janelle had written in black Magic Marker in a flowing hand across the lower third of the photo, "you're as handsome as your cousin Nick was. Don't break as many hearts, Love and kisses, J."

"Well how *did* she act at Stu's house last night?" Junior asked over her shoulder, trailing into the street after the triplets again.

"Tory didn't go *over* to Stu's house last night," Del answered for me, disgusted. I'd already heard, several times, how stupid it had been to send Janelle to the Feed and Seed Store in the first place.

"Why in heaven's name not?" Junior asked, surprised. "Debbie made a special point to invite you."

Generally, I did not wait for an invitation from Debbie Fischbach to go to Stu's house. But wild horses could not have dragged me there after her coda about admiring my courage in leaving a recently separated man in the exclusive company of the beautiful Janelle, who, as Debbie sweetly added, had aged so much better than *some* of us.

"I was tired," I said primly. I had also turned off the telephone, covered my head with a pillow, and vainly tried to sleep.

We waved at a scraggly bunch of cowboys, Davy Crocketts, señoritas, and diminutive pioneers carrying foil-covered stars and large yellow crepe-paper roses. The second-grade interpretation of Texas.

"Oh look." Junior pointed down the street. "Here comes the king and queen. And there's Debbie across the street, talking to Ron Adler."

Ron's tow truck had been one of the first parade entries. He'd already completed the entire eight-block parade circuit and could watch the rest of the spectacle in front of his own business.

Debbie, wearing jeans, a turtleneck, and a Delphi sweatshirt emblazoned with the traditional bust of Apollo, stood next to Ron and waved excitedly at Cameron and Sandra, who were perched on the upper edge of the backseat of Neil's precious blue and white '61 Impala convertible. The royals waved impartially from under the weight of their velvet robes and heavy crowns, though when Cameron spotted his mother, his face lit up with a genuine smile.

Neil, who was driving his own collector car, couldn't wave because his free hand was busy flinging large numbers of foil-wrapped mint patties into the crowd.

"And there's Hugh Kincaid, over in front of the church," Junior continued her running commentary on mutual acquaintances.

"Yeah, and look who he's talking to," Del said darkly, pointing as Neil's car pulled even with us.

Through the crowd across the street, I could see Doug Fischbach talking vehemently with Hugh Kincaid. Hugh shrugged and then touched Doug's arm lightly and pointed toward Cameron, whose smile died, and wave faltered, when he saw his father.

"Isn't that interesting?" Del said as Doug glowered at his son, and then stalked off in obvious disgust.

"Where's he going?" Junior asked absently, rubbing her lower back with one hand and waving with the other at assorted third-graders dressed as Wisconsin, in cow and cheese costumes.

"Arguing with Debbie, looks like," Del said, straining

to see over a suddenly excited and agitated crowd. The float with J. Ross Nelson had just turned the corner and was heading our direction. "Dammit," Del muttered through clenched teeth as people closed in all around her.

"I'll see if I can get a better view," I said, pushing my way to the front of the crowd. The noise level rose as the float got nearer.

Across the street, the Fischbachs were having a vehement discussion. Doug's face had a flat and nasty look as he grabbed Debbie's arm roughly. She tried to pull away. He said something that made her flinch as if struck.

"Hello there," said a chuckly voice that belonged to a brightly painted face with a huge red nose, which popped up directly in my line of vision. "Have you been Saved?"

"Huh?" I asked, trying to see past his green and white polka-dotted shoulder. Or at least I thought they were dots. But each time I moved to get a better view of Doug and Debbie, the clown stepped in front of me again, and I realized that his suit was covered with little white crosses.

"Klowns for Krist," he said in a voice that was a jolly combination of Bullwinkle and Pat Buchanan, his large nose flashing on and off. It was also painted with crosses, as were the dozen or so helium-filled balloons whose strings he clenched with a cross-emblazoned white glove.

"Not interested," I said, still trying to see across the street, catching only a glimpse of Doug's jacket through the crowd. "Thanks anyway."

"No, excuse me," he said, stepping in my way again. "But, have *you* been Saved?"

That's the sort of question that I would consider impertinent even if Mr. Klown and I had been properly introduced. And in the present situation, the intrusion was most unwelcome.

Unfortunately, it was already too late. The crowd parted again briefly, but the Fischbachs were no longer in sight. I glared at the intruder. Even as a child, I was not enamored of clowns—there always seems to be a hint of the lunatic around those red-rimmed eyes.

"Remember that Jesus loves you," he chortled, holding out a pamphlet.

"Oh go turn the other cheek," I said, disgusted.

The clown shrugged and continued on, pausing to give each of Junior's triplets a balloon as she beamed down on them.

"What happened?" Del shouted in my ear. It was the only way I could hear her—the crowd was roaring.

"Couldn't tell," I yelled back. "They were arguing. But that dipshit got in my way and I lost them."

I would have continued bitching, but we were suddenly caught by the amazing sight of the famous J. Ross Nelson perched on the hood of a red and white '57 Corvette anchored to the back of a hay trailer hitched behind a brand-new pickup truck.

Del surveyed the float, shaking her head. "It took them all week to put *that* thing together?"

Stapled here and there around the edge of the otherwise undecorated trailer were banners extending good wishes to the current football team, from the 1965–1975 Delphi alumni. A few halfhearted burgundy and black crepe-paper streamers fluttered from the back of the trailer. The committee must have decided that no one would notice peripheral details with J. Ross Nelson on board.

They were right. Janelle commanded the attention of everyone assembled, looking every inch the movie star in a long spangled gown that appeared to consist of glitter and paint. The simple ponytail had been replaced by Big Hair, a wind-impervious do that I'm betting will pop up on a few local ladies next week.

Before, Janelle had looked attractive in an average sort of way, at least from a distance. Here and now, she was the epitome of everything we lumpy, out-of-style mid-westerners were not. Just watching her, I felt myself growing shorter and fatter, and less sure of Stu's affection.

The movie star smiled, waved, and made eye contact with every third person on the parade route, including me. I could swear she dropped a wink my direction.

While Junior could not help but be impressed by the glamour, she was a good deal more involved in people watching. "There's Stu," she said to me, pointing across the street.

Stu's truck had passed by long ago in the parade, and he was now leaning back against the Feed and Seed building, arms crossed and expression unreadably sober.

Though it was hard to tell from my angle, with all the cameras in the way, I thought Janelle had also spotted Stu. She turned slightly in his direction, and I could swear she waved a little less impartially.

Stu remained impassive, though he turned to watch as Janelle's float disappeared around the corner.

"What do you suppose *that* meant?" Del asked, smiling now at assorted fourth-graders, evidently representing a state made up entirely of the Statue of Liberty and the Mets.

I pretended to be absorbed in the Right to Life car, from which determinedly perky supporters tossed candy and flyers with equal enthusiasm. Junior pocketed a handful of each.

"My, my, my," Junior said, pointing. "Will you look at that."

We turned to see a concoction of flashing lights and sparklers attached to a metal framework that spelled the words "Delphi Rules." The whole apparatus was at least ten feet high. It rotated on a turntable perched over a vehicle that looked like an army tank without the gun turret. The school song blared from loudspeakers attached to either side. Every so often, paper cylinders shot up and out of a white plastic pipe set upright in the center of the turntable. In the air, the cylinders themselves popped open in a shower of confetti, glitter, and burgundy tissue-paper stars.

Everyone "oohed" like it was the Fourth of July.

"They said it was gonna blow our float out of the water," Del marveled, shaking her head, "but I didn't think it could."

"Silly girl," I said, watching the float constructed by Delphi's more recent alumni rumble past. "Neil can do anything."

We were so absorbed we nearly missed the fifth-grade Eskimos and gold miners marching by. Junior's oldest daughter Tres waved to us frantically from the middle of a group of saloon girls.

The sixth-graders were evidently too old to enjoy the silliness of dressing up and marching. Most wore their usual school clothes, and nearly all of them scowled.

"Someone already did New York," Del said, puzzled.

"What state are they, anyway?" Junior asked.

"Premenstrual, it looks like," I said, getting ready to go home.

Since the sixth-grade marchers traditionally signaled the end of the parade, the sound of a gunning motor and squealing tires surprised everyone.

Around the corner roared an evil-looking vehicle, brushpainted a flat black. It would have been traveling too fast even if Delphi's main drag had not been packed solid with absentminded people jaywalking home.

"Jesus Christ, what is that?" Del asked.

Junior didn't even frown at the blasphemy. She quickly grabbed the hands of two of her toddlers and shoved the other in my direction. "Says 'Better Safe Than Sorry' on the side," she said, squinting.

It also had "Safety Commitee" and "Be Preparred" misspelled on the hood. Each motto appeared to have been unevenly spray painted in large white letters.

"Do you suppose they're Boy Scouts?" Junior asked, trying to see who was driving.

"Not likely," Del said.

The car's three occupants wore furry animal costumes that covered their heads completely. They pulled even with the cafe, idled briefly, seemed to consult with one another, and then reached for something on the seats beside them. The crowd was nearly silent, caught completely off-guard by the car's unexpected appearance and behavior.

The driver, a moth-eaten beaver as far as I could tell, gunned the engine again, and all three motley animals furiously tossed small foil objects into the crowd.

Though the parents were still confused, the children weren't. Little ones, including Junior's, knew the drill.

They rushed into the street to fill their buckets with the multicolored shiny packets.

"What the hell are they throwing?" Del asked, suspicious.

"Peppermint Patties," Junior said, watching her three. "Just like Neil threw."

"I don't think so," said Del, shaking her head, as the first of the children showed the new treasures to their parents, who reacted with confusion and then surprise.

With one last blast of smoke, the car squealed away, heading straight out of town, instead of turning south at the corner as the rest of the parade entries had done. I'd already noticed that there were no front license plates, and as the car fishtailed out of sight toward the highway, I saw that there were no rear plates either.

The adult disgust had quickly turned vocal.

"What the hell is going on?" Junior muttered, grabbing a bucket from one of her beaming children. She picked up a couple of objects, frowning. She flipped them over in concentration, then uttered a small scream and dropped the whole bucket, spilling it on the sidewalk.

Joshua, or Jessica, or Jeremy—I could never tell them apart—burst into tears and wailed loudly. To prevent toddler looting, I bent down to gather the scattered candies.

Unanimous adult grunts of outrage could be heard all around. Or nearly unanimous, anyway. Here and there, I heard a subversive chuckle. The loudest was right behind me.

"Hey." Del poked me in the back. "Don't forget to give the kid these." She handed me more of the foil packets. "He's gonna need them in a decade or so."

Across the street, Stu laughed outright with Ron Adler. Behind me, Del was wiping her eyes, and even Aphrodite grinned. Up and down the sidewalk, smiles played around the mouths of men who strove mightily to keep straight faces.

Junior was tight-lipped and unmistakably furious.

Here and there, small children had torn open their new

toys and were curiously inspecting transparent disks. One or two had even figured how they unrolled and were flapping them at each other.

The TV cameras rolled merrily, recording our collective reactions. Crews grinned as on-air personalities somberly displayed some of the squares they'd retrieved from the street. Brightly colored packages, with names like Trojan and Lifestyles and Sheik on them.

"On second thought," Del said wickedly, "give 'em back to me. I got a hot date tonight."

16

Homecoming

I'd like to believe that there are cities with bookstores, and more than one movie theater, and restaurants whose wine cellars are not exclusively devoted to the output of Sutter Home or the brothers Gallo. Places where the television is turned off and conversation is the order of the day. Where adults consort with adults, and high school activities are entertaining only to other high school students, and possibly their parents.

If such places do exist, they're far outside the borders of the Midwest, since here, attendance at high school sporting events is not only considered proper for the entire community, it's practically required. Delphi prides itself on the fact that most of the citizens turn out to encourage (and berate) our collective young along the Path of Victory.

Not that any team from Delphi had trodden the Path of Victory in recent years, but our hearts, and voices, are in the right place. If standing along the sidelines, screaming at bumbling high school kids, is considered the right place.

Of course, *my* place was in the stands, along with the rest of the wives, girlfriends, and mothers, and the pep band. But the notion of sitting anywhere near pregnant, pennant-waving Junior for two hours, while she pumped me for information about Stu and Janelle, or bitched about whoever had tossed condoms into the crowd at the parade, was too depressing.

So I broke rank and wandered the sidelines with the restless men who would follow the line of scrimmage up and down the field for the entire game. Normally, my rebellion would have been noticed and commented on, but the game crowd, like the earlier one at the parade, was both larger and more filled with out-of-towners than usual. A fair number of people carried cameras nonchalantly, peering over shoulders and around corners, pretending to watch the game when they were really waiting for the arrival of J. Ross Nelson.

"So is she coming tonight or what?" I asked Stu. We stood at the fifty-yard line as the gray evening faded into a damp dusk that threatened rain.

He watched the field for a minute. I thought he was going to say something stupid like "Is who coming?" Instead he shrugged, and without looking at me, said, "I don't know. She didn't file an itinerary."

I considered the shrug, and the fact that he hadn't actually looked at me, and that we had been standing for fifteen minutes without a smile or a touch.

"Well," I said cautiously, looking straight ahead, "I don't expect you to be able to account for her every move. But she's staying at your house. I assume you talk to each other."

Stu finally turned to me, green eyes somber. "Look, Tory, I know it's weird that she's at my house. But it wasn't my idea. She sleeps in Walton's room, and she's gone most of the time. I hardly see her at all, and when I do, we don't talk. We're not friends." He turned his attention back to the game.

Someone did something good on the field, Stu and the rest of the guys cheered wildly and moved, en masse, down field about six yards. I chewed my lip and followed behind. I had not been alone with Stu since Janelle's arrival—our date for the homecoming game, arranged long ago, was our first opportunity for talk, though trying to talk seriously with an ex-football player during a high school homecoming game was sheer folly.

Because I had no idea how he would react to Janelle as a houseguest, my overheated imagination had supplied me with several equally unpleasant scenarios. I had prepared myself to endure either pointedly innocent enthusiasm over their reunion or feigned anger over the imposition. His gloomy ambivalence threw me for a loop.

Something else happened on the field—Ron Adler beat Stu happily on the back as the crowd cheered. The speaker boomed, "Fischbach, number 69, with the sack. Patriots' ball, third and fifteen."

Wearing number 69 like his father before him, Cameron Fischbach was having a great game. "We're making homecoming history here, folks," the loudspeaker droned. "A Fischbach dynasty is born."

The crowd cheered wildly again. We were actually ahead of the powerhouse Hitchcock-Tulare Patriots, something that hadn't happened in more than a decade. However little I liked Doug's coaching methods, he was producing results, to the delight of the hometown fans.

The mercury lights around the field buzzed and glowed weakly. Stu talked mostly with Ron and the others. I couldn't tell if he was entirely wrapped up in the game, or if he was ignoring me. I felt like a fool trailing after him.

The crowd erupted again. "Punt blocked by number 69, Fischbach," the speakers blared.

I tapped Stu on the arm, trying to get his attention. "I'm going to get myself a hot chocolate," I shouted. "Want anything?"

"Huh?" he shouted back, still watching the field.

"Never mind," I mimed. "I'll be back."

He nodded absentmindedly and turned to the game again.

I made my way through the crowd, catching sight of Presley as he dodged between people on the sidelines, chasing a bunch of his junior high buddies. They paid a good deal more attention to the cheerleaders than to the game.

"And what can I get for you?" Hugh Kincaid asked from inside the rickety wooden concession stand.

"A cup of hot chocolate," I said, surveying the line of candy bars arrayed on a shelf along the back wall, directly under a display of overpriced Delphi banners and sweatshirts, "and a Three Musketeers. How come you're working in here?"

"Anything to get out of chaperoning the dance." He grinned, filling a Styrofoam cup with Swiss Miss and hot water from a thirty-cup coffeepot. He placed the candy bar and cup on the narrow counter. "That'll be a buck fifty, ma'am."

I dug change out of my pocket and handed some to him. The people in the stands roared again. "Quite a game," I said, sipping gingerly.

"Young Master Fischbach is acquitting himself admirably," Hugh said. "I hope his father will be pleased. Doug should be flattered that Cameron is wearing his old jersey."

Someone had realized that Doug in high school, and Cameron now, had both been assigned the same team number. The principal suggested that Cameron wear his father's old jersey, preserved in a trophy case in the main hallway of the school, as a good luck charm for the homecoming game. It seemed to be working, though I thought it would take more than sentimentality to impress Doug.

"His mother is delighted, anyway," I said, hearing the Fischbach name again announced over the loudspeakers.

Though she didn't wander with the men, a perfectly groomed Debbie Fischbach stood along the sidelines, hooting wildly for her son. As we watched, a heavyish blond woman approached Debbie and tapped her on the shoulder.

Debbie turned to the woman, squinted for a moment, then squealed suddenly and hugged her. They talked excitedly.

"I think that's Lisa Franklin," Hugh said, squinting himself.

"Lisa Franklin Hauck-Robertson," I amended, guiltily

squashing a hint of satisfaction over the ex-cheerleader's weight gain.

"The place is crawling with almost familiar faces," Hugh commented, attending to the popcorn machine as we talked. "Alumni, I suppose, in town for the big party tomorrow night."

"I expect you'll see most of them," I said, remembering all the info sheets that had mentioned Mr. Kincaid as a favorite teacher. "Have you talked to our J. Ross Nelson yet?"

"Haven't had the pleasure, I'm afraid," he said. "I did rather expect her to make an appearance at the game tonight. Do you know if she is coming?"

Since there was no use pretending not to know why Hugh thought I'd know Janelle's plans, I just shook my head. "I talked to her a couple of days ago at the cafe, but I haven't seen her since, except at the parade this afternoon"—I took a deep breath—"and Stu says she doesn't check in with him." I shrugged.

Hugh shrugged back, with a commiserating smile, and then turned to wait on the halftime crowd that converged on the stand. I waved and made my way back to where I'd left Stu, though he was nowhere to be seen.

Of course, neither were any of the other guys he'd been standing with. They were all probably clustered around assorted trunks and tailgates in the parking lot, surreptitiously mixing drinks in large insulated mugs. Alcohol was forbidden at any school function, but as long as the imbibing was discreet, and the imbibers were obviously of age, no one made a big deal of it.

I peered wistfully into my hot chocolate, shivering in the damp chill, thinking that a shot of schnapps would be lovely.

"First Nick Bauer, then Stuart McKee—you seem to have captivated every handsome man Delphi had to offer," a throaty voice said in my ear. "Why didn't you tell me that you were seeing Stu?"

Minus the big hair, spangly dress, and '57 'Vette, Janelle Ross was almost ordinary enough to go unnoticed in a crowd. At least if the crowd was paying attention to an exciting football game. And if the ones who weren't watching the game were looking for a movie star, instead of an uncommonly attractive woman who used to be from around these parts.

She wore jeans and a brand-new Delphi sweatshirt, and carried a Styrofoam cup of steaming coffee and a bag of popcorn. Her hair was again tied back in a simple ponytail.

"Didn't seem germane to the conversation." I shrugged. I was doing a lot of that lately. Besides, keeping company with handsome, unfaithful, married men wasn't something I wanted listed on my resumé anyway. "I figured he'd tell you if the subject came up," I lied.

"The subject came up all right," Janelle said, carefully sipping her coffee.

She stood there, calmly surveying the scene, lost, I suppose, in her own memories. I was amazed that the camera-carrying hopefuls walked past her without a second glance.

"And he let me know right away that he was in a relationship," she continued. "That's why I wanted to talk to you tonight."

"To tell me that Stu considers himself to be in a relationship?" I asked, a little sharply. If that was so, why was he so distant? So glum?

"No, goofus," Janelle laughed. "To invite you out to the river after the game."

"What? Where?"

"I know some things have changed, but the river is still where it used to be, isn't it?"

"Yeah, but—" I stopped, confused.

"A few of us are getting together later tonight. It didn't seem appropriate to have another party at Stu's house." She nudged me. "And Doug and Debbie have too many kids to party at their place. So we thought we'd hang out at the river. Just like old times. It'll be great."

This was weird—Janelle Ross suggesting that we all congregate on the banks of the James River to relive the good old times before she mysteriously disappeared. Good old times like when she was caught in a backseat with her best friend's boyfriend, and later had to distract a potential child molester while I hustled two drunken thirteen-year-olds away. Good old times when Doug punched Stu, and Nick set the tone of our marriage by being unfaithful on our first date.

I had no desire to relive a single one of those memories, and it must have showed on my face.

"Come on," Janelle said quietly. "You and Stu are the only ones who aren't idiots or phonies. If you don't go, I won't have anyone to talk to. And I can't get out of going. Please."

She looked vulnerable and lonely, like she honestly needed a friendly face to help her get through the ordeal.

"Well," I said slowly, wondering what Stu would think when I told him we were expected to serve as J. Ross Nelson's bodyguards.

"Come on, you gotta," she wheedled, smiling. Then her face turned suddenly hard, her eyes tight and narrow. "Jesus Christ, what's he doing here?" she said under her breath.

"Who?" I asked, turning around quickly. A short, solid, balding man was pushing through the crowd, heading straight for us.

"Look," Janelle said hurriedly, "whatever you do, *don't* tell him about the river tonight. I gotta go now. See you later." And with that, she melted into the crowd.

"Where'd she go?" the short man demanded, grabbing my arm. He wore a patterned shirt open a couple buttons more than necessary, a heavy gold necklace, and a big diamond ring on the hand that was squeezing my arm.

"Excuse me?" I asked, pointedly pulling away.

"You heard me, toots," he said, extracting a wallet from a back pocket. "Where'd she go?"

"I don't know what you're talking about," I lied primly. People milled around us but Janelle had disappeared completely. Must be some kind of movie star trick.

"Yeah, right," he said, squinting through heavy-rimmed glasses. "This trigger your memory any?" He deftly folded a wad of cash—more money than I took home in a week—and held it out to me, looking around to see if anyone was watching.

The crowd ignored us completely, engrossed in the halftime formations of the marching band. They were playing "Louie, Louie."

"Still don't know what I'm talking about?" he asked.

I looked him right in his beady little eyes, barely regretting the cash, shook my head, and said, "Sorry, can't help you."

He stared back, snorted, and stuffed the wad in his pocket, shaking his head. "Piss on it. I'll find her, with or without your help. How many places can she hide in a burg like this anyway?"

I assumed that was a rhetorical question. I asked a question of my own. "Who are you, anyway?"

"Don't you recognize me?" He smoothed sparse, wavy hair back from an already high forehead.

I searched his face and mentally thumbed through my high school annuals, looking for a match. I came up blank. Ditto on the info sheets Junior and I had collated. If this guy was a former classmate, he'd changed too much for me to guess his identity without a hint.

"Of course she doesn't recognize me," he said to the sky. "A state like this doesn't even have newspapers. The shit-kickers here probably can't even read."

We may not be literate but there's nothing wrong with our hearing. Several bystanders turned and glared at the guy.

"Listen, honey," he said to me, more quietly than before, "don't you at least get magazines in the outback? *Us? Entertainment Weekly? People?"*

His mention of *People* magazine triggered a faint memory. I examined him again, matching the face against the picture I'd just remembered.

He smiled, a predatory grin with far too many perfectly white teeth. "You got it now, sweetie. That's why I need to find Ms. J. Ross Nelson," he said. "I'm her husband."

17

Nine-Man

In the long run, I don't think the adult psyche is well-served by having been popular in high school. I suppose that sounds like sour grapes, since I was always on the outside looking in, but my belief in that basic truth comes from observation, not resentment.

Most of us were born ordinary, and we are destined to spend ordinary lives doing ordinary things—our modest successes and unsurprising failures stem from the sheer ordinariness of our lives. We should be content with that lot.

Unfortunately, Americans are drilled from infancy in the magnitude of our own potential—infected with the notion that each and every one of us can do whatever we want, if only we try hard enough.

That's a heavy burden, even for those whose idea of a good day involves not spilling coffee down anyone's back and having the cash register balance at the end of a shift.

It must be even more difficult for someone who once stood in the spotlight, in front of cheering crowds.

Take Doug Fischbach (as Henny Youngman would say,

please), a man who spent his high school years lionized. Supremely cocky, he left for college with great fanfare, and the town's high hopes, only to disappoint himself and his supporters with a mediocre football performance that left him no chance to make it in the pros.

There is a nasty homily that states that those who can, do, and those who can't, teach. The unspoken corollary to that is: Those who can't, coach.

Back in Delphi, older and not yet wiser, Coach Doug Fischbach seemed to focus his entire being on wringing a winning season from a group of boys in a town that had grown used to losing.

A diminishing rural population made it impossible for Delphi to field the usual eleven man football team. We played now in a league composed of even smaller communities who struggled to find, and keep healthy, the nine players required for regulation games. The smaller team size in no way negated the rabid interest of adults in the athletic pursuits of adolescents.

The small towns of Hitchcock and Tulare had consolidated their gene pools to form a powerhouse nine-man team that was currently, and unexpectedly, ranked second in the standings, right behind Delphi.

And Coach Fischbach was determined to keep them there, fired not only by the need to prove his own abilities, but to reenact the triumphant homecoming game of 1969. The one that sealed four-year football scholarships to good Minnesota universities, for both him and Stu McKee.

The present third quarter had concluded much the same as the first half—a tight game with Delphi barely in the lead, Cameron performing spectacularly, and Doug furiously unhappy with every play and player, regardless of who had the ball. He shouted at, insulted, and humiliated each member of his team—calling into question their intelligence, masculinity, and parentage in a way that bordered on obscenity.

"Why do the kids put up with that kind of treatment?" I asked Stu, whose halftime drinks had mellowed him. He stood next to me, arm settled comfortably around my shoulders between on-field excitements.

"All coaches do that." Ron Adler blinked from my other side. "It's just a way to get the kids' attention. No one takes it seriously."

Cameron, sitting on the bench, helmet off and towel draped over his head, shoulders rounded in dejection, looked as though he took his father's abuse seriously enough.

"Ron's right," Stu said to me, watching the field intently. "Kids won't listen unless you shout at them. Besides"—he pointed at Cameron, who headed back into the game as Doug shouted instructions at his back—"they're big boys. A few bad words aren't gonna hurt 'em."

"Well, if it was my kid, I'd put a stop to it," I said darkly as Doug screamed, spittle flying, in the face of another unfortunate player.

Stu turned and said gently, "Believe me, Tory, kids hate overprotective mothers a lot more than screaming coaches."

"No shit." Ron blinked.

"And how would you know?" I asked Ron, irritated. "You didn't play football."

"I wrestled," he said with injured dignity. "Same thing."

The conversation was going nowhere, which was just as well, because Delphi had kicked a thirty-five-yard field goal, making it impossible for the Patriots to win unless they gained a touchdown in the final minute of the game. The hometown fans were on their feet, roaring, the stands a sea of waving pennants.

The men on the sidelines stood together, a near-critical mass of flailing arms and Y chromosomes—a masculine bonding that swept up even usually sedate and uncompetitive guys like Neil Pascoe and the Reverend Clay Deibert.

I could not see over, or through, the solid wall of hooded sweatshirts, satin team jackets, and baseball hats. I mimed to Stu that I was going over by the concession stand for a better view. He barely nodded.

I was not the only one unmesmerized by the possibility that the Oracles might actually beat the Patriots. The man who had claimed to be Janelle's husband prowled through the crowd. Here and there, he tried to ask people questions, but most were too engrossed in the game to talk to him.

Del was also paying attention to something other than football. With elbows crossed on the counter of the concession stand, and ample breasts propped comfortably on the elbows, she laughed and shook her hair back. Del, who eventually dallied with every eligible man (and some not so eligible), had finally gotten around to Hugh Kincaid.

Ever polite, Hugh chatted with Del, though he was obviously keeping one eye on the game. She raised an eyebrow in my direction and started to say something to him, but was interrupted by a cheering crowd whose volume knob had been cranked all the way up.

"Another sack for Fischbach. What a night, folks, what a night," the announcer said, excitement ringing in his voice. "Patriots' ball, second and twelve. Oracles call for a time out."

Hugh, cheering inside the stand, didn't even pretend to pay attention to Del. She shrugged and walked over to me.

"No luck, huh?" I asked, watching the field. Doug was kneeling at the center of a huddle of sweaty, dirty boys, many of whom held their helmets in their hands.

"I don't get it," she said. "The average man spends three-quarters of his time bitching about not getting any—and then when some is staring him right in the face, he'd rather watch a stupid game."

"Must be a guy thing," I said. "Maybe testosterone should be declared a toxic substance."

All evening I'd had no luck getting Stu's attention for serious conversation, even after mentioning Janelle's invitation to the river. He'd nodded absentmindedly and mumbled, "Whatever."

"Say," Del, tuned to my wavelength, asked "you heard anything about a party tonight after the game?"

Play had resumed on the field. The Patriots gained four yards. The crowd groaned. Time out was called again.

"Yeah. Ms. Nelson herself invited me," I said. Del had been pissed the last time I talked to Janelle without telling her. I was not going to make that mistake again. I ran down my conversations with her and the "husband."

"Weird."

"No shit," I said. "You gonna go?"

She shrugged. "Depends."

I figured it depended on whether Hugh's attention could be secured more easily after the game than during.

"Mom, can I have a couple bucks?" Presley popped up between us. His cheeks were flushed and his dark hair was plastered to his forehead by sweat. He'd been running around with his friends, ostensibly cheering the team, but mostly watching for the occasional flash of cheerleader underwear. Which probably accounted for the flush.

"Sorry, kid, fresh out." Del shrugged.

Presley turned to me and batted his eyelashes. As a rule, I do not fall for that kind of flirtation, especially from a thirteen-year-old, but I felt a small wave of tenderness for this unfortunate testosterone time bomb. He didn't ask to be a Y chromosome carrier.

I handed Pres a five. He thanked me and disappeared in the crowd.

"Wasn't he supposed to be grounded?" I asked his mother.

"Yeah, well, it's homecoming," she said.

Which explained everything. At least to a South Dakotan.

As we talked, the time clock ticked down. Delphi still led Hitchcock-Tulare by four points, and in less than twenty-five seconds, were going to beat the Patriots for the first time in our history.

Stu and the rest of the guys hovered right at the line of scrimmage, close to the Patriots' goal. I was not totally immune to the drama myself. Del and I stood a little farther downfield, next to Debbie Fischbach, who was pacing nervously.

The teams lined up again and snapped the ball. Our guys had only to hold the Patriots back for one more play—something they'd done competently the entire game.

I watched as the play evolved as if in slow motion. The Patriot quarterback, whom Cameron Fischbach had sacked three times already, sidestepped neatly around him. Cameron twisted, leaped, grabbed air, and landed with a thud as the quarterback sprinted, unhindered, the final ten yards to the goal as the clock ticked down to zero.

The Patriot cheering section erupted, and the Delphi fans stood, pennants motionless, in stunned silence broken only by a single piercing wail. Debbie Fischbach, hand over mouth and deathly pale, howled as Cameron slowly stood and stumbled back to the Oracles' bench.

The pain in her voice shocked the rest of us into remembering to be good sports. We shouted encouragement to our boys for a good effort. A really good effort. At least Del and I and the moms and cheerleaders did.

The guys along the sidelines hung their heads in shame and dejection, disappointment obvious on their faces. A couple of them were genuinely, and vocally, angry that their self-image had not been collectively upheld by a bunch of teenage boys.

The jubilant Hitchcock-Tulare team members hugged and high-fived one another.

The smiling Patriot coach strode across the field, hand extended. Doug stared at him, frozen, spun around, and stalked to the bench where Cameron sat, head down.

"That's it for tonight, folks, a heartbreaking squeaker, but a truly amazing game for number 69. Let's hear it for the coach and Delphi Oracles. And let's hear it for the undisputed star, number 69, Cameron Fischbach."

The crowd, finally realizing that a homecoming loss was not the end of the world, roared in approval of the undisputed star, whose furious father reached down and jerked him up roughly, then threw him bodily over the bench before storming off the field.

18

The Mighty Jim

The James River, which winds its way from central North Dakota all the way to the southeastern corner of South Dakota, where it joins the Missouri River, is an unnavigable, uninspiring trickle. Even in the pioneer days, with water a precious commodity, few settlements clung to its banks. And most of them withered and died when the technology emerged to tap wells into the underground waterways formed by the vast Ogallala Aquifer that lies under the state.

Narrow and shallow, twisted by oxbows and sharp bends, the river's main attraction lay in its tendency to freeze in the winter, providing the local snowmobilers a surface for their noisy sport without the danger of being decapitated by barbed-wire fences.

During the summer, the water levels often dropped enough to restrict the water flow entirely, creating stagnant pools that even sheep will not drink from. In the spring and occasionally in the fall, rains swell the river, sometimes to alarming proportions, carrying downstream pesticides and tons of silt washed from fields, along with the occasional farm implement or dead cow.

That said, the Jim River does have the kind of rustic appeal associated with the books of Laura Ingalls Wilder. Grassy banks slope from endless windswept prairies, the great bowl of the sky meets the horizon in a 360-degree view marred by nothing but power lines and what passes for hills in these parts.

A few tree species hardy enough to thrive without human assistance grow along the riverbanks—cottonwoods, willows, and chokecherries provide shade in the summer, a riot of gold and yellow leaves in the fall, and shelter for wildlife in the winter.

They also adequately screen the banks from the prying eyes of county deputies patrolling the back roads, which made the Jim a perfect place for teenagers to hold keggers.

Not that anyone gathered at the oxbow four miles east of Delphi would be mistaken for a teenager. If wrinkles, gray hair, and expanding waistlines were not enough to give our age away, the general reluctance to sit on the ground and drink sloe gin and Coke would.

"Did anybody bring blankets?" Gina Adler asked, squelching nervously in the mud. "I forgot it'd be so wet."

"I got a tarp in the back of my pickup, want me to get it?" Stu asked her.

"That'd be great." Gina grinned. She followed him over to the box of his truck, whispering over her shoulder, "He's sooo cute. Do you know how lucky you are?"

I didn't answer her. Stu had been unnervingly quiet on the drive to the river. As always, he was polite and charming, but I had no idea what he really thought. About anything. The realization that I did not know him in any way other than the biblical sense did not seem particularly lucky.

"Are we having fun yet?" Del said in my ear.

"Can't you tell?" I asked. "Nothing like a group of middle-aged midwesterners stumbling around in the dark, pretending they're still young enough to enjoy getting drunk outside in the cold, instead of in their own living rooms."

Six or eight vehicles, headlights on low, were parked in a semicircle around the outer perimeter of the area, though the lights did little to permeate the damp darkness. There were cars and trucks parked behind the front row, and, periodically, others pulled in. Someone had plugged Mary-Chapin Carpenter into a cassette deck and punched the volume up.

"So where's the guest of honor?"

"I haven't seen her yet, but that doesn't mean anything," I said, remembering her patented Hollywood now-you-see-me-now-you-don't act.

"Suppose she'll stage a replay of the backseat action with Doug Fischbach?"

"I doubt it," I said with distaste. "One of the advantages of being grown up, not to mention rich and famous, is never having to have sex in a car."

"Oh, I don't know." Del grinned. "Leather upholstery always makes my heart go pitter-pat."

"I can deal with leather," I said. "It's door handles and gearshift knobs that I object to."

"You just haven't had enough practice," said the expert.

"Are you planning to fine-tune your skills tonight?" I asked.

She arched an eyebrow in reply and took the arm of Hugh Kincaid, who'd stepped out from behind a clump of trees carrying a couple of paper cups, one of which he handed to Del with a smile.

They walked off together toward the riverbank, out of sight. Though I made a rule never to ask Del for details, the faintly Oedipal connotations of this pairing had me curious.

Everyone else was curious too—there were several pointed stares, and a couple of frowns, following the teacher and his former pupil.

"Disgusting," Junior muttered, helping Gina straighten out a blue tarp on the uneven ground.

"I think it's romantic." Gina giggled, settling herself cross-legged on the tarp. She picked up an open can of Bud and took a swig.

"It should be illegal," Junior said darkly. She lowered herself carefully to the ground. "Think of the example this sets for the schoolchildren." Junior was always ready to throw the power of the legislature behind her notion of correct behavior.

"There are no children here to influence one way or another," I said. "And Doug's behavior at the game set a much worse example for our impressionable youth than a couple of mature adults on a date."

About fifteen feet away from us, Doug knelt on the wet ground, trying to assemble a bonfire. His face was set in an angry scowl lit by the feeble glow of a pocket lighter. Debbie stood behind him, arms crossed and tight-lipped. He turned and said something to her. Without changing expression, she nodded and headed back toward the vehicles.

"Hey ladies, what's going on?" Ron Adler blinked jovially. He carried a nearly full six-pack by an empty plastic ring. He handed another Bud to Gina, and one to me. He popped his own can open and folded himself into place next to his wife.

"We were just talking about how romantic this place is," Gina said, leaning her head on Ron's shoulder. "I met Ronnie right here, you know," she announced to us.

"Yeah, I remember," I said.

Junior, who still claimed not to remember that night, remained silent.

"And you had your first date with Nick," Gina continued. "And Doug and Janelle disappeared from here together, which is kinda romantic too." She took another swallow of beer. "And the magic is still working. Delphine Bauer and Hugh Kincaid are right this very moment walking along the riverbank, enjoying their first date."

"Oh yeah?" Ron blinked darkly. "You sure about that?"

Gina looked to me for confirmation, a small gleam of

triumph in her eye. Gina's mood had probably been boosted by the fact that Del was out of Ron's reach for yet another night.

"'Fraid so," I said. "Chalk one up for student-teacher intercourse."

Ron and Junior both glared at me.

"And lookee there." Gina pointed. "If that's not romance, I don't know what is." She took another beer from the six-pack and set it next to her.

Neil had pulled up in his convertible, the car he drove only for special occasions, like homecoming parades. Sitting in the front seat with him was Rhonda Saunders.

Gina waved frantically and Rhonda waved back. Neil grinned in our direction.

"I'm amazed he drove the '61 out into the country," I said, ignoring the knot I seemed to get whenever I saw Neil and Rhonda together. "He treats that car like it's his baby."

"Maybe he's celebrating something," Gina said playfully.

"Yeah, maybe," I said glumly, and then, seeing that Neil and Rhonda were headed in our direction, stood up hastily. I brushed off my backside and said, "I suppose I should go and find Stu."

"He was standing by his pickup last time I saw him," Ron said.

Doug finally had the bonfire roaring. It threw sparks high in the air, and lit the area enough to allow the headlights to be turned off. James Taylor sang from someone's loudspeakers now. That voice could usually smooth the wrinkles in my forehead and ease the turmoil in my heart. But tonight, even "Sweet Baby James" didn't help.

In the dark I could barely make out Stu leaning against the pickup box. His hat was pushed back on his forehead, he had one hand in a pocket, and the other held a plastic glass. He stood, staring out at nothing.

"What's up?" I asked softly, taking position next to him against the truck, keeping a small but careful distance between us.

"Nothing," he said, remembering to smile. "Just thinking."

"About what?" Though I wasn't sure I really wanted to know.

"Old times," Stu said quietly. "And high school. You grow up, you go away, and you come back, and nothing ever changes." He gazed at the sky. "Do you ever want to relive your past?"

"God no," I said hastily. Relive being the fat girl? Being married to Nick?

He stared into his empty glass for a moment, then grabbed a quart of Southern Comfort from the truck box behind him and refilled it. To the brim.

Stu was a moderate beer drinker. I'd never seen him hitting the hard stuff. He took a large swallow.

"Listen, Tory," he said slowly, not looking at me, "I gotta tell you something . . ."

I held my breath; my heart froze. James Taylor's voice filled the night air. He's going to break up with me, right in the middle of "Fire and Rain," I thought. He's going back to Renee. Or running away with Janelle.

Either option seemed equally possible, and equally terrible. I realized I was breathing again, in shallow gasps. I struggled to keep my face even, in case Gina was watching us for more evidence of the romantic powers of the James River.

Suddenly the fact that I hadn't known what Stu was thinking seemed like a good thing—a circumstance I had no desire to change. While JT mournfully thought that he'd see Suzanne one more time, I wished for a freak tornado, or a flash flood, or instant, irreversible deafness.

Anything to keep from hearing what Stu was going to say next.

"I know I should have . . ." he continued.

A rumble sounded in the distance.

Stu paused and sent a quizzical glance skyward.

For a second I thought the noise was a harbinger of the tornado I'd been praying for.

But the rumble got progressively louder and closer. And lower to the ground.

Stu was looking toward the road now, and so was everyone else. Ron and Gina stared apprehensively into the distance. Doug, an expression of reptilian satisfaction on his face, said something to Debbie, and then laughed out loud. Even Junior lumbered to her feet and peered out into the darkness.

The rumble increased to a roar. People nodded and pointed as a pair of headlights swung into the gravel and headed to the front of the line of parked cars. A 1957 red and white Corvette convertible, engine gunning, spun in a half-circle before it came to a stop not too far from Stu's tarp.

19

Now You See Her

If she was aiming for a memorable entrance, Ms. J. Ross Nelson calculated correctly with her loud and fashionably late arrival on the banks of the James River, in her spiffy little collector car.

However, if she was looking for favorable attention for herself, Janelle Ross proved that she had been gone too long from the prairies of South Dakota.

The women, who congregated around Stu's pickup, were irritated by her willingness to be the center of attention, her fame, and her high, firm bosom.

And while the men certainly appreciated all of the above, they were far more interested in the car.

"Must be nice," Gina Adler muttered, watching Ron edge shyly over to the 'Vette, as if drawn by a magnet.

"Told you they were fake," Del said. Hugh had also joined the male throng.

"Who does she think she is?" Junior asked, glaring at the men, the car, and Janelle.

"The 1969 homecoming queen," Debbie Fischbach said nastily. "The most popular girl in school. Don't you remember?" Doug had trotted over to the convertible even before the engine died.

Like Janelle, former cheerleader Lisa Franklin Hauck-Robertson seemed to have the ability to materialize at will. I had not seen her arrive—she was just suddenly there, in the middle of the crowd at the river, looking even less well-preserved in the flickering firelight than she had at the football game. She sipped from a plastic water bottle but said nothing.

The women watched resentfully as all the men, except Stu, gathered in an admiring circle. Occasionally one would reach out and stroke the car softly, but mostly they stood, hands in back pockets, a small but reverent distance away. A couple of them asked polite questions, which Janelle answered from the driver's seat with a laugh.

Doug watched the others with a smirk, then sauntered around to Janelle's side, leaned down, and said something in her ear. In the fading light of the bonfire it was difficult to gauge her expression. He laughed loudly, then gave her neck a squeeze. Or a caress, I couldn't tell.

I heard a small, sharp, intake of breath, and out of the corner of my eye, saw Debbie stiffen. Then suddenly she was in motion, patting her hair, pulling down her sweatshirt, grabbing a beer from the six-pack on the tarp. Anything but watching the circle of men.

Lisa stepped out of the circle of women and said something to Debbie, who laughed quietly and bitterly.

From the center of her admiring crowd, Janelle perched herself on the back of the seat, swung her long legs over the side, and stood up, stretching. She mimed a shiver and pointed at the fire. Everyone nodded and followed. "Hey you guys," she called to us, on the way past. "What are you waiting for? Come on over and get warm."

Gina hesitated. "What do you think?" she asked quietly.

"It beats standing around with our thumbs up our butts," Del said. Used to an exclusive hold on the male attention in Delphi, she was not sharing the spotlight easily.

"I was thinking of going over there anyway," Junior said. "I *am* kind of chilly."

Debbie sighed. "Can it be avoided?" she asked Lisa.

"Unlikely," Lisa said. They headed toward the fire, bright and patently phony smiles on their faces.

"What about you, Tory?" Rhonda asked. She was the only one young enough to be unthreatened by J. Ross Nelson's intoxicating presence.

"In a minute," I said, shooting a look at Stu, who was still leaning against his pickup, an unreadable expression on his face. "You go ahead, I'll catch up."

I opened another beer for courage as the rest regrouped around the bonfire. The wind had died and sparks floated up lazily on columns of hot air. Someone had set up a dozen or so lawn chairs, and people arranged themselves, talking, drinking, and laughing comfortably.

"You were saying, before we were so rudely interrupted?" I asked Stu, as lightly as I could. Someone had replaced the James Taylor tape with Garth Brooks. At least I wouldn't have to associate the heartbreak I felt sure was coming with my favorite singer.

He reached out and ran a gentle finger down my cheek. "It'll keep," he said with a small shrug. "Go, meet the actress."

"I met her already," I said. "Sure you wouldn't rather talk instead?"

"Nah," he said, looking at the ground. His glass was still full of Southern Comfort, though I didn't know if it was the same drink, or if it had been refilled.

"Tory Bauer," Good Ol' Girl Janelle called. "Get your ass over here. And bring me a beer while you're at it."

"Better go," Stu said softly. "Her Majesty is calling."

I hesitated, wondering if I should force the issue or wait until Stu felt more comfortable about dumping me. Janelle called again. Stu insisted that I go, and I finally agreed, though the reprieve weighed heavily.

With a last, solemn glance backward, I walked over to the fire, pausing only to grab a full six-pack of beer from Ron's cooler. In the shadows, except for occasional sips from his glass, Stu's silhouette was motionless.

"It's about damn time." Janelle laughed, pulling a beer can from the plastic ring, pointing to an empty chair beside her. "A girl could thirst to death in this crowd."

"You only had to ask." Ron blinked gallantly, standing by.

"Yes, honey, I know." Janelle winked at me and patted Ron on the butt.

Gina frowned.

Ron blinked wildly.

Del scowled.

Though Janelle was the center of attention, others were carrying on their own conversations, mostly about the football debacle. Janelle tried to fit in, to be treated like an ordinary human. She laughed at jokes, oohed and aahed at pictures of kids, and listened to everything everyone had to say. Maybe only an insider would spot that everyone treated her with deference, and more than a little awe. No one interrupted her, no one contradicted her. No one brought up probing or embarrassing questions. And only the bitter attempted sarcasm.

Neil was still interested in her car. He had studied the body and engine, and was now asking about the hard top, the single headlights, and the top-end speed.

"Have you always lived here?" Janelle asked Neil, instead of answering him. "I don't remember you from high school."

"That's because he was a child when we graduated," Debbie said sweetly, finishing her beer in a final gulp. She opened another. Lisa laughed.

"I remember *you,"* Neil said gallantly. "And I have most of your movies at the library."

"That's right," Janelle said, tilting her head speculatively, "you're the librarian. The millionaire."

Neil blushed. His bank account was not something he announced at parties. "I run the library. And I restore old cars. Mostly Chevys. You say your engine is original?"

"Yup, a 283 fuel-injected, 300-horse, Hurst transmission with a reverse lock-out," Janelle said, in car code. She darted a sideways grin at me, then continued with

Neil. "So, are you in love with Tory here too? Like every other man in town?"

"We all love Tory," Rhonda piped in. "Who could resist?" She threw a companionable arm around my shoulders. "Right, everyone?"

Everyone laughed, a reaction that did not exactly signal agreement.

"Hey, we're runnin' outta beer," Doug interrupted loudly from the other side of the fire. His voice was slurry, and a little hoarse. "Tory," he shouted, "be a good lil' waitress—run an' get us some more beer. Then we can all go swimming."

"Now why should Tory get *your* beer?" Rhonda demanded indignantly.

"She don't mind, it's her job. Do ya mind, huh Tory?"

"I'm not on duty at the moment," I said with the little dignity I could muster, "but no, I don't mind." I would even wait on a drunk Doug Fischbach if that would get me away from the fire and everyone's scrutiny. "Anyone else want anything?" I asked.

Ron, still reeling from the fanny pat and oblivious to the tension, said, "There should be at least four more six-packs left in my cooler—why don't you bring 'em all. Then you won't have to make another trip."

"Sure," I said woodenly, determined to ask Stu to take me home.

Unfortunately, he wasn't standing next to his pickup. Or anywhere else that I could see.

"Tory, wait up," Janelle called. "I'll help you carry."

"I can get it," I said, elbow-deep in Ron's cooler. It's my job, I thought. I pulled a couple six-packs from the ice, but could not find any more. "Ron must have miscounted, there're only two left."

"You'd think an alkie like Doug would bring his own beer," Janelle said in disgust. "You know what the creep said to me when I got here? He asked if I wanted to go skinny-dipping with him. He said he'd piss Debbie off so she would go home early, and then we could get together after the party."

"Ick," I said, though I did remember a time when Doug

had not been so repulsive to Janelle. Right here at the river, no less. "That wouldn't be a good idea even if it was summer—the river is near flood stage. Besides, Doug doesn't have any skinny to dip."

"You got that right," Janelle said, tucking one cold six-pack under each arm with a smile. "By the way, thanks for coming tonight. It's nice to have at least one real person to talk to."

"Sure," I said, pleased, disarmed, and slightly embarrassed by my earlier jealousy.

"While we're up, I need to go behind the little girls' tree and pee. Think you could stand guard?"

I imagine that movie stars have to be careful when they go to the bathroom in public; the paparazzi are everywhere, hoping for that once-in-a-lifetime shot.

No one around the fire was looking our way. "All clear," I said. She ducked around a clump of chokecherries, and I heard the sound of shifting clothing and some other unmistakable sounds.

I hummed a little to myself along with Garth and his friends in low places, so as not to eavesdrop. The bushes rustled.

I hummed some more, idly wondering why the bushes were rustling since the wind had died down long ago. Then the bushes giggled.

"Tory," Janelle said from the other side of the chokecherries. "I think you better come over here."

20

Déjà Vu

Not being well-acquainted with psychic phenomena, I don't know if déjà vu is traditionally accompanied by a sinking feeling or not. Actually, I don't even know if the term *déjà vu* was appropriate for this particular situation, since it was not a case of just "sensing" that I'd been in a similar position before.

I knew damn well I'd done this already.

"I think we got us a problem here," Janelle said, trying to stifle a laugh.

I knew that. I'd recognized one of the giggles.

On the damp ground in front of us, barely visible in the intermittent moonlight, sat Presley Bauer and homecoming king Cameron Fischbach, both of them laughing and obviously drunk. Empty Bud cans littered the ground around the boys. At least eight of them.

"Now we know what happened to the rest of Ronnie's beer," Janelle said.

"Hey, Tory," Presley drawled. "You know something? I might be kinda drunk."

"No shit," I said, sighing. "What the hell are you doing here?"

"We wanted to see an old fart party." Presley laughed. "It's pretty damn dull, but I gotta admit the beer's fine."

Cameron seconded that notion sloppily.

Janelle and I looked at each other and shook our heads.

"These fine inebriated fellows belong to Del and Doug respectively, right?" Janelle asked me. "That complicates things. Both of their parents are here—it's gonna be difficult to sneak them out of here."

"I vote we let 'em take their lumps. Maybe they'll learn a lesson," I said, deliberately ignoring my usual instinct to protect Presley.

"What'll happen if they get caught?" Janelle asked, eyeing the partially subdued pair.

"First of all, they'll be suspended from extracurricular activities at school for a while," I said, racking my brain for the rules and regulations.

"That'd really break my ol' man's heart," Cameron slurred. He'd showered and changed to blue jeans, though he still wore a dirty number 69 jersey. The one that had been his father's in a long-ago victorious homecoming game.

"They'll have to meet with a probation officer and do community service. At least that's what'll happen to Cameron. Presley is only thirteen, there may be a different procedure for him."

"Thirteen!" Janelle shouted, then remembered that we were trying to be quiet. "What the hell are you doing getting a thirteen-year-old drunk? Are you both idiots?" she demanded in a whisper.

"Hey, I got myself drunk," Presley said indignantly.

"I'm watching out for him," Cameron said at the same time.

"Yeah, right," I said as the boys tried unsuccessfully to look repentant.

"You two stay there," Janelle commanded, pointing at the ground. She then beckoned me to the edge of the bushes and peered around at the fire.

"You know what kind of scene there'll be if Doug catches Cameron here," she said quietly.

I agreed. "At the very least, Doug will have no choice but to throw Cameron off the football team."

It occurred to me that being thrown off the team might have been Cameron's whole purpose in showing up at the river.

"Should we get Delphine?" Janelle asked.

Del sat next to Hugh at the fire, laughing and talking and flirting. She looked like she was having a wonderful time. Hugh seemed to be enjoying himself too.

"Better not," I said. I'd known the maternal thing would kick in sooner or later. "She's here with a teacher, and teachers are required to report any suspicion of chemical use to the principal too."

"With a teacher?" Presley whispered, theatrically aghast. "Which one?" He scrambled ahead to look.

"Pipe down," I said sternly, pushing him back. "You want to get suspended?"

"Mr. Kincaid?" Presley wailed. "I'm on the annual staff. How will I ever show my face at school again?"

"While you're dying of humiliation, you might remember that you weren't invited to this particular shindig," I said. "If you'd stayed home where you belong, you'd never have known."

"But Mr. Kincaid is my—"

A sudden series of shouts from the other side of the chokecherry clump interrupted Presley.

At the fire, Doug Fischbach was standing, furiously arguing with his wife. He said something that I couldn't understand, though the nastiness of the remark was reflected in the shocked faces of those nearby. Including Stu, whose face was worked into a mixture of anger and complete loathing.

Debbie said something sharp and equally repugnant to Doug, who responded with a powerful open-handed blow that sent her reeling.

The crowd stood in stunned silence.

"Mom!" Cameron howled, and rushed from behind Janelle, where he'd been peeking around her legs.

Before anyone had a chance to register Cameron's sudden and unexpected appearance, he had tackled his father, knocking them both almost into the fire. Everyone jumped into action as Cameron furiously pummeled his father. Ron tried to pull Cameron away. Debbie sobbed and shouted. Stu tried to restrain Doug and got another flailing fist in the eye for his trouble.

"Oh shit, oh shit, oh shit," intoned Presley.

"Here." Janelle hurriedly dug in her pants pocket and handed me a set of keys. "Take my car. Maybe I can divert them long enough for you to get Presley home before anyone sees him."

The logic of her suggestion was inescapable. There was nothing I could do for Cameron. The consequences of this little drinking binge were going to be heavy indeed, a fact that seemed to be dawning on Presley, who was turning green around the gills.

I nodded and took the keys, déjà vu settling in with a dull thud. Is it homecoming that triggers this kind of stuff? I wondered. Or the river?

A separate thought occurred to me. "Stu . . ." I said.

Janelle misunderstood. "Don't worry, he'll take me home," she said over her shoulder as she trotted away.

I filed that statement away for later consideration and ushered a visibly shaken Presley to Janelle's '57 Corvette, hoping no one at the fire would think to look around.

"Hey," Presley said just before he threw up the first time, "cool car."

21

Now You Don't

SATURDAY

I'm not entirely certain when it became clear to me that teachers had a separate existence outside the classroom. Their identities were so indelibly entwined in the small routines and dramas that composed the ordinary school day that a life away from chalk dust, pop quizzes, and fire drills was inconceivable. I remember surreptitiously peeking into the flyleaf of a book on the desk of my second-grade teacher and the shock of discovering that her first name was "Mrs. John."

In high school, when I understood that they all had first names, I still wasn't completely able to assimilate the fact that their body parts functioned in the same manner as those of ordinary mortals (notwithstanding concrete evidence in the form of children produced by them).

Even now, the notion of grappling naked with a former teacher left me slightly queasy. Queasy and, I'm ashamed to admit, curious.

"What do you mean, nothing happened?" I asked Del for the third or fourth time.

She sighed and picked up a couple of dinner specials from the counter. "Exactly what I said, nothing happened."

I trailed her from the counter. "Oh come on, Del. With you something always *happens,* and you know it. Even on a date where nothing happens, *something* happens."

I would not have been that direct if Del had not, for the past couple of decades, forced the intimate details of every encounter on me. I knew whereof I spoke.

Del abruptly deposited the specials in front of slightly surprised patrons. "For the last time," she said, meeting my gaze defiantly, "nothing happened. Hugh and I are just friends. We talked. He brought me home. End of discussion. All right?"

She swung past me, waitressing her little heart out as I sorted through her lies. Del did not have any male friends—she considered the men either as past, or future, conquests. She had no dates where "nothing" happened, and she was never interested in conversation.

Most importantly, she had not come home last night. I know because I sat alone with her retching son until he finally dropped off to sleep, just before I went to work.

With Janelle's car, and her help distracting the crowd, I had been able to sneak Presley away from the river without anyone being the wiser.

And now Del was lying. And she didn't know that I knew she was lying. I decided to keep quiet about Presley until I could figure out why she wanted me to think she'd been home all night.

Del bustled about efficiently, chirping at the customers, ignoring me completely.

"It's guilt, you know," Rhonda said in my ear.

She still worked occasionally on weekend mornings. Since the near constant rain showers had done nothing to deter the extra-heavy reunion crowd, we were glad to have her.

"That's why she doesn't want to talk about what happened with Mr. Kincaid." Rhonda, well-aware of Del's reputation, was too newly graduated to call Hugh by his first name.

"You suppose?" I asked, still eyeing Del as she joked with a couple of older alumni.

"Yup," Rhonda said seriously. "It's an oedipal thing—making love to a father figure breaks all of society's taboos and has dire consequences in the world of the subconscious."

"Are you taking psychology too?" I asked.

"That's beside the point," Rhonda said. "You notice Mr. Kincaid hasn't come in for breakfast either."

She was right. Hugh, a Saturday morning regular, had not yet made an appearance.

Actually, Hugh wasn't the only regular missing. We'd also not seen Ron Adler, who was generally banging on the door when we opened.

Stu had arrived, though, looking bruised and weary as he slid into an empty booth. Any anxiety I'd felt about our relationship was smothered by the overwhelming urge to give him a hug and draw him a warm bath.

"Some night, huh?" I said softly, setting a cup and pot of coffee on the table in front of him. I sat opposite in the booth.

"Yeah," he said shortly, rubbing his forehead, the newest shiner glowing malevolently. He looked out the window, scowling at the rain.

"You okay?" I asked, though the answer was obvious.

"No, I'm not okay," he growled. He paused another minute, then glared at me. "Where in the fuck did you go last night? I looked for all over for you."

I sat back, surprised. "I took Presley home. In Janelle's Corvette. Just like she told me to."

"Coordinating rides must be one of Miss Hollywood's hobbies," Stu said, stirring his black coffee. "While Ron and I were trying to hold Doug down, she waded right into the middle, walked off with Cameron, and ordered me to take Debbie home immediately."

"Well, there wasn't time to tell you myself," I said, feeling defensive. With an attitude like that, Stu could draw his own bath. "Besides, Janelle told me that she'd ride back into town with you, and that she'd explain where I went and why. She didn't tell you?"

"She didn't tell me shit. All I know is that I looked for you, and couldn't find you. And then I looked for Debbie, but she'd already left. Everyone else was leaving, so I gave up and went home. Alone."

"Me too," I said. "Well not completely alone." I gave him the condensed version of Presley's appearance at the party and what fun it had been to hold his head over the toilet all night. "So you can tell Janelle that the keys to her car are here with me, and that it's safely parked behind the trailer."

That Stu showed no interest in the fact that I had actually driven a movie star's '57 Corvette was an indicator of his foul mood

"You two are such good friends, you can tell her yourself," he said, not looking at me.

"You'll probably see her first," I said slowly and distinctly, "since she is staying at *your* house."

"I never see her at all," Stu said carefully. "I didn't hear her come in last night, and her door was closed when I went to work this morning. Maybe we'll be lucky and she'll disappear completely."

"Hey guys," Rhonda leaned over the table and said quietly, "sorry to interrupt, but check this out." She nodded at the window that faced the street.

A determined and slightly disheveled Lisa Franklin Hauck-Robertson emerged from Adler's Garage into the drizzle, Ron Adler in tow. She motioned him to the passenger window of a pickup truck to talk to a shadowy figure sitting inside.

"That's Coach Fischbach's truck, isn't it?" Rhonda asked quietly.

Stu nodded, watching intently. Ron, partially obscured by the cab of the pickup, was gesturing and nodding emphatic negatives in the rain.

"She's done that up and down the whole street. For fifteen minutes now I been watching—she goes into a store or whatever, stays inside for a couple of minutes, comes out—sometimes alone, sometimes like with Ron over there—talks to whoever is in the truck, and then goes to the next place."

"Del, come here a minute," Rhonda said over her shoulder. "What do you think of this?"

Ron was still shaking his head, blinking madly into the truck window. Hugh Kincaid rounded the corner and was waved over to join the conversation.

Del peered out the window, tightened her lips, and said, "I think we're too damn busy to worry about what anyone else is doing." She narrowed her eyes at Rhonda and me and said archly, "Would either of you ladies like to lend a hand here? I'm running my ass off while you two gaze out the window."

She spun on one heel and left before either of us could reply.

Rhonda raised an eyebrow. "See what I mean?" she whispered. "Guilt."

I shrugged. Del was right—we were too busy for two-thirds of the staff to stand around gawking.

"Who's the other person in the truck?" I asked, with one last glance across the street. The pickup windows were tinted; the passenger could not be identified from our angle.

"Suppose it's the coach?" Rhonda asked.

"Let's hope not," Stu said darkly. "Every time I see him, he takes a swing at me. Next time, I'm throwing the first punch."

"Well, whoever it is, we'll know in a minute," Rhonda said, nodding at the window.

Lisa, grim and determined, was splashing across the street toward the cafe.

We busied ourselves carrying dirty dishes, taking orders, and measuring coffee grounds into fluted paper filters. Anything to keep the door to our backs when Lisa entered.

Out of the corner of my eye, I saw Lisa, damp and agitated, slide into the booth with Stu.

Belatedly remembering that I had not taken Stu's order, and looking for an excuse to eavesdrop, I sauntered over to them.

"Can I get you anything?" I asked brightly, pen and pad in hand.

"Nothing for me, thanks," Stu said, eyeing me meaningfully. He knew what I was up to.

"Just coffee, please," Lisa said.

"Yes indeedy," I said cheerfully.

"Just a second, Tory," Lisa said, "maybe you'd know."

"Know what?" I asked.

"Where Doug Fischbach is," Lisa said. "He didn't come home last night, and Debbie is out of her head with worry."

I don't know which surprised me more—that Lisa thought I might know Doug's whereabouts, or that Debbie was actually worried about him. Especially after last night.

"I haven't the foggiest, Lisa," I said. "He hasn't been in the cafe this morning. Sorry."

Lisa sighed and ran a hand through her damp, overdyed hair. "And you, Stuart?"

"I hope I never see that son of a bitch again," Stu said.

"What about Janelle?" Lisa asked.

"Personally, I don't care if I ever see her again either."

"No, that's not what I mean." Lisa smiled. "Do you think Janelle might have seen him?"

"Ask her yourself," Stu said wearily. "Try the house, she's probably still sleeping."

"We did already," Lisa said. "She's not there. Her car is gone too."

"I can explain that . . ." I said.

The cafe door burst open, and a short, wet, heavy, balding man burst in and charged up to me.

"You!" he shouted, jabbing a finger into my chest. "Where is she? I know you know. You were talking to her last night."

All conversation in the cafe stopped. Aphrodite left the kitchen to stand menacingly at the till, within arm's length of the wall phone. Stu slowly stood behind me, a protective arm on my shoulder. Del and Rhonda stared openmouthed.

"You know this guy?" Aphrodite demanded.

"I saw him at the football game last night. He was looking for Janelle," I said loudly. For everyone's benefit.

"I'm Benny Nelson," he said smugly, "Janelle's *husband.*"

Amazingly, he held a damp, hairy hand out for me to shake. I just looked at it.

"Listen." He grabbed my arm.

I pulled back. Aphrodite lifted the phone from the receiver. Stu's hands tightened on my shoulders. Lisa watched silently, with a smug expression on her face.

"Listen yourself," I said, more forcefully than I felt. "Keep your hands off or we'll call the police."

He stared at me for a long moment and then dropped his eyes. "You rubes are sure touchy," he said, to himself mostly.

"What do you want?" Aphrodite asked.

Still looking at me, he said, "I can't find Janelle. She didn't stay in her motel room. No one in this dipshit town has seen her. I need to find her."

To our absolute astonishment, his face crumpled and he started bawling right in the middle of the cafe, great heaving sobs. "I'm so afraid something has happened to her. I gotta find her." He appealed tearfully to everyone. "You gotta help me."

The dead silence that followed was broken by a laugh, amused, bitter, and completely genuine.

"They did it again." Lisa wiped her eyes. "They fucking did it again."

I looked at Stu, who shrugged, bewildered.

"Don't you see?" Lisa asked Stu. And Del. And me. "It's just like before." She grinned. It was a nasty, humorless expression. "They're staging an encore performance of the Doug and Janelle Disappearing Act."

22

Encore Performance

Whatever 1969 might mean in the larger historical context of America as the year of Woodstock, Teddy Kennedy's automotive plunge from a bridge on Chappaquiddick Island, the visit Charles Manson's faithful followers paid to actress Sharon Tate, and man's first walk on the moon, it will now, and forever, be remembered in Delphi as the *first* time Janelle Ross and Doug Fischbach disappeared together.

As a committee member, I was required to arrive at the All-School Reunion early for last-minute preparations. One class was in charge of the bar. Another group adjusted the microphone and sound equipment on a small stage platform at the far end of the room. Some were taping up last-minute banners and decorations. We were supposed to hand out reunion booklets, and since no one had yet arrived to claim one, I had plenty of time to dissect, with the other locals, the only occurrence as fascinating as the first time Janelle Ross and Doug Fischbach had disappeared.

"Don't you think the similarities are amazing?"

Rhonda asked, concentrating soberly over a paper cup of fruit punch. If the get-together had been held at the bar, Rhonda could have enjoyed an underage beer. And though this little soiree, staged in the school gymnasium, had a special dispensation to sell and serve alcohol, Rhonda would have had a hard time convincing the bartender that she was over twenty-one.

"Thanks, Mrs. Saunders," I said, handing over a couple of bucks for an overflowing cup of Michelob drawn from a keg packed in a washtub full of ice.

"See you later, Mom," Rhonda said over her shoulder, leading us away from the small crowd at the makeshift bar. She returned to the subject that had caught everyone's attention. "You *all* went to an after-homecoming party at the river—just like last night. And *everyone* got drunk."

"Wrong," Del said, sipping a beer. She stood with us, but her eyes swept the room constantly. "The only drunks last night were members of the Fischbach family."

"Not entirely," I said hesitantly. She still didn't know about Presley. "Debbie drank several beers, but I wouldn't have said she was drunk. But Gina Adler was a bit tipsy." Del herself had downed several cans in quick succession between her arrival with Hugh and the fight that ended the party.

"My point," Del said, "was that last night wasn't anything like that party in 1969."

"Of course it was," Rhonda insisted. She'd spent all day questioning us endlessly about both occasions. She ticked points on her fingers. "It was homecoming. The weather was icky and the river was high. Doug Fischbach punched Stu McKee."

There was another similarity that Rhonda didn't know about—both parties had been witnessed by drunken thirteen-year-olds, and I'd had to clean up the aftermath.

"At each party, Debbie Fischbach was upset and left early, without Doug." Rhonda grinned, working up to her finale. "And Janelle Ross and Doug Fischbach were last seen together at the river."

"Yeah, and both of them had vice presidents named

Johnson," Del said tiredly. "Aren't you forgetting one major point?"

"Oh yeah, at both parties, people spent time with other people they really shouldn't have." Rhonda winked at me; she was teasing Del.

Del's lips tightened. "No, dipshit. This time, there are no dead bodies."

"Just wait," Rhonda said, nodding. "I have a feeling."

"That's silly," I said. Rhonda was determined to turn a nasty little affair into an intrigue. "Everyone has been accounted for."

"Everyone, except for Doug and Janelle," she said, pointedly.

"You think they killed each other?" I asked, trying not to grin. Though I have been known, on occasion, to jump to some pretty wild, and mostly erroneous, conclusions about cause-of-death in Delphi, I generally had the minimum evidence of an indisputably dead body.

"Well, one of them might have killed the other one," she chirped. "For all we know, they both might be Jack the Rippers." Rhonda frowned and tried again. "Or would that be Jacks the Ripper?"

"I'd be more worried about the Teds Bundy and the Jeffreys Dahmer," Neil Pascoe said, carrying a glass of punch. He'd come in a while ago and had worked his way slowly around toward us. "I assume you are discussing this evening's Hot Topic."

"What else?" I laughed.

"How thoughtful of the movie star and the football coach to provide us with a conversational ice breaker," Neil said.

"So have you come up with anything new?" Rhonda asked Neil.

"Not really. Debbie hasn't been seen since this morning when she and Lisa whatsername made the rounds in town. Ditto Cameron. It's too soon to file a missing person report with the police, and besides, everyone thinks Doug and Janelle are just knocking off a few for old time's sake."

That seemed to be the general consensus. Small groups

broke and reformed all around the gymnasium. Some newcomers had arrived. Nicely dressed alumni of various ages, each wearing a name tag that also stated the year of graduation, earnestly discussed Coach Fischbach's latest breach of athletic etiquette. It's not that they were any easier on Janelle, it's just that, since she was a movie star and all, they never really expected proper behavior from her.

"What's Stu think about all this?" Neil asked me quietly.

I shrugged. Our conversation at the cafe had been too much like a fight for either of us to make a firm date for the evening. Stu was on the reunion planning committee; I assumed he'd show up sooner or later. And then we'd talk. Maybe.

Good friend that he is, Neil didn't press.

"Gina Adler is sure taking it hard," Rhonda nodded toward a small group a few feet away from us.

Gina, pale and drawn, had obviously been crying, though she flashed a wan smile in my direction. Ron hovered around her like an anxious moth.

"She's probably worried about Debbie. They worked together a long time on this reunion," I said, watching as Ron took Gina's punch cup to be refilled.

"She's probably hungover," Del said shortly.

"It's probably guilt," Rhonda corrected. "After all, Gina helped to bring Janelle back to Delphi in the first place."

"Not according to Doug," Neil said, watching them closely.

Hugh Kincaid had joined Gina's group and was talking quietly with her. She briefly laid her head on his shoulder as he said something comforting in her ear.

"Nope," Rhonda said, "it's pure guilt." She turned to Del for confirmation, or a little more needling, but Del had stalked off without even a cursory good-bye. "A lot of that going around lately."

People poured in steadily, the conversations became more animated, and the subject turned from recent scandals to past glories. Women, especially from the later classes, squealed in recognition of each other. They hugged, laughed, and drank beer. And went to the bathroom in groups of at least four.

I found myself straining to recognize faces as people claimed their reunion booklets, but discovered it helped more to squint and concentrate on postures and profiles while searching the memory banks. Unfortunately, everyone I thought looked about my age was actually quite a bit younger.

Once I narrowed myself to attendees with grayer hair and larger waistlines, I began to recognize former classmates without referring to name tags.

Gerald Messner, still tall and goofy-looking, but goofy-looking in the debonair way of millionaire software designers, stood with a possessive arm around a very young, very blond, very large-chested young woman. The fabled Monique. She would have given Janelle a run for her money in the Most Beautiful Woman in the Room Department.

If Janelle had been there, of course.

Rhonda had drifted off to squeal at others from her class, and Neil was schmoozing with some oldsters a few feet away.

I was deep into a one-sided conversation with a woman a couple years younger than me, learning more than I ever wanted to know about her children, her job, and her recent spiritual reawakening, when I noticed a change in the timbre of the conversations in the gym.

A small pause of hushed expectation swept the room as Lisa Franklin Hauck-Robertson propelled a frail and exhausted Debbie Fischbach toward the stage.

Debbie looked years older than she had last night. An expert makeup job obscured, but did not completely hide, a new bruise on her cheek. Only slightly shaky, she mounted the stairs and approached the microphone.

She surveyed the crowd for a moment and then spoke. "As chairwoman of Delphi High School's All-School Reunion, classes 1965–1975, I'd like to welcome each and every one of you back to dear old Delphi High," she said in a careful voice, completely neglecting to mention

Gina Adler, who, as co-chair, had done most of the actual work.

Lisa stood at the foot of the stage, watching the crowd warily, as Debbie continued her speech, a standard self-congratulatory message that no one would have paid attention to had not the speaker's husband recently disappeared with the evening's guest of honor.

If Gina minded being left out of the credits, it didn't show. She stood calmly on the sidelines listening, arm linked through Ron's, as his face worked itself through an amazing array of blinks and contortions. Pregnant Junior was a little farther away, with a few others from the committee, their faces, like those of most of the crowd, avidly curious. Rhonda watched the stage raptly, occasionally whispering comments to Neil. Del stood a little behind the Adlers, face unreadable.

I had to admire Debbie's courage in facing the room head on—she must have known she'd be an object of curiosity.

The speech finally ended, and Lisa forced everyone into a round of applause a good deal more enthusiastic than the crowd might have bestowed without her glaring example.

"Tory." An urgent male voice in my ear startled me. "Can you come here a minute? I think it's important."

Without waiting for my assent, Stu grabbed my arm and pulled me toward the gymnasium door. Framed there, in the dim light of the lobby, stood Presley, pale and obviously upset, wringing something between his hands.

"What's going on?" I asked Stu. "Is something wrong with Pres?"

"I don't know. I found them wandering around outside. They wouldn't tell me anything. Presley insisted that I come and find you. Not his mother. Just you."

Thirteen years old, taller than me now, though still impossibly young, Presley paced back and forth in the lobby as a very anxious, pale, and blinking John Adler—Ron and Gina's son—stood near the emergency exit.

Irritation at being unceremoniously yanked from the

reunion changed to concern, which changed to apprehension as I recognized the object Presley held in his hands.

It was an old and dirty Delphi Oracle football jersey. Imprinted with number 69.

"I was feeling better, Tory, so John and I rode our bikes back out to the river where you guys were last night, to check for stuff. You know, dropped money or leftover beers. Stuff like that," Presley said in a rush. His voice, which had not yet changed, rose a notch. "I'm sorry. If I'd known, I never woulda went back there. But I didn't know." He was perilously close to tears.

In the background, John, still pacing, wheezed a high-pitched confirmation.

"Known what?" I asked Presley, heart sinking, not wanting to hear his answer.

"We didn't know *he'd* be there," Presley said desperately.

"Who?" Stu demanded.

Pres closed his eyes, summoning his courage. "Coach Fischbach," he said in a small voice threaded with anguish. "Coach Fischbach is down at the oxbow. In the water. And, oh God, Tory—he's dead!"

23

Rhonda's Obsession

Some people rise to every occasion with that famous pioneer can-do attitude. They gird their loins, grit their teeth, put their shoulders to the wheel and noses to the grindstone. They embody every cliché for human nobility. And what's more, they do it with a song in their hearts and a smile on their lips.

I am not one of them.

I do what I have to do, sure—I'll even make the leap to self-sacrifice, but I will not smile as I tread the long and winding road.

And I sure as hell won't be singing.

Everyone else was, however. Inside the gym, someone led the reunion attendees in a rousing off-tempo version of the Delphi school song. It kept them focused on the stage and not on the lobby while the four of us tried to figure out what to do.

Or at least two of us were figuring. The other two stood silently.

"Are you sure?" Stu demanded unnecessarily.

The boys' faces confirmed their own awful suspicions.

"I'd better get Del," I said quietly to Stu.

"No!" Pres said vehemently. "Mr. Kincaid is in there with her. See?" He pointed into the gym. "If he finds out that I was at the river today, he'll find out that I was at the river last night too. I'll get suspended."

Sure enough, Del and Hugh were singing amiably on the edge of the crowd. Del took Hugh's arm companionably and they walked off together.

"Can't you do it?" Pres asked me, scrunching down so no one would see him. "You're a grown-up."

"Do what?" I asked, not liking the turn of the conversation.

"Go back to the river and check it out," Pres said, as though that should have been obvious. "We're just kids. We can't call the sheriff. They won't believe us. You have to. After you're sure."

"What do you think?" I asked Stu. "Should we at least get Debbie? She's Doug's wife, she deserves to know."

"I don't think *we* should do anything," Stu said quickly. "I vote we call the police right here and now. It's not our business."

Unfortunately, with Presley involved, it *was* my business. Pres still refused to make the call, and I didn't think I should do it until their story had been confirmed.

"Are you sure you don't want me to get your mom instead?" I asked Pres, sighing.

"No. Please."

I chewed my lip, trying to decide what to do. Stu tapped his foot impatiently.

"What's up, guys?" Neil asked, stepping out into the lobby. He wrinkled his glasses up on his nose, cheerful but alert.

"You're here. Good. Maybe they'll listen to you," Stu said to Neil.

I shot Stu a sharp look of exasperation, and then in as few words as possible, explained the situation to Neil.

"You're absolutely certain?" he asked Presley, who nodded almost imperceptibly. "Well then . . ." He paused, working his mouth in concentration. "I guess we better go and see."

"Thanks," I said gratefully. No matter how little I enjoyed the prospect, driving out to the river seemed the best course of action.

"Jesus, Pascoe, I thought you had some common sense," Stu exploded. "If these kids are wrong, it's just a wild-goose chase. If they're right, it could be dangerous. Maybe Doug needs medical attention. You run a library, not a hospital."

"When did you find him?" Neil asked the boys.

Pres looked over at John, and then back at Neil. They both shrugged. "About an hour ago."

"Another ten minutes won't make much difference then," Neil said calmly to Stu. "But you have a point. If we're not back in half an hour, call the sheriff."

"And what am I supposed to do in the meantime?" Stu asked sarcastically.

Neil ignored the tone and answered the question. "Watch out for Debbie, if you can. Someone else might have been to the river already. They might be less discreet about making sensational announcements."

"Anything else?" Stu asked, anger barely contained beneath the surface of his voice.

"Yeah, find Junior and ask her to hand out reunion booklets for me." I added quietly, pleading for his understanding, "I'll be back as soon as I can. I have to do this."

Stu locked eyes with me but said nothing. Torn, and hating the situation, I glanced at Neil, but found no help in his carefully neutral expression. I knew it was my call, and I'd already made my decision. I turned to explain, plead with Stu again, but he spun on one heel and stalked back into the gym.

There was no time to sort through the undercurrents of that last exchange, or why I was relieved that Neil was going, instead of Stu.

"Come on," Presley said, grabbing John's arm and pulling him out the lobby door.

I sighed and followed them. We loaded ourselves into one of Neil's refurbished pickup trucks—Neil and I in the cab and the boys settled in the box.

I knew Neil would not bring up Stu unless I did, and I had no intention of doing so. "You think Doug is really dead?" I asked as we sped along the familiar gravel road.

"It's pretty hard to mistake dead for anything else," Neil said simply. "As you know from experience."

"Everyone figured Doug and Janelle ran away together again. You think she's there too?" I asked. "Dead?"

"The boys didn't say anything about finding another body," Neil said, "and I don't suppose that's the kind of detail they'd leave out."

"This'll make Rhonda's day," I said sadly. "She's been pestering everyone about the similarities between that party in 1969 when Butchie Pendergast drowned and last night. She swore we'd find another body."

"Well," Neil said, "now we know Doug and Janelle didn't run away together again."

"Rhonda's vibes are more tuned than mine," I said. "She was bound and determined to uncover a mystery in all this. All I've done is try to talk her out of the notion."

"We all did." Neil shrugged. "She even asked me who discovered the Pendergast boy's body. I didn't know, do you?"

We turned off the road onto the gravel bank at the oxbow. "I guess that detail got lost in the uproar about Doug and Janelle disappearing together for the first time." I paused. "For the only time."

Neil killed the engine and I sat, as the sun neared the horizon, remembering last night. And 1969. Caught in Rhonda's obsession about similarities between then and now.

He sighed and swung open his door. Presley jumped from the box and pointed to a clump of chokecherries just past the bend in the river.

"Over there, down in the water." He hesitated, waiting for us to take charge.

"We'll go first," Neil said, confirming the decision with a nod. "You boys follow, and tell us if everything looks the same as when you were here earlier. Don't touch anything."

"Oh shit," John said, speaking for the first time. "We already did. Presley picked up that old football shirt."

Pres, who was still holding the jersey, squealed and dropped it. "It wasn't with the other stuff. We picked it up before we saw, uh . . . the . . ."

"Too late to worry about that now," I said over my shoulder as Neil rounded the tree clump. "Just put it back about where you found it and don't forget to tell the sheriff."

"Oh jeez," Pres said mournfully.

With a backward glance at them, I stepped through the weeds to the riverbank.

Neil stood, back to me, shoulders slumped and head bowed. Without turning around, he said quietly, "You don't have to come any closer if you don't want to. It's Doug."

I inhaled deeply, wishing I was anywhere but on the bank of the Mighty Jim, stepped beside Neil, and looked down.

Doug Fischbach, ghostly white, naked and bloated, lay faceup, partially submerged in the swirling brown water. He didn't seem to be injured. Except for being dead, that is. He'd apparently snagged on a small outcropping of rock that had been exposed when the high water washed a portion of the bank away. Tree branches and other debris bobbed gently, trapped in the small pool formed by his body.

I stood silent for a moment, absurdly aware of each breath I took. Inhale, exhale, inhale, exhale. I was alive, and Doug wasn't. I blew out all my air and asked, finally, "Can we at least close his eyes?"

I hadn't liked anything about Doug Fischbach—as a coach, he was vindictive; as a husband and father, he was abusive; as a human being, he was totally reprehensible. But, like Butchie Pendergast before him, Doug did not deserve to be so completely stripped of dignity.

"We better not," Neil said softly. He wrinkled his glasses up again and turned to face the pale and very subdued boys standing on the bank. "Does everything look the same to you?"

They nodded. "I think his clothes are on the other side of that tree over there." Presley pointed a small distance upriver. "We saw 'em but we didn't touch 'em," he assured us quickly.

The haphazard clothing pile seemed to contain everything Doug had been wearing last night—pants, shoes, satin Delphi Oracle jacket, socks, and underwear. Littered around the site were assorted pocket change, a knife, and a wallet. The last rays of sunset caught a small sparkle in the mud a few feet away. I bent down to see—it was a gold circle pin with rhinestones dotted around the perimeter, the kind worn by high school girls in the fifties.

"Nice," Neil said, looking over my shoulder at the pin. "Suppose Doug had that with him too?"

"Who knows? Doesn't seem the kind of thing he would carry around. Someone else could have dropped it," I said, straightening up, checking my watch. "We've been gone more than twenty minutes already. We better get back, before Stu gets worried."

Neil harrumphed slightly. "The sheriff is going to want to talk to the boys right away. I think you should drive back into town by yourself and make the call. I'll wait here. With them. Keep an eye on things. Just in case."

I didn't want to think about any "just in cases," and I didn't like the idea of leaving him, or the boys, but I saw the sense in his suggestion.

"I'll go straight to the gym," I said reluctantly, "see Stu, and then call it in. What about Debbie? Should I tell her? Or anyone else?"

Neil frowned. "Better not. Doug has obviously been dead awhile; it won't hurt to leave Debbie with a couple more hours' peace of mind."

I felt like a coward leaving Neil behind. I felt even worse knowing that I was, in effect, withholding the awful news from Doug's next of kin.

"What about Rhonda?" I asked. "She'll be horrified that her prediction came true."

"Her prediction *hasn't* come true," Neil said, "all we have is a dead football coach. Not a mystery."

I sighed. Neil was right. Doug could have died from any

number of causes, and for any number of reasons. None of them sinister. And none of them connected to 1969.

So why was I reluctantly starting to think that Rhonda was right too?

Neil put an arm around my shoulder and planted a soft kiss on the top of my head.

"Drive carefully, be brave, and, most important," he said, "keep your eyes open."

24

Incidents and Accidents

It occurred to me, while driving back to town in Neil's truck, that this was exactly the spot in horror flicks where plucky females, often played by J. Ross Nelson, came to a nasty end.

You know the kind of scene I'm talking about—where the idiot woman goes into a dark basement alone, having left the fifteen-inch kitchen knife in the foyer next to the telephone table. The kind of scene where movie patrons yell helpful advice at the screen when they realize a bloodbath is coming.

Under most circumstances, such a thought would not have spooked me, but leaving Neil alone at the river with the boys, and a body, did not sit well. And the gnawing suspicion that Rhonda had been on the right track left me even more unsettled.

As a diversion, I grabbed a random cassette from the box on the dash and plugged it in. I was immediately caught in the rhythm of Paul Simon. He and his bodyguard accompanied me safely back into town, where I resisted the urge to head straight to the trailer and crawl back into bed.

I also resisted the urge to sit in the parking lot awhile before going inside since Stu had a clock on us and would be calling the sheriff soon himself if I didn't check in.

The lights were low, and the program was well under way. Groups of people were seated at long trestle tables scattered around the gym. Onstage, awards were being given to the alumni who had traveled the farthest to attend the reunion. Since Gerald Messner wasn't up there, I assumed he'd flown in from the West Coast, not from his villa in France.

I stood in the doorway, sorting through the crowd, trying to find Stu, and finally spotted him at a table along the wall, seated with most of the reunion committee members and a bunch of others I vaguely recognized. Del, Junior, and the Adlers were all there. Unfortunately, so was Debbie Fischbach, seated in the middle between Stu and Lisa Franklin Hauck-Robertson.

Stu glanced up and saw me, his eyebrows rising in a silent query. I shook my head slowly. No, it wasn't a wild-goose chase. No, the boys weren't wrong. No, there was nothing we could do for Doug.

He locked eyes with mine for a long, solemn moment which was broken by the laughter of the crowd. Then he turned back to the stage, a stiff public smile on his face.

As someone got an award for having eleven children and thirty-five grandchildren, I dialed 911 on the pay phone in the lobby. I said what I had to, thanked the dispatcher kindly, and rejoined the All-School Reunion.

Stu carefully looked the other way, and since there wasn't a spare chair beside him, I found one behind the booklet table and wearily sat down, hoping for a minute to regroup before facing anyone.

"Where have you been?" Junior whispered, sharply annoyed, pressing a hand into the small of her back. I hadn't seen her standing in the dark, behind the table. She still had months before delivering, but I swear she was getting bigger by the minute. And testier. "You were supposed to be here early to help. We've been absolutely swamped."

Evidently, she had not been mollified by Stu's cover story, and I could not defend myself without giving away more than I wanted to. "Sorry," I said, "something came up that couldn't be avoided. But I'm here now. Why don't you sit and I'll take over for the rest of the evening."

I was no longer in a reminiscing mood anyway, and the booklet table was a good vantage point from which to follow Neil's advice to keep an eye on things.

Junior was still miffed. "Not much left to do *now,"* she mumbled, sitting down.

The program dragged on for what seemed like hours, though it was probably only forty-five minutes, during which nothing of interest happened, either on the stage or off. I jumped at every shadow in the lobby, expecting the sheriff to appear suddenly and ask for Debbie. Onstage, assorted speakers droned, and I tried not to remember the reason for my anxiety.

At one end of the committee table, Gina clung to the arm of a comically stiff and wide-eyed Ron Adler. Del, who was sitting alone a few chairs down from them, methodically dismantled an empty beer cup and added the pieces to the growing pile beside her. At the other end, Stu leaned over and said something into Debbie's ear, but did not look in my direction. Debbie repeated what Stu had said to Lisa, who laughed quietly and shot a glance at me.

From her table, a few yards away, Rhonda motioned to me surreptitiously. I ignored her. She got up quietly and squatted next to Del for a whispered conference. Del caught my eye, raised an eyebrow, and shrugged.

As the speaker droned, Rhonda made her way back. "It won't do you any good to ignore me," she said, peeved.

"Ignore you? What do you mean?"

"Cut the bullshit, Tory," she said, eyes narrowed. "Something's up. Spill it."

I sighed. Stu wouldn't look at me, Neil was stuck at the river with a couple of adolescents and a dead body, Del sat there shredding every piece of paper she could get her hands on, and Rhonda was trying to play tough guy.

"Listen, I'll tell you as soon as I can," I said, opting for the truth, "but you'll just have to be patient for a little—"

A blur of activity at the gymnasium door caught my attention. This is it, I thought. This is where the evening gets really interesting. And awful.

But no tan-uniformed officers stepped in to break the terrible news gently to Debbie Fischbach. Instead, Benny Nelson, sweating and obviously agitated, burst into the room, ran down the aisle, and jumped onto the stage. He grabbed the microphone from a startled oldster who was accepting an award for being the earliest attending Delphi graduate.

The high whine of feedback filled the suddenly silent room.

"Everybody stay calm," he said in a rush, "I have terrible news for you all."

Oh shit, I thought. Oh shit.

Finally Stu looked my way, but there was nothing we could do now. He placed a gentle hand on Debbie's shoulder. Rhonda grabbed mine in a death grip.

"I knew it. I knew it," she whispered fiercely.

"My wife, the woman you knew as Janelle Ross, is missing," Benny said mournfully.

Everyone was silent. We knew that already.

"And now I'm afraid she may be dead," Benny continued.

This time there was a collective and audible gasp in the room.

"What did I tell you?" Rhonda asked, letting go of my shoulder.

"You need to split up into groups," Benny ordered, "and spread out along the river to search for her. And you need to start right now, before it gets completely dark."

"What for?" someone hollered. "We're a whole lot more apt to find her shacked up in some motel with Coach Fischbach."

Debbie closed her eyes, frozen in humiliation.

"That's just it, you idiot," Benny shouted back. "She isn't in some jerkwater motel with your jackass coach."

"What makes you so sure?" the same voice hollered back.

"Because . . ." Benny said, a glint of malice in his squinted eyes, and hollow sorrow in his voice.

I knew what was coming and stood up quickly, trying to get around the table and to Debbie's side before Benny could finish his sentence.

". . . I just came from the river and your football coach ain't going to be shacking up with no one ever again."

People were beginning to whisper furiously. Some stood up. Benny didn't notice the commotion. Or he didn't care. "Your coach is dead. He drowned, you asshole. That's why we need to search for Janelle. She could be hurt. Or dead too."

This time the room erupted in a welter of noise and agitated conversation. From the corner of my eye, I saw that the deputies had finally arrived. One made for the stage in a purposeful stride, and some helpful soul headed the other two in Debbie's direction.

Stu grabbed the nearly catatonic Debbie and held her tightly, twisting away, using his body as a shield to protect her from the sudden crush of curious commiseration.

Rhonda stood shocked and immobile. Gina buried her head on Ron's chest. Del stared at them in disgust. Lisa stood, looked from Stu to me and back again.

"You knew," she said, so quietly that I don't think anyone else heard. Then her eyes rolled back and she wilted, smacking the back of her head on the table as she collapsed, unconscious.

25

Hints and Allegations

MONDAY

Under normal circumstances, Doug Fischbach's drowning would have occupied everyone's attention completely. But the intoxicating addition of a missing, almost-respected movie actress, with irrefutable ties to the deceased, turned what would have been avid small-town speculation and theory-mongering into a sideshow.

The early breakfast crowd at the cafe was wide-eyed with a weekend's worth of unsubstantiated rumor and local press coverage.

"Maybe she wouldn't run away with him again," Rhonda, who had no morning classes at the university on Mondays, said thoughtfully, pouring coffee into already full cups. She'd forgiven me for holding out on her Saturday, and was spending every free moment in the cafe. "Maybe he was despondent and killed himself because Janelle was the only woman he ever loved."

"If *despondent* means 'drunk and nasty,' that describes Doug." Ron blinked. "Though I can't imagine him killing himself because he was a jerk."

Ron did not belong to the School of Speak Well of the Dead.

"That doesn't explain why Janelle is missing. If she wouldn't run away with him, why isn't she here? And if she did run away, why did she go? And when?" asked Neil, who had been spending more time than usual at the cafe too. "Besides, I don't remember anyone saying anything about suicide."

"I suppose they can't rule it out entirely," Hugh Kincaid said, just finishing up his breakfast. "Since there really isn't a question as to cause of death, what else is there to talk about? And when it comes to suicide, who's to know what will trigger a decision like that?"

"Well, actually," Rhonda said, "there have been numerous studies on the causes of suicide and it's been pretty well-documented—"

"What's the school's take on all this?" I interrupted, hoping to forestall a rehash of Rhonda's psych class. "Seeing as how Doug was an employee."

"I expect we'll get the official reaction this morning." Hugh stood and handed me his usual tip. "But the superintendent called each teacher personally and asked us not to give interviews or speak to the media. I know he's frantic to downplay any connection between the school and all this.

"To give him his due, I think he's really more concerned about Cameron and the other Fischbach boys than collateral damage to the reputation of Delphi High School."

"How is Cameron, anyway?" Neil asked. "And his mother?"

"I went out to see them yesterday, and they're doing about as well as could be expected."

"The poor kid was publicly humiliated by his father at the football game, and then got into a fistfight with him the very same night," Rhonda said, ready to resume her lecture. "And then the father dies before any of those issues can be resolved. Cameron is going to carry that baggage around with him for a long time."

"Rhonda's right," Neil said, smiling at her. "Even if the death is ruled accidental—and with Doug's blood alcohol level, and the fact that he mentioned skinny-dipping earlier in the evening, it's pretty well a given—Cameron is going to have a rough time."

"I'll be keeping as close an eye on him as I can," Hugh said, at the door. He was still the senior class adviser, and he took his assignment seriously. "I just hope he hangs in there until a little time passes and everything falls into some sort of perspective."

The fascination with Doug's death only heightened the interest in Janelle's whereabouts. No trace of her had been found along, or in, the James River. Her motel room appeared not to have been used. Though Stu wasn't actually talking about the situation, he had given everyone to understand that Janelle had not slept in her bed on Friday night.

Of course, he didn't say that to me. Since Saturday, he had not spoken to me at all.

The officials were treating Janelle's disappearance carefully. They didn't really think she was dead, but they could not rule out that possibility, and so an investigation into her disappearance was ongoing. A check of local airline reservations had not turned up anyone matching Janelle's description or known aliases. She seemed to have dropped off the face of the earth.

Benny Nelson, however, was wailing and sobbing for the benefit of every camera and microphone he could find. His current theory was that she had been kidnapped. He'd made tearful pleas for her return.

"What do you make of this guy?" Rhonda pointed over Ron's shoulder at a photo of mournful Benny in the paper.

"Phony as a three-dollar bill." Ron blinked. "I saw the letter Janelle wrote to the reunion committee, and she didn't mention no husband."

"Yeah, but I do recognize him," I said. "I've seen pictures. In magazines and stuff. I'm pretty sure it's the same guy. But when we saw him at the football game,

Janelle was desperate to avoid him. She made me promise not to say anything about the party at the river."

"I seem to remember a divorce mentioned somewhere," Neil said, getting ready to leave. "I'll go home and check this Benny Nelson out, and see what I can find."

"Great idea," I said. "Whatever he is to Janelle, I don't trust him. Or his crocodile tears."

Janelle's status as a semicelebrity had vaulted the story into immediate regional airplay, and the nationals were beginning to express interest. And unfortunately, someone had uncovered the fact that Janelle and Doug shared a rather colorful history.

"It's in the paper and everything." Ron read aloud, " 'A teenage beer party held in the exact same spot in 1969, also after a homecoming football game, resulted in the tragic death by drowning of sixteen-year-old Lawrence Pendergast.' " Ron turned the page and continued, " 'The death of that young man and the disappearance from Delphi of J. Ross Nelson (then 1969 homecoming queen) and Douglas Fischbach (1969 homecoming king) have long been considered Delphi mysteries. This new drowning, under conditions suspiciously similar to the earlier accident, reopens questions that have never been adequately explained. Perhaps it is time for a new investigation of both incidents.' "

"That's what I've been saying all along," Rhonda crowed triumphantly.

I hated to encourage Rhonda, but I was also starting to think that there were just a few too many coincidences to ignore. "It would help if we knew where in the hell Janelle was." I sighed.

Though nothing had been confirmed, there had been numerous alleged "Janelle sightings."

"It says here," Ron read, "that someone bearing a striking resemblance to J. Ross Nelson was seen boarding a flight to Denver at the Aberdeen airport."

"She could be dead," Aphrodite weighed in from the kitchen, sliding a couple of burger platters across the counter for me.

"She could be anywhere—she had plenty of money, and a talent for melting into the background when she wanted to hide," I said, ferrying burgers.

"I bet she's still around," Rhonda said, chewing a lip.

"No one in their right mind would abandon a '57 'Vette." Ron blinked.

Janelle's car was still parked behind our trailer, and the keys were still in my pocket.

"A trucker I know said he heard one of his buddies picked up someone who looked a lot like her on the highway and gave her a ride into St. Paul," Del said, startling us all. She was not on duty for another couple of hours and we had been so intent on our conversation that we had not seen her come in.

Looking tired and a little frazzled, she poured herself a cup of coffee and slid into the booth opposite Ron, who rattled his papers, cleared his throat, and for the first time in history, ignored Del completely.

26

....

A Real Good Scout

In 1969, prevailing wisdom dictated that the way to deal with trauma and grief was to indulge in one good cry and never think about it again. In those days, "put it out of your mind" was a credo inflicted on young and old alike. Dwelling on sorrows was considered an unacceptable self-indulgence. Amnesia was encouraged.

In school, we were not allowed to talk about our feelings. Indeed, we were not supposed to think about the mysteries of Butchie Pendergast's death, the unexplained disappearance of the most popular girl in the school, and the equally unexplained reappearance of the football co-captain.

For a very short time, Mr. Kincaid had allowed students from any grade to come to his room during his free period and talk. The death of a fellow student, even one as unlamented as Butchie, had stirred up a generalized malaise and a heightened awareness of our own mortality. But the administration, backed by worried parents and concerned clergy, forced him to steer conversations with students to less morbid subjects, thinking that surface cheeriness would erase the inner turmoil.

In contrast today, grief, loss, and sorrow are thoroughly acknowledged and dissected. The school system takes its place at the forefront of politically correct caution and concern by engaging counselors and psychologists to console students any time anything untoward happens.

While I understand that denial has a limited clinical appeal, I'm not entirely sure that microscopic attention to every nuance of feeling is any more effective in dealing with the very human bewilderment of sudden loss and irreversible change.

I sat at the Formica table, alone in the trailer kitchen shortly after the end of my shift at the cafe, contemplating another pile of medical bills and the impossibility of ever repairing my credit record, when Presley came in.

He dragged himself into the living room, dropped his books on the floor beside the vinyl couch, flopped onto it, and turned on the TV, without much more than a cursory nod my direction.

"What are you doing home so early?" I asked, deciding not to think about unpayable bills.

Without looking at me, flipping through the channels, he said, "They had this dorky woman in to talk to the whole school about Coach being, you know, dead. Then they called all of us football players into the locker room and she talked some more. And then she said we could go home, if we were really upset."

"And are you really upset?" I asked.

He shrugged. "Not so upset that I felt like crying in front of the rest of the team like that counselor lady wanted us to. I mean, Coach was a good coach and all, but he was kind of a jerk." He finally looked at me, small, pale, and not nearly as nonchalant as he wanted to be. "You know?"

"Yeah," I said. "You don't have to pretend to like him just because he's dead."

"It's not that," Pres said, looking down again. "I didn't like or not like him. He was the coach—nothing else mattered. But I didn't want him to be dead. And I didn't want to be the one to find him."

I'm an adult, and the sight of Doug, dead and floating in the river, had completely spooked me. How much worse had it been for thirteen-year-old Presley?

Since we were alone, I risked an affront to his dignity and sat next to him on the couch and put an arm around his shoulder. And since we were alone, he risked a little more of his dignity by laying his head on my shoulder.

"I know what you mean, kiddo," I said softly. "Finding a dead body isn't nearly as much fun as people think."

"Everyone kept asking me about it all day. 'Was it cool?' 'Did he have his eyes open?' 'Was he really naked?' 'Were you scared?' " Presley repeated plaintively. "It was awful. I couldn't wait to get out of there."

"I can imagine," I said, tightening my arm a little. "People say really dumb things when they're uncomfortable, and dead bodies make them uncomfortable. Did they at least wait until Cameron was out of earshot before bringing up the subject?"

"That's the worst thing of all," Pres said, genuinely confused. "Cameron cornered me in the bathroom and asked most of that stuff himself."

"Well," I said, wishing I could peek in Rhonda's psych book for backup, "I imagine he thinks he can count on you for the truth. No matter how awful their relationship was, Doug was still Cameron's father, and that's the kind of stuff no one else will tell him."

"You think so?" Pres asked, relieved enough to lean down and pick up his stack of books.

I took the hint and removed my arm. "Especially since the last time they saw each other they got into that terrible fight. Sometimes people say horrible things that they don't mean, but can't take back." I was thinking of the names Doug called Cameron at the football game.

"Yeah, Cameron probably feels bad for what he said too," Pres said, arranging a geography book on his lap and opening a spiral notebook to a page of notes with the circled words "Be Preparred" written in felt pen across the header.

"What?" I asked, frowning, wondering why that phrase rang a bell.

"After the football game, at the river, before you found us, when we were, you know, kind of drunk," Pres said, skimming a paragraph in the book. "I'm sure Cameron didn't mean it when he said he wanted to kill his dad. That he couldn't wait until his dad was dead."

"He probably feels guilty for even thinking something like that," I said, still wishing for that psych book. "I know none of you like talking to the grief lady the school hired, but maybe Cameron should talk to Mr. Kincaid. He's a good guy, he might be able to help."

Pres's lips tightened.

"And even though you're not in high school, I'm sure you could go in and talk to him yourself, if this stuff is still bothering you," I added.

"No, I couldn't," Pres said vehemently. "For crying out loud, Tory, he's dating my mom."

I'd forgotten about that.

"Well, for what it's worth, your mom says they're just friends," I said.

"Yeah, right. Besides, I was drunk and he's a teacher. He'd have to report it. That is if Mom hasn't told him already."

"So far, your mom doesn't know you were at the river," I said. "Or that you were drinking."

"Really?" he said, brightening.

"Don't get your hopes up," I said severely. "She's going to know sooner or later. It would be the mature thing if you told her yourself. Especially since you're studying to be a Boy Scout."

"Huh?" he asked, confused.

I pointed at the circled note to himself, smiling a little at his blushing reaction.

The phone rang.

"Got some interesting news," Neil said without a preamble.

I'd have to wait until later to tell him the interesting news I'd just realized about Presley.

"About Doug or Janelle?" I asked. They were the only other interesting subjects in town.

"Neither," he said. "Well, I suppose it's about Janelle too, but mostly it's about her husband."

"Oho, so Benny Nelson *is* Janelle's husband."

"That's where the 'Nelson' comes from, in the J. Ross," Neil said. "But that's not the interesting part. The interesting part is that they've been divorced for five years now."

"Funny. He never once put an 'ex' in front of the word 'husband'. Not even for the cameras," I said. For the past two days, we had watched Benny's tearful mug, wailing on TV about his missing wife.

"Not only that, but in the divorce proceedings, Janelle alleged that he absconded with several of her millions while acting as her manager. And . . ." He paused, excited. "Our Mr. Nelson has been such a bother, wanting to renew both the personal and professional relationship with Janelle, that she filed a restraining order against him. Benny Nelson is forbidden to come closer than two hundred feet to his ex-wife."

"So that's why she was anxious to avoid him at the football game. He must have followed her here to Delphi," I said. "How'd you find this out?"

"The tabloid shows are picking up on the story. One of them uncovered the divorce papers and the restraining order. They're starting to hint that Doug's drowning wasn't quite as accidental as it looked. Mr. Nelson has a history of jealous rages. And they're speculating that perhaps Janelle is hiding, in fear of her life, from an abusive ex-husband."

"It makes you wonder if she really is hiding," I said, for the first time seriously beginning to consider that Janelle might be dead.

"You know, the sheriff had already arrived at the river on Saturday," Neil said thoughtfully, "and the boys and I were standing around, waiting to be dismissed, when Mr. Benny drove up and conveniently learned enough to rush back to town and make his announcement at the reunion.

Has it occurred to anyone to wonder exactly why he drove out there to begin with?"

"It will soon," I said, "or I don't know Delphi."

27

Speculation à la Mode

TUESDAY

Guess what? I do know Delphi.

It took less than a day for us to run through the possible (and impossible) permutations of the Doug/Janelle/Benny trio. By the end of my shift on a slow Tuesday, we had thoroughly dissected every logical scenario, and were starting to consider the illogical ones.

"Maybe Benny killed Doug *and* Janelle." Ron blinked. "You know, in a fit of rage. Ex-husbands feel that way sometimes, you know."

I can speculate with the best of them, but that seemed a little farfetched. "If Benny killed Janelle, where is her body?" I asked. "And just how did he drown Doug? Even naked, Doug was a good six inches taller and at least forty pounds heavier."

"I don't think Janelle drowned," Del pronounced, refilling Ron's cup. "I mean, Doug got hung up along the riverbank right next to the oxbow, but *she* just disappeared—without a trace? I'd be more willing to believe that she killed Doug."

Though the search was ongoing for Janelle, officials weren't putting as much effort into it as earlier. They seemed to be dismissing the notion that she was dead.

Local opinion was pretty evenly divided on the question.

"Tory's argument against Benny drowning Doug goes double for Janelle," Neil said, trying to inject a note of sanity into the conversation. "I tend to think she's alive, somewhere."

"Doug could have killed her, and then fell in and drowned," Aphrodite said, in one of the longest sentences I'd ever heard from her.

She was sitting on a stool at the counter, smoking a cigarette and listening avidly. There were no burgers to fry, no orders to take, and no reason to try to look busy. There was absolutely nothing to do, except rehash old theories and dream up some new ones with all the cafe regulars.

All the regulars except for Stu, who had not been seen in the cafe for a record three days.

"Someone on the news said that if Janelle is alive, she has a duty to come forward and help with the investigation," said Ron, finishing up the last of his apple pie à la mode. "Why should Janelle hide? I think she's been murdered."

"Someone, my ass," Del said, disgusted. She and Ron were no longer ignoring each other, but they were not on their usual terms either. "That wasn't 'someone,' that was Junior Deibert, mouthing off for the camera."

"Well, I heard it on TV," Ron said, pouting.

"You could have heard everyone in Delphi on TV, but that wouldn't mean that anyone knew anything worth listening to," Del said.

The local media, and some of the minor national media, had been interviewing as many of us as they could get to stand still and talk for them. Which was nearly everyone.

"How come we haven't seen Tory on the air?" Ron blinked, teasing.

"Because she has more sense than that," Neil answered

for me. "And the teachers have held to their agreement not to blab to the reporters."

"I hear they keep trying to get Debbie for an interview. And I know they've asked Lisa. She's about the only one of the reunion people who hasn't gone back home," I said.

"I hope Debbie sticks to her guns," said Neil severely. "It is not necessary for her to parade her grief for the entertainment of the state of South Dakota."

"Maybe she has a better reason not to talk," Del said slyly, lighting a cigarette. "She and Janelle were rivals, remember? And they were both screwing the same guy. Maybe Debbie found the perfect opportunity to get rid of her jerk husband *and* his old girlfriend at the same time."

"Nonsense. Debbie was gone long before Doug drowned on Friday. She left just after me," I said, letting my mouth run ahead of my brain and regretting it immediately.

"Yes." Del narrowed her eyes at me. "I've been meaning to ask you about that. Just why did Her High and Mightiness send you into town with her precious automobile?"

"Well, ah . . ." I said, backpedaling. I firmly believed that Del should know about Presley's drunken appearance at the party. And soon. But I didn't think she should hear about it in front of an audience.

"Tory wasn't feeling well, and Janelle generously offered her car since she wasn't ready to come back to town yet," Neil lied. He already knew the particulars of Presley's indiscretion. And he knew that Del would be thoroughly pissed.

Del harrumphed in disbelief.

"You know, I'm starting to wonder if Rhonda isn't on the right track," I said quietly, settling in with a Diet Coke. "There really are an awful lot of similarities between what happened back in 1969, and what happened Friday."

"She was *way* ahead of us on all this." Ron blinked. "Maybe you should pick her brain a little more."

"Rhonda isn't the one Tory needs to talk to," Del said, looking Ron right in the eye. He stared back at her.

"Well, bothering Debbie isn't the answer either," Neil said disapprovingly.

"I didn't mean Debbie, though I *would* love to hear what she has to say," Del said, facing me with disingenuous look on her face. "We keep forgetting that we have a perfect source of information right here in town. Someone who knew everyone in 1969, and who was right in the thick of things both times. Someone who knew Janelle then, and had ample opportunity to get reacquainted. Someone who, so far, hasn't said shit about anything."

"And who might that be?" Ron asked, blinking.

"Stuart McKee," Del said sweetly to me. "Don't you think it's time you talked to him?"

They all looked at me.

28

Nasal Passages

Confrontation is not my long suit. I do not rock the boat, make waves, or mess with the status quo. As an only child, raised on a farm by my strong-willed mother and completely loopy grandmother, I learned early on that it was easier to give way than to make a stand, or a fuss.

That lesson was reinforced by my fear of losing Nick Bauer. So lonely had I been, and so amazed was I by his love, that I forced myself to overlook how easily distracted he was by other women. I felt my hold on him was too fragile to ask, much less demand, that he stop screwing every breathing female who said yes.

In the end, compliance and complaisance got me nothing—I lost Nicky the only way I could.

I still avoid confrontations whenever possible.

So why was I sitting on Stu McKee's rustic couch while he concluded yet another telephone conversation with his estranged wife?

Partly, I knew that Del was right. There were things that Stu would know about the people at both parties that the rest of us could not. He had been a *real* insider. His take on events, past and present, would necessarily be different from ours.

Maybe I realized that whatever our relationship had been (and in the three months of its existence, we had not bothered to define or quantify it), it was surely a mess now.

However little I enjoyed the notion of tackling either subject head on, anything was better than the way we had been dancing around the perimeter of each other's lives for the past few days.

In order not to hear Stu say ". . . talk to you next week then . . ." in that cheerfully unperturbed voice, I plugged *That's Why I'm Here* into the stereo, grateful as always that James Taylor realized his purpose in life was to entertain me.

"I figured you wouldn't mind if I played some music," I said carefully as he hung up the loon phone. I figured it was safe to start with a neutral subject.

He came in and sat in one of the overstuffed chairs that matched the couch—the one that was furthest away from me—with his eyebrows knit and lips clamped in a straight line.

"Whatever," he said, looking away. "Though . . ." He trailed off.

"Though what?" I asked.

"Nothing."

"No, it's definitely not 'nothing.' If you have something to say, say it."

The conversation was already going from bad to worse.

"All right," he said, nodding slightly to himself. "Fine. Go ahead and play some music, but does it always have to be James Taylor?"

That confused me. "But I thought you liked James Taylor."

"I do. But not every minute of every goddamn day."

"But you bought these so I could play them here," I said, instantly forgetting what I had intended to discuss.

"I didn't think he'd be the only singer you'd ever want to listen to. I am sick and damn tired of that nasal whiny voice of his. Morning and night. All the time." Stu's voice had an edge I'd never heard before.

I suppose, in the back of my brain, I understood that he wasn't actually angered by the quality of James Taylor's voice, but the sudden attack, coming from such an unexpected direction, had me flummoxed.

"His voice is *not* nasal," was the only reply I found.

"It is too," Stu said, contempt dripping from his voice. "He's so nasal that even his fucking guitar is nasal."

"Fine." I ejected the tape and rummaged furiously through the box and came up with another, one I'd brought from home. "We'll listen to something else."

I nearly had *Negotiations and Love Songs* in the slot when he said, "And not Paul Simon either."

"So who do you want?" I spun around. "A little Reba or Wynonna? Or some other country chick with big hair and big tits? That's what you like isn't it?"

"What?"

"Big hair and big tits. There've been enough of both around lately. Right here in this house, as a matter of fact!"

For a woman with little experience in confrontation, I was getting the hang of it pretty quickly.

He stared at me wide-eyed. "So that's what this is about? You picked a fight with me because of Janelle?"

"Just a minute, buster, I didn't start this fucking fight," I shouted. "But since you brought her up, let's just talk about Janelle for a minute."

"There's nothing to talk about," Stu said, standing now, shouting too. "She invited herself here. No one cared what I thought about having her in this house. No one offered her another place to stay. I was stuck with her, and now you've been acting weird all week!"

"*I've* been acting weird?" We were at the stage where we were parroting each other's dumbshit statements back and forth. "*You're* the one acting weird. Ever since Janelle showed up, you've been moody and crabby. And you haven't been in the cafe for days."

"And what about you?" he spat.

"What about me?"

"You and Neil Pascoe traipsing out to the river to see a dead body together was certainly weird. And every time I look across the street from the store, he's in the cafe. And there the two of you are, yakking away, just like this is some kind of game or something.

"Well, I'll tell you, Tory, whether or not there is more to Doug's drowning than we know right now, I can assure you that it's *not* a game. And I'd bet my house that Janelle had something to do with it. The whole town has been treating her like she's some kind of royalty, just because she's an actress. Well, she's always been an actress. She's been playacting for as long as I've known her! Janelle Ross never had a real emotion in her whole life, or showed her real face. She *always* got what she wanted. And she *never* cared who she used, or who got hurt on the way . . ."

The phone rang. Stu stood his ground, breathing heavily, for another ring, then turned abruptly to answer it. The vehemence of his anger astonished me. I had assumed that Stu and Janelle had been just friends in high school, but bitterness that deep had to have been born of something a lot more complicated.

Shoulders tense, and facing away from me, Stu talked quietly into the phone. Probably another call from Renee, she of the impeccable timing.

"Sure," Stu said with no inflection in his voice. He turned to me, holding out the phone. His eyes had lost their furious glare, his face was lined and tired. "It's for you."

"Sorry to interrupt," Neil said in a rush, "but you better get over here quick. It's important."

Physiologically speaking, there isn't much difference between anger and fear. One second I was shaking furiously with the notion that Stu's taste in music was dictated by his preference in bra size. The next I was trembling in the certainty that Presley had been injured. Or killed—drowned perhaps, the same as Doug Fischbach.

My overtaxed brain could supply no other reason for Neil to track me down at Stu's and demand that I rush to his house. A tragedy had occurred, no doubt. One too horrible to detail over the phone. One that that I could not survive without Neil Pascoe's strength and reassuring physical presence.

I left Stu immediately. I was too frightened to do more than register his resigned expression.

Neil was watching for me. He opened the front door of his huge Victorian house the minute I mounted the front porch and ushered me in, locking the door after.

Neil's door is never locked. Even when he goes out of town.

"What's going on?" I demanded, breathless. "What's happened?"

"Upstairs," he said cryptically, and motioned for me to follow him up to his living quarters on the second floor.

He was outwardly calm, though his eyes, behind horn-rimmed glasses, danced merrily. He did not look bereaved.

He looked delighted.

Which sped the transition from fear back to anger.

"Do you have any idea how much you frightened me, Neil Pascoe?" I demanded, following him upstairs.

"Sorry." He laughed. "There wasn't any other way to get you here, and I couldn't tell you anything over the cordless phone. Anyone with a scanner can listen in."

"This better be good," I muttered.

First Stu, and now Neil. Every guy I knew was acting strangely. All at the same time.

"It's good all right," he said, standing aside at the doorway to let me enter his gleaming kitchen first.

"It can't possibly be worth all this—" I crabbed, and then stopped dead in my tracks.

I stood, mouth hanging open, eyes popped, for a full minute.

"See what I mean?" Neil chuckled.

"Funny thing," I said, finally, to the woman who sat at Neil's kitchen table, sipping a glass of very nice California wine. "I was just talking about you."

29

Just a Hometown Girl

It is always a short-lived thrill for a Delphi native to know something that the rest of the town doesn't. Very few secrets actually stay secret around here, and possession of one is jealously guarded for as long as possible.

Of course, Neil's locked door would suggest to any Delphi rationalist that *something* was going on in the library, though everyone would automatically assume that the "something" was sexual in nature.

No one would ever guess that Neil Pascoe currently harbored one of the most fascinating secrets in town, who, herself a Delphi native, let us not forget, harbored some of the longest-kept secrets in our memory.

"First things first," Neil said, rubbing his hands together. "Would you like a glass of wine, Tory?"

"Uh, sure," I said, still nonplussed by the whole situation.

"The Simi all right with you?" he asked, reaching up to slide another stem from the rack suspended over the countertop. "Or should I open a bottle of Riesling?"

"Chardonnay is fine," I said, watching Neil pour a glass from the half-empty bottle sitting on the table.

I raised an eyebrow at him, asking a hundred questions. He answered with a small shrug.

"I imagine you're wondering what I'm doing here," J. Ross Nelson said, in the throaty voice that made her the darling of slasher-movie fans.

"That, among other things," I said, sipping the wine.

A couple of hours ago, I would have been thrilled to sit with an impeccably groomed, casually dressed, obviously alive and well J. Ross Nelson, and drink from Neil's private reserve cellar.

But so soon after the fight with Stu, with his indictment of her still ringing in my ears, and a million unanswered questions of my own, the best I could manage was a closely guarded curiosity.

"Well, to start with," Janelle said, hands cupped around her wineglass, "I feel terrible about Doug. I didn't know anything about it until I heard on the news that he was dead. You can imagine how surprised I was to find that everyone thought that we had run away together, and that I was now either dead myself, or some sort of drowning-murderess."

She laughed softly, eyes sad and sincere. I've seen that expression before, on the big screen.

"So, if it isn't too personal to ask, where the hell have you been? People *are* wondering," I said. The only way to keep from being sucked in by her charm was to be brusque.

"So I hear." She grinned, stretched, and scratched her head. "Late Friday night, I got a message from my agent about a Saturday audition for a serious breakthrough role—the kind I've been waiting twenty years to get. So I took the first flight to California that I could, intending to return in time for the reunion. But something went wrong with the casting director's schedule, and the audition was delayed a couple of days. As sorry as I was to miss the reunion, I decided this role was just too important to jeopardize." She stood up, reached for the wine bottle, and refilled her glass. "I'd already ridden in the parade, so I didn't think anyone would notice if I didn't show up on Saturday."

That statement was too ridiculous for comment. Neil and I sat silently.

"I like to go into isolation to prepare for an audition," she continued, "so that was the perfect opportunity. By the time I turned on a TV, the shit, as they say, had already hit the fan."

Her explanation was almost reasonable and borderline logical, which was why I mistrusted every word.

"How did you get back into town from the river on Friday night? I had your car," I said, pulling the keys from my pocket and dangling them in the air. "And how did you get to the airport?"

"We were all upset and confused—what with Doug's kid starting that brawl, and Ronnie Adler's little wife crying off to the side, and everyone else shouting and angry. There didn't seem to be much point in sticking around. Debbie wouldn't let me help her, even if I could. You"—she pointed at me—"were already gone and Stu was occupied with trying to settle things down. I just walked back into town."

Neil and I exchanged looks. A movie star had walked four miles, in the dark, with rain threatening?

She interpreted the look correctly. "Hey, I run five miles a day to keep in shape. Exercise is exercise. Besides, Delphi hasn't changed that much. I still remember the way."

"And then?" Neil prompted, peeling the foil from the neck of another bottle of wine. His cats, Elizabeth Bennet and Mr. Darcy, circled his legs.

"Stu wasn't home when I got there. I called my service for messages, found out about the audition, and tried to find a cab to take me into Aberdeen."

All three of us laughed at that one. Taxis are pretty well nonexistent in these here parts.

"So how'd you get to the airport?" Neil asked from inside his refrigerator, where he was rummaging. He emerged with a slab of Colby, grabbed a box of crackers from the pantry, and set them on the table with a cheese slicer and a stack of paper napkins. The cats followed expectantly. "Sorry, I didn't know I was going to entertain."

"This is great, thanks." Janelle flashed a thousand watt-smile at Neil, who looked inordinately pleased.

Since Neil appeared to be falling for Janelle's story, hook, line, and sinker, I vowed to maintain an aloof impartiality. As a reminder, I kept Stu's hurt and angry face in my mind's eye.

"The airport?" I prodded.

"Oh, yeah," Janelle said with her mouth full. She managed to look beautiful even then. "I hitched a ride in a semi."

"You hitchhiked all the way to Aberdeen with a slime-ball trucker?" Neil was aghast.

"No, I hitchhiked all the way to St. Paul with a very nice trucker, and flew out from there." She paused, seeing our expressions. "Don't look that way. It's not like I haven't done it before. Besides, the character I auditioned for was a drifter—I thought of it as research."

"Why didn't you just get your car from me at the trailer, instead of taking that kind of chance?" I demanded. Even in sparsely populated, rural South Dakota, hitchhiking is stupid. "And why didn't you tell anyone where you were going?"

"Well, first of all . . ." She poured another glass of wine. Her fourth or fifth. "I figured I'd be back the next afternoon. Second, Stu had been kind enough to offer his spare room for me to use, and he and everyone else had been so good about giving me my privacy that I didn't think anyone would even notice I was gone. Third, and most important, I didn't want that asshole Benny to know I'd left Delphi. The pisser followed me here, and he would probably have followed me right back to California."

"Why didn't you call the police when he showed up?" Neil asked. "You do have a restraining order against him."

"Listen, if the cops in L.A. can't keep him away from

me," Janelle said, something hard and sharp and undeniably real in her voice, "what are the boondock cops going to do? I've learned to live with it—I just go about my life and avoid my psycho ex-husband as much as possible.

"Which is why I'm lying low for a while. And why I am going to ask you the huge favor of not telling anyone that I'm staying with Neil for the next couple of days. It would never occur to Benny to look for me here."

She broke a piece of cheese in half and delicately fed it to the cats.

I shot a look at Neil, which he avoided returning.

Janelle wiped her hands and continued, "My agent advises me to let the fuss die down a little. He's worried that all this adverse publicity will affect my chance of getting that role."

"You forget what life is like in a small town," I said, helping myself to some cheese and crackers. The cats watched avidly. "The fuss *might* die down nationally. But you've provided Delphi's most fascinating diversion in a long time. People are obsessed with you and your life. And they're already beginning to connect this drowning and disappearance with 1969 and Butchie Pendergast."

I didn't add that I was one of those people.

She shook her head ruefully. "I had no idea there was anything for people *to* remember about 1969. I didn't even know that Butchie had died, for almost a decade.

"Doug and I were eighteen, for chrissakes, when we decided to embark on our little fling after that homecoming kegger. It seemed so romantic and dangerously grown up to sneak away from the river together, on the spur of the moment like that. I learned too late that infidelity, even the high school variety, has a very long half-life," she said sincerely, elbow on table, chin in hand. "But we were in love, or at least we thought we were. By the time we realized that neither of us was thinking with our heads, it was too late for me to go back to Delphi. Doug decided that he wanted to make a go of it with Debbie." She shrugged. "I never saw, or heard from him again, until last week."

"Were you and Stu a hot item in school?" I asked,

trying to sort out exactly whom Janelle had been unfaithful to.

"We dated a couple of times, but it was nothing serious," she said lightly. "We were friends then. And we're friends now."

Not according to Stu, I thought.

"That still leaves a lot unaccounted for," Neil said calmly. Maybe he wasn't as taken in as I had thought. "A month before the reunion, Doug bragged that he was responsible for bringing you back to Delphi."

"That's nonsense," Janelle said, with thoroughly convincing indignation. "Debbie and Gina Adler wrote to my agent, who forwarded their letter to me. I'm in between projects right now, and luckily had enough free time to make it back. I thought it'd be a hoot to see the old stomping grounds."

"Some hoot," I said with a raised eyebrow.

"No kidding," she agreed.

"You probably have no idea how wild the speculation is. Maybe if we work out some sort of itinerary of where everyone was on Friday night, we can slow down the rumor machine without giving away anything about your present whereabouts," Neil said to Janelle, pushing his glasses up on his nose. He pulled a pad and pencil from a drawer and prepared to take notes.

He wrote his own name at the top of a page, and then transcribed his testimony underneath. "Rhonda had asked me for a ride, and we arrived at the river in the '61 convertible. You came." He pointed at Janelle. "We all talked about cars, etc. Cameron charged out of the bushes and tackled his father at the fire. Stu McKee and Ron Adler tried to separate them. Tory disappeared right about then, though everyone was so agitated, I don't think they even noticed that the Corvette was gone. I didn't see Cameron after that. I assume he went home."

"Cameron wore his dad's old football shirt," I interrupted. Presley and John Adler said that they found the dirty number 69 Oracle jersey at the river, a little distance away from Doug's clothes. "Did you see him take it off?"

Neil focused on the middle distance, concentrating.

"No, but that doesn't mean anything." He continued writing. "Things calmed down, and I took Rhonda home."

He turned the page and wrote my name. He knew my story already and wrote it down with a minimum of additions from me.

We looked at Janelle.

She exhaled. "I got to the river a little bit late. While I was still in my car, Doug made a nasty suggestion about getting rid of Debbie so he and I could go skinny-dipping later. I told you about that at the river, right, Tory?"

I nodded.

"We all stood around the fire. I talked to Mr. Kincaid for a while, which was nice since we didn't get to talk much when I saw him the day before." She stared at the ceiling. "Delphine and Ronnie Adler were whispering a little ways from the fire, and his wife didn't like it."

"That's par for the course," I said.

"Then Doug cornered me again and said a strange thing about having something of mine that I'd probably want back."

This was new to me. Neil too, by the look on his face.

"Did he tell you what it was?" I asked.

"He showed it to me. It was one of those circle pins that girls wore a long time ago. He had it in his pants pocket."

Neil and I looked at each other. "Was it gold, with rhinestones around the outer edge?"

"Yeah," Janelle said. "Did he show it to you too?"

"No. We saw it at the river," I said, "on Saturday. It was stomped into the ground not far from Doug's other stuff."

Janelle cocked her head to the side, the tilt she'd perfected in high school. "That's weird. I mean, I don't think it was valuable or anything."

"Looked like costume jewelry to me," I said. "The kind my mother and aunt wore when they were young."

Janelle continued, "Anyway, it wasn't mine. And I have no idea why Doug thought that it was." She shook her head, then returned to the timeline. "Soon after that, Tory and I went to get beer from Ronnie Adler's cooler, and the fight started. And then I left. I never saw or talked to Doug Fischbach again. The rest you already know." She drained her glass and yawned. "It's been a long day. I know it's early, but do you mind if I turn in?" she asked Neil.

"I have to go home anyway. I work in the morning," I said, standing and stretching. "I'll keep checking the Friday itineraries. It's all anyone wants to talk about at the cafe, anyway."

"Great idea," Neil said heartily. "I'll walk you down."

I said good night to Janelle, amazed, again, to find myself in the position of J. Ross Nelson's friend and protector.

"So what do you think?" Neil asked quietly outside his front door.

"I don't know," I said, truthfully. "Everything she says sounds logical, but something about her story doesn't jibe. It just doesn't feel right."

"I know what you mean," he said, standing in the dark on the porch with me. "She showed up tonight after supper and somehow or other hornswoggled me into inviting her to stay here." He grinned, glasses and teeth gleaming.

"Like you mind," I said. "How often do you get to serve wine to a Hollywood star anyway?"

"Well, I'm glad that she asked me to find you—it wouldn't have been any fun at all if you weren't in on it," Neil said softly.

"I don't know that I *am* in on it," I said, thinking through everything that had happened in the past few days. "Why is she so buddy-buddy with me? I wasn't her friend in high school. I didn't even know her."

"Ah, but you gave her the magic nickel," Neil reminded me. "And maybe that was enough to garner her eternal gratitude."

"All it garnered me was a dislike of cheerleaders, and a distrust of skinny, beautiful actresses," I said, laughing.

Which was why I decided it would be a good idea to talk to *everyone* about Friday night. Not just the cafe crowd, but Debbie Fischbach and Lisa too. Even

Cameron, if I could manage it. I'd mention that pin and watch their reactions.

Janelle wasn't the only one I didn't trust.

30

South Dakota Curiosity

I harbor no ambition to grow up and be Miss Marple. Like everyone else in the state, I have the normal complement of nosiness genes—the same batch inbred in every midwesterner. But that sort of prying usually confines itself to bank balances and bedroom activities.

Investigating alibis and cross-checking stories for discrepancies was not generally on my list of things to do. And I have no false illusions about the accuracy of my hunches or conclusions. Except on the printed page, I am not fascinated with death. But I do know the difference between the artfully posed literary deceased, the puzzle painstakingly crafted for the enjoyment of the masses, and the real thing.

The real thing, unfortunately, haunts my dreams and dogs my waking hours with questions that I can't answer by myself.

For instance, why is J. Ross Nelson back in Delphi?

If she is just "lying low," why couldn't she do it in California—a place infinitely more suited to blending into the scenery? Or better yet, did she really leave Delphi at all? Janelle offered no evidence to back up her weekend trip to La La Land.

While I couldn't think of a single reason for Janelle to come back, there were several good ones for sticking around and hiding. None of them pleasant.

Which is how I ended up on the Pascoe/Bauer investigative team again.

And why I intended to cross-examine everyone I knew, starting with Hugh Kincaid, who, as luck would have it, emerged from our trailer just as I crossed the street from Neil's library.

"Well, hi there, Tory. Nice evening, not too cold. No rain at least," Hugh observed, a normal South Dakotan conversational opener.

"Better enjoy it while we can. Winter's coming," was my typical rejoinder.

Chitchat about the weather freed my brain, which was frantically seeking a method to grill Hugh about last Friday without giving away any of the secrets I was charged to keep.

"So what brings you to our neck of the woods?" I asked, blundering into what could be a sensitive area. Obviously, Hugh was visiting Del—perhaps making that all-important second date.

"Well, actually I'm on sort of a triple mission—first I wanted to see Delphine." He grinned. "And I needed to pick up Presley's account of the junior high homecoming activities for the yearbook. He missed his deadline, and I need those pages immediately.

"But just as important, or maybe even more so, I wanted to see him on a personal basis. Cameron Fischbach came in today, and he said that he was worried about how Presley was dealing with this whole situation. Presley is younger than most of the kids I advise, but he is one of my students, and I'm concerned about him."

"The aftermath of finding Doug's body was tough," I said, relieved that Hugh was taking the time to try to get through to Pres. "Did he talk to you?"

"Not really," Hugh said sadly. "He's a little hostile,

which I can't figure out since he isn't usually afflicted with the attitude problems that plague boys his age."

"Well, the fact that you're dating his mother probably colors his reaction," I said gently, surprised I had to point that out, until I remembered that Hugh didn't know that Presley had seen him with Del at the river.

That stopped him for a moment. "I hadn't taken that into consideration."

"It's nice that Cameron has the energy to worry about his friends," I said. "How's his girlfriend taking it?"

I was thinking of Rhonda's sister Sandra. Since she and Cameron had been elected homecoming king and queen, I had assumed they were a couple.

"As far as I know, Cameron doesn't have a girlfriend. He's something of a late bloomer, I think." Hugh smiled. "But he's a loyal friend, and that's more important. He's genuinely worried about what Presley saw at the river."

There was the perfect opening to the subject I really wanted to discuss with Hugh. "While we're on that, Neil Pascoe and I were talking about last Friday night. You probably heard that Presley and John Adler also found Doug's old football jersey on the riverbank. Everyone remembers the fight, of course, but no one seems to remember when Cameron took the jersey off."

"Everything was such a jumble," Hugh said, thinking back, "I couldn't swear, but I'm pretty sure the jersey was on the ground when I left. Why don't you ask Delphine? She might remember, since she stayed out of the fray better than I managed to."

"I'll do that," I said, pleased to get the answers I needed without resorting to lies.

"You know," Hugh said, "Neil Pascoe, Rhonda Saunders, and I are the only ones who attended Friday night's bash who weren't also at the one back in 1969."

"Well, Rhonda wasn't even born then, Neil was in elementary school, and you were our teacher—it would have been weird for you to show up at a student social occasion. Especially a party where everyone was drunk." I laughed.

"Yes, but I can't help wondering how many wheels were set in motion at that single event. I'll tell you a secret, Tory," he said sadly, "I knew about that party before it took place. All of the teachers did. We just didn't interfere, in those days.

"And for whatever reason, that night seems to have been a watershed moment for everyone who attended. I can't help but wonder how the evening would have ended if I *had* driven to the river. I considered it, you know," he said softly. "And I have always regretted my decision to stay home. If I'd shown up, the party would have dissolved, and a death might have been prevented."

I was beginning to realize that Rhonda was right. There were undeniable parallels between 1969 and now. Cause and effect were a closed circle.

Without the frenzy of homecoming, would Doug have been less apt to brawl? Would he have punched Stu? Would he have cheated on Debbie?

And if Doug and Janelle had not actually been caught in the backseat of Butchie Pendergast's car, would they have decided to run away together? And if not, would Butchie be alive now? Would Doug?

If Del, Nicky, Ron, and I had not driven a very young and inebriated Gina Eisenbiesz home, would she have fallen in love with a man who was terminally infatuated with another woman?

If I had not slipped into a lopsided relationship with Nick Bauer at that party, would I have been as apt to begin another lopsided relationship with Stuart McKee more than twenty-five years later?

All of those questions piqued my curiosity. I just hope that curiosity doesn't kill the South Dakotan.

31

Old Hurts, Old Habits

WEDNESDAY

I considered my pseudo-interview with Hugh Kincaid as sort of a practice shot with a friend who voluntarily led the conversation into the territory I wanted to explore. He provided a baseline experience from which to launch the rest of my inquiries, a reason to hope that I could ask specific questions without giving away the hottest secret in recent Delphi history.

In the trailer last night, I'd tried to broach the subject with Presley, both to see if he had any information that I'd missed earlier and to smooth his ruffled feathers. Unfortunately, he barricaded himself in his room and spoke not a word to his mother or me.

Del was uncommunicative herself, last night and this morning, eyeing me narrowly every time I tried to bring up either homecoming party.

"I'm beginning to find the subject of Doug Fischbach, in any stage of decomposition, supremely boring," she said darkly. "I'll be glad when the rest of his family gets here tomorrow, so we can finally bury the son of a bitch. Can't you find something else to fixate on?"

"I'm not fixated," I said, loading dirty dishes onto the rolling cart. "I'm just curious. Neil and I were trying to figure out exactly when Doug's old jersey ended up on the ground at the river. Hugh said he thought it was there when he left, and maybe you'd remember for sure." I rolled the cart through the low swinging door that divided the cafe from the kitchen and said over my shoulder. "Do you?"

"Do I what?" Del lit a cigarette, purposefully obtuse.

"Do you remember the jersey lying on the ground when you left the river on Friday night?" I asked, being specific so she could not misconstrue the question again.

"I didn't pay attention to the ground," Del said, blowing smoke out the side of her mouth. "But the kid told Presley that he went home right after the fight, so it must have been there." She shrugged. "I don't see what difference it makes, one way or another."

Del was in one of her moods, and I knew from long experience that it would do no good to pressure her. I turned to Ron Adler, finishing up breakfast in his usual booth. "What about you? If you left the river after Del and Hugh, you might be able to clear this whole thing up."

Ron shot a blinking scowl at Del's back. "I can't say that I noticed when *Mr. Kincaid* left the river."

The mix of disgust and sarcasm in his voice finally explained the strain between Ron and Del. It was so obvious that I should have understood immediately—Ron was jealous. He'd watched Del go from man to man, standing wistfully on the sidelines. But seeing Del with a former teacher, one she'd had a crush on in high school, was evidently too much for him.

If his bitterness was this visible to us, how awful it must be for his wife. Poor Gina. No wonder she'd been sad and weepy lately.

Back still to Ron, busily swabbing the counter, Del snorted. Ron blinked some more, threw a couple of bills on the table, and stalked out.

I decided to let it go. The private eyes of America need not lose sleep over competition from me. When Lisa Franklin Hauck-Robertson came into the cafe alone, the person who served her concentrated only on her waitressing duties.

"What can I get you?" I asked, pen and pad in hand.

"I don't suppose I could get a latte?"

"Sorry. But I think Aphrodite has a tin of Café Vienna somewhere in the storeroom, if you want me to dig it out," I said. "It's instant. Only take a minute to fix."

She shuddered. "No thanks. How about a cup of coffee, black. And Tory"—she lowered her voice—"could you sit for a minute? I'd like to talk to you."

The Investigation Gods work in strange and mysterious ways.

"Sure," I said, grabbing a Diet Coke for myself while I was at it.

Like every woman of a certain age, Lisa had tiny lines and creases snaking from her eyes and the corners of her mouth, the legacy of a midwestern youth spent squinting into the summer sun, and against the winter wind.

We were all a little worse for the wear. Except Janelle, of course, whose face and figure could be attributed to lucky genes, hard work, and a shitpot full of money. The rest of us had to carry our years. Lisa's looked like a heavy burden.

I sat in her booth, folded my hands, and waited for Lisa to begin, since she had requested the conference.

"We'll get right to it," she said, grimacing at the coffee. "I want to know how you knew that Doug was dead before that creep Benny Nelson announced it at the reunion. Don't deny that you knew in advance—you and Stuart McKee both."

There was no reason to deny anything. "Actually, it was Neil Pascoe, Presley Bauer, John Adler, Stuart McKee, and me," I said, and then gave her a condensed version of the boys' discovery, ending with Hugh Kincaid's concern about how Presley was dealing with it.

"Delphi is lucky to have Mr. Kincaid," Lisa said, her face and voice softening. "I don't think I would have survived my senior year if not for him. If I have any good memories of this godforsaken town, it's because of Mr. Kincaid. He was that rare adult that you could tell anything to. He treated students like they were fellow human beings, and friends."

I remembered Doug's nasty comment about how well Mr. Kincaid "got along" with all the girls. There was a disparity in how former students viewed him—the women went gooey at the mere mention of his name, the guys were hard and cynical.

Lisa continued, "He's the reason I do what I do. And that's why I'm away from my practice longer than I should be, because I'd like to help Debbie and her children get through this."

"You're a doctor?" I asked, surprised. I didn't remember seeing that on her reunion info sheet. Of course, I didn't remember seeing anything that would account for the hyphenated last name, either.

"Specifically a relationship facilitator," Lisa said. "My work involves helping splintered families repair themselves." She smiled wanly. "Hoping to do for others what I could never seem to do for myself."

The world was a hard place. Pretty cheerleaders grew up to be multiple divorcees. Football stars became less than heroic men, juggling wives and families, and occasionally girlfriends, simultaneously. The school bad girl grew up to be the town bad girl.

"It's a tough life for everyone," I said, shrugging.

"Well, some of us have had it easier than others," Lisa said, voice hard.

"No one around here, believe me," I said, defending everyone I knew, in one fell swoop.

"I wasn't talking about anyone who lives here," Lisa said.

"Oh." She meant Janelle.

"Yeah, *oh,*" Lisa repeated. "Debbie's been dragged back through some really awful memories because of our precious ex-homecoming queen."

"Well, Doug had something to do with it too," I

reminded her. "In fact, if anyone is going to take the blame, I'd be more inclined to lay it on him."

"Actually, it's both of them. One way or another, they are responsible for a great deal of unhappiness. My very earnest hope was that they had run away together, this time permanently. And if it wasn't for the fact that Doug is dead, I'd say our tragically missing actress was staging this whole thing as a publicity ploy."

I wasn't so sure that Lisa was wrong about that, but of course I couldn't say so. "Debbie and Gina Adler did all the reunion organizing. I don't think that Janelle and Doug were in contact until after she arrived in Delphi."

"I wouldn't count on that." Lisa poured more coffee into her cup. "I stayed at the Fischbachs' for a couple of days before the reunion. Doug did absolutely nothing to help around the house, or with the kids, except bitch when they didn't perform to his standards. But he drove to the post office to pick up the mail. Every single day. He made such a big deal about that little chore. I wondered if he wasn't getting letters from somewhere and didn't want Debbie to know."

Lisa nodded like a conspiracy buff with proof that JFK had been shot by aliens.

"Stu hasn't said anything about Janelle either sending or getting mail while she was at his house," I said.

"Yeah, well, you wouldn't expect him to be objective about Janelle, would you?" Lisa asked with a small laugh.

There was no objectivity in Stu's bitter anger. But that didn't explain Lisa's cryptic statement. "What do you mean?"

"Oh come on, you were around then. Don't you remember? Stu and Janelle were the hottest couple in school—they went together the whole summer before their senior year. Janelle thought she was in love with him. He was supposed to be homecoming king, until word got out."

"Word got out about what?" I was genuinely confused. I had been so wrapped up in my own world of books and Nicky Bauer that the love lives of the school big-wigs hadn't registered.

"That Stu couldn't keep it in his pants, of course," Lisa said. "That's why Doug Fischbach punched Stu at the river that night. You were there, you must remember that much at least."

I did. And I remembered Nick gleefully preparing to repeat whatever Doug had said to Stu, when we were interrupted by giggling, drunken Junior.

Nick never did get around to telling me exactly what was said that night.

"You were there too, right in the middle," I said to Lisa. "Did you hear what Doug said to Stu?"

"Damn right I heard. I remember it word for word." She lowered her voice in imitation of a furious high school boy. "Doug said, 'You're not happy screwing the prettiest girl in the school, you gotta make the rest of them too.' "

I sat back in the booth, wind knocked out of my sails. Not only was Stu's relationship with Janelle deeper than I remembered, deeper than he, or she, had admitted, but he'd been unfaithful to her.

That would explain Doug's enmity. And revenge would explain Doug and Janelle's fling. I remembered now that Doug hadn't thrown that punch until after Debbie had rushed into Stu's arms.

"So Stu was sleeping with Debbie?" I asked.

"Among others," Lisa said, looking down.

Another shock. "You too?"

"That's one of the hurdles that Mr. Kincaid helped me to clear. I had, and still have," she said, with a small deprecating laugh, "a tendency to fall in love with every man I sleep with. Mr. Kincaid taught me to look forward, and not back. To use each experience as a building block for the future. All that sounds pat and silly now, but believe me, I never would have made it without him."

I'd have spent a few moments ruminating on Hugh Kincaid's long-established ability to help adolescents traverse the thorny path to adulthood, if another of his statements hadn't been ringing in my head.

He'd sat in the cafe, the morning after Doug decked Stu in the bar. Like everyone else, he'd talked about the fight.

Though I hadn't heard the particulars of Doug and Stu's pre-punch conversation, Hugh had.

With a sadness that settled around my heart like lead, I was suddenly afraid to wonder if Doug had had good reason to say to Stuart McKee, "You never change, do you?"

32

Head Cheerleader

If my life had been the subject of a made-for-TV movie, the main character (played by a woman taller, prettier, thinner, and more than likely younger than me) would have reacted to the news that her married boyfriend had a long history of infidelity with an epiphany. She'd have stared into the middle distance for a full thirty seconds, then resolved to go and sleep with married men no more.

After all, the only surprise would be how very much she was surprised.

Alas, my life is just my life, not a cinematic compilation tidily sliced into twenty-three minute segments, with a satisfying resolution to tie it up at the end.

I realized immediately that Doug had made his accusation about "never changing" *before* Janelle arrived in Delphi. He must have been referring to his own wife. A woman, I now realized, who had a little excess baggage of her own.

On the other hand, Doug was, and had always been, a sadist who enjoyed inflicting pain for no better reason than that it amused him.

He could have been guessing. He could have been lying. He could have been right on the money.

I didn't know.

So I girded up my curiosity and did, for all the wrong reasons, what I should have done a few days ago.

I paid a condolence call.

"Thank you, Tory, for the casserole," Debbie Fischbach said, pale and subdued, but otherwise in control. "That was so thoughtful of you."

"Actually, it's from all of us at the cafe," I said. I'd browbeaten Aphrodite into whipping up something for me to take. One does not arrive on this sort of visit empty-handed.

"That's even nicer," Debbie said. Bereavement had taken the hard edge off her personality. "Won't you come in and visit for a while?"

Since that was my entire reason for driving out to her house, I didn't hesitate to follow Debbie into her spotless living room and sit in one of her perfectly coordinated rocker/recliners.

She smiled faintly, sipping from a glass of ice water, as we stumbled through the usual things one says at a time like that. I cast about the room, looking for something else to talk about, something that might lead to any of the thousand impertinent questions I wanted to ask her, when I spotted a gold circle pin on the glass-topped coffee table.

"That's a pretty pin," I said, rather surprised to see it there.

Debbie leaned forward and picked it up, turning it this way and that as if inspecting the rhinestones. "Yes, it is rather nice. Isn't it? The sheriff gave it to me with the rest of Doug's, um . . ." She hesitated. ". . . effects."

"Was it yours?" I asked, fairly sure that I knew the answer, since Doug had assumed it belonged to Janelle.

"Actually, I'd never seen it before. It's a little old-fashioned, rather like the kind of thing my mother wore when she was young."

"I think everyone's mother had a pin like that," I said.

"Perhaps it belonged to Doug's mother," Debbie said. "In any case, I intend to keep the pin. It will remind me of Doug's little mysteries." She smiled at me crookedly. I began to wonder if there was water in that tumbler, or something else. "You might be surprised at how many mysteries our Doug had."

Here was my opening. "Actually, Doug's mysteries have been a hot topic around town lately."

"I can well imagine."

"I know this is difficult for you," I said, "and if I'm overstepping my bounds, please let me know, and I'll shut up immediately."

She laughed softly. "It will be a pleasure to talk honestly about Doug. People have been so kind, so sympathetic. But I can see that they are itching to ask about all those rumors. Maybe if I talk to you, you'll spread the word, we can all rest a little easier."

There was a bit of the old, nasty Debbie peeking through, but I didn't hold it against her. She was entitled to a cheap shot at Delphi's expense.

"The timing of Janelle's return and the coincidence of Doug's death has everyone, at least everyone around our age, thinking about high school again, and all that happened back then," I said, still skirting the edges of what I wanted to say.

"What's really amazing, Tory," Debbie said, swirling the liquid in her glass, "is that for a good many years, the name Janelle Ross was never, ever mentioned in our house. It's not that she was a taboo subject, or that we were uncomfortable about old memories. I think we actually, and honestly, forgot about her. Until we moved back home to Delphi." She chuckled sadly.

"Well, one of the things that has people confused," I said slowly, "is why you invited Janelle to the reunion in the first place."

"It wasn't my idea." She shook her head. "As I said, Doug never seemed to remember Janelle at all until a few months ago. Maybe just being here put her in his head again. He insisted that we invite her to the All-School

Reunion. And when Doug insisted on something, it got done.

"Suddenly, she was all he could talk about. Janelle this and Janelle that. How he knew a rich and famous movie actress, and he made absolutely sure that everyone understood that he meant 'knew' in the biblical sense. How he and the future starlet had shared three wild days of sex in 1969, just before her big break."

Debbie's calm exterior did not mask the pain in her eyes as she continued, "And he made sure to tell everyone, even the children, that it never would have happened if I hadn't betrayed and humiliated him."

I had known that Doug was less than admirable, but this shocked me anyway. I instantly forgave Stu and Debbie for anything they might have done together.

"That's awful," I said softly. "There was no reason for your children to have to know that stuff."

"Doug saw it differently. He didn't care that Stuart McKee had at least a small excuse for doing what he did. Doug hated Stu."

"Stu had a reason to cheat on Janelle?" I asked, not sure there was such a thing.

"Well, at the time everyone thought so," Debbie said. "There was a rumor that Janelle was sleeping with someone else, though no one seemed to know exactly who the lucky fellow was. For a while, I actually suspected Mr. Kincaid. Janelle used to spend a lot of time at his house. But since Hugh is still here, still teaching and highly respected, I expect I was wrong about that."

She looked into her empty glass, excused herself, and walked over to a cupboard, from which she pulled a half-gallon vodka bottle, and poured a refill. No ice this time. "At any rate, if Doug and Janelle arranged the river scene to get revenge on both of us"—she toasted me with her glass—"it worked."

"Well, whatever happened between Doug and Janelle after they took off together, I'm certain they weren't having sex at the river *that* night," I said, thinking back to the scene in the girl's bathroom on coronation day in

1969. "Janelle got her period just before the assembly where they announced the homecoming candidates. I gave her a nickel for the Kotex machine. Remember?"

"There's more than one way to have sex, Tory." Debbie cackled softly. "They didn't call her the 'head cheerleader' for nothing, you know."

She took a large gulp of vodka and continued. "Doug had never been an ideal husband or father, but once he entered this Janelle phase, he was even worse. He became more abusive, verbally and physically. He ranted about Janelle and continually reminded me about my indiscretion. He accused me of carrying on an affair with Stu now. That's why I arranged for Janelle to room at Stu's house. I thought it might mollify Doug. At least about Stu and me.

"But of course it didn't. He became obsessed with winning the homecoming football game, as a way of repeating the past. Of showing Janelle, and Stu, and everyone else, that he was still the great Doug Fischbach. And he put incredible pressure on Cameron. No matter how hard Cameron tried, he never lived up to his father's impossible standards. Doug called him terrible names, said he'd never grow up to be a 'real man.' I think seeing his father hit me at the river on Friday snapped something inside him. Something that had been brewing a long time."

She sat for a moment, staring into her glass.

"Cameron was already here when I got home last Friday night," Debbie said. "I will never forget the wrenching sound of that child sobbing. We sat up all night, comforting each other, jumping at every noise, waiting for Doug to show up, drunk and even more furious. We slept on the couch.

"And of course Doug didn't come home. It wasn't the first time he'd stayed out all night, and, frankly, I was relieved to put off the confrontation. It wasn't until the next morning that we began to be worried."

She shrugged and continued to drink in silence. By Saturday, it was already much too late for worry.

I didn't ask her if, as Doug suspected, she and Stu really were having an affair.

I didn't ask her if she saw the jersey on the ground before she left the river on Friday night. Whether or not it was the truth, I knew what her answer would be.

I realized, after listening for over an hour, that the most important person in Debbie's life was not her husband, or any alleged boyfriend, but her oldest son.

For the first time, it occurred to me to wonder if either mother or son had conspired to relieve the other of the incredible burden of Doug Fischbach's continued existence.

33

Funeral Feast

THURSDAY

Here in the Midwest, we're acutely aware of our reputation for extending a friendly hand, lending assistance without being asked, and pitching together to ease one another's burdens.

And with very little prodding, we usually meet our own and the country's inflated expectations of proper behavior. We build barns, bake cakes, shovel sidewalks, and curb our natural tendency to talk about one another when propriety demands.

One place you generally will not hear anything bad about a person is at his own funeral. And certainly everyone put a great deal of effort into conversation appropriate for a standing-room-only memorial service.

But after the Reverend Clay Deibert's uplifting eulogy; after Stu, Ron, Neil, Hugh, and a couple of late-arriving out-of-town relatives had carried Doug Fischbach to his final resting place; after we all trooped back to the dining room in the Lutheran Hall to sample the repast laid out by Junior and the church ladies, it was a different story.

Not that anyone was blatantly muddying the name of our late football coach. It's just that, try as we might, no one could think of anything good to say about him.

It had been like that after Butchie Pendergast's funeral too. While there was a great deal of commiserating with, and for, the family over the loss, and the usual lament about the deceased being so young, and having so much left to accomplish, there was little said about anyone actually missing the dear departed.

"I feel kinda weird," Rhonda whispered to me, nibbling from her Styrofoam plate filled with the usual funeral fare—thinly sliced ham on dinner rolls, Jell-O salad, sliced dill pickles, carrot sticks, and chocolate cake baked by the Lutheran Women's Guild. "I mean the service was sad and all, and I could just cry whenever I look at those poor kids, especially Cameron. But otherwise, I'm sorta relieved that I don't have to wait on him anymore. Or worry if he's gonna blow up in public and start calling names and punching and stuff."

"I know how you feel," Presley agreed, slurping down another cup of fruit punch. He'd already devoured two plates of food. I'd had to remind him that this was not an all-you-can-eat buffet. "I wasn't even gonna come, but they let school out and everything, and it seemed chicken not to." He lowered his voice and said, "I was worried that he was gonna look like he did at the river. But I saw him in the coffin, and it wasn't so bad. He looked sorta calm. Peaceful-like."

"Something he never seemed to manage when he was alive," I said.

I felt only marginally guilty about my own additions to the whispered, but persistent, Doug-bashing. After all, I had been charged, by the widow herself, to spread her version of the last few months of their marriage.

"Maybe he's coaching in heaven now," Rhonda said wistfully.

Del crunched a pickle spear. "There's a thought: Doug sitting on a cloud, calling the angels fags for not hitting the devils hard enough."

"Too bad for her, though," Aphrodite said, pointing across the room at an impeccably groomed and properly sorrowful Debbie.

Debbie seemed to have weathered the service well and was stoically enduring the obligatory feeding of the mourners. Wearing a simple but tasteful dress adorned with no jewelry except the gold and rhinestone circle pin, she made it a point to speak to everyone.

"She looks better than I would have expected," Rhonda said, watching Debbie work the room.

"She's doing all right," I said. Even with Debbie's blessing, I couldn't bring myself to say, at the man's own funeral, that his wife was probably better off without him.

Someone had cranked the heat up in the Lutheran Hall. I was hot and thirsty, and it was too soon to pay our last condolences and leave. "I'm going to get some more punch. Anyone want anything while I'm up?" I asked.

Once a waitress, always a waitress.

"Sure." Aphrodite handed me an empty cup with a bright red lipstick imprint on the rim.

Junior, who had been directing operations out of sight in the kitchen, now stood behind the loaded trestle table. Almost everyone had been served at least once, and those gathered around her were intent on seconds and more hot coffee.

"Where's Stu?" Junior asked me.

"He had to go back to work right after the service," I lied. I actually had no idea what Stu was doing, but I didn't want to get into that with Junior. Or anyone else.

"You know, this reminds me more and more of a long time ago," Ron Adler said quietly, behind me. He'd been picking over the sandwiches and the last of the cake. "Everyone was at Butchie's funeral too, except for Janelle."

"And Doug," I reminded him. "They were both gone right after the party at the river, remember? Neither one was here for the memorial service."

Something about that statement, something that had to do with Ron, almost danced into view, and then disappeared. I narrowed my eyes at him, concentrating.

"Uh-huh." He nodded, blinking. He was watching Del in the corner, not really paying attention. Then he shook his head and turned back to me. "You know, we still have that blue tarp of Stu's. We brought it home with us after the wingding at the river on Friday night. What with all this going on"—he blinked, mouth full, indicating the room with a finger—"it kinda slipped my mind, but it's in the back of my pickup whenever Stu wants it. You tell him, okay?"

He didn't wait for my answer, but ambled off to talk to Neil, who was standing in the corner, observing the crowd for the still-hiding Janelle. Unless, of course, she was in the room, wearing one of her blend-into-the-wallpaper disguises.

"That's not all that slipped his mind," Junior said darkly, watching Ron's back.

"What do you mean?"

"I don't know who this 'we' is that he talks about, taking things home last Friday night, but it certainly wasn't Gina."

"Sure it was," I said. "Ron and Gina left not too long after the fight broke up."

"Well, Ron might have left then, but he forgot Gina," Junior said, still scowling.

"Huh?"

"Ron left the river on Friday night *without* his wife," Junior said slowly, so even an idiot like me could understand. "He forgot to take her, and he forgot to tell her he was leaving. Poor Gina wandered around for twenty minutes looking for him, like a forlorn puppy. We finally persuaded her to ride home with Clay and me."

"But I'm sure Ron said . . ." I trailed off, trying to remember exactly what Ron had said.

Debbie stepped up to the table and handed an empty cup to Junior, which she refilled with a perfect preacher's-wife smile.

Junior held the cup out, momentarily dropping her eyes to the pin on Debbie's dress, and froze. She stood, stock-still, hand extended, not breathing. The color drained from her face. "That's a nice piece of jewelry." She swallowed, striving to keep a small waver out of her voice. "Where did you get it?"

Debbie, perhaps fortified by a couple of glasses of Kamchatka ice water, looked down at the pin, then directly into Junior's eyes, and said, "Doug picked it up somewhere. Do you like it?"

34

An Unbroken Circle

Though we try to practice public stoicism, we are not British. We encourage a stiff upper lip, but are neither surprised, nor contemptuous, when we fall short in that department. We mist up at graduations, sniffle at sad movies, and cry outright at weddings. We do not expect to come through a funeral unscathed.

So no one was shocked when Junior, overcome with emotion, excused herself and made her shaky way out of the hall and onto the couch in Clay's office.

No one except Debbie and me. Debbie was startled by Junior's reaction. She watched me escort Junior from the room with a quizzical expression.

It seemed so unlikely that Junior had a connection to Doug, or that particular piece of jewelry, that I was willing to chalk the whole thing up to vapors.

"Here, drink this. It'll make you feel better," I said, handing Junior a glass of water. If she hadn't been pregnant, I'd have scouted around for something stronger (though the chance of finding liquor in the Lutheran minister's office was slim to none).

Junior sipped, nodded, closed her eyes, and moaned a little.

"Are you all right?" I asked, alarmed. Maybe she'd gone into early labor.

"I remember now," she said faintly. "My mother had that pin."

"If you're talking about the pin that Debbie was wearing," I said, "everyone's mother had one like that."

"No," she said, fixing me with a frantic look. "My mother didn't have a pin like that. My mother had *that* pin. That exact pin."

I sat in the swivel chair behind the desk and stared at Junior. "What makes you so sure that *exact* pin belonged to Aunt Juanita? They made gazillions like it in the fifties. They were a dime a dozen," I said.

"That isn't a 'dime a dozen' pin,'" Junior said, eyes closed. "It's one of a kind. Daddy had it designed specifically for Mother. Solid gold and diamonds. It was an engagement gift. One of her prized possessions."

Diamonds? Solid gold? Shows you what I know about jewelry.

"If it belongs to Aunt Juanita, how did Doug Fischbach get it? Did she report it stolen?" I could just imagine the fuss Aunt Juanita would make when she discovered that Debbie Fischbach was now wearing her engagement gift.

"It wasn't stolen," Junior said miserably. "It was lost."

"Well, Debbie's been trying to find out where it came from; she'll probably be willing to give it back," I said, "if Aunt Juanita can prove that it was hers. Especially if she lost it recently."

All of this was fascinating, but it did not explain Junior's overreaction to seeing her mother's heirloom. Or how it came to be in Doug's possession. Or why he thought it might have belonged to Janelle Ross.

"Mother didn't lose that pin," Junior said, closing her eyes tightly. "I did. More than twenty-five years ago."

I rocked back in the chair, hands locked behind my head, and waited for her to continue.

Junior swallowed. "I always loved that pin. It was so beautiful, and it was so romantic of my father to have it specially made for my mother. I used to beg to wear it, but mother said I wasn't old enough. That I wouldn't take proper care of it. That I'd lose it." Junior chuckled weakly. "Guess I proved her right there."

"I don't get it," I said. "If you lost it that long ago, why was it with Doug's things now?"

"I don't know," she shook her head. "I had forgotten all about it. I mean completely. But seeing it pinned to Debbie's dress brought it back. Oh Jesus, it brought *all* of it back. All at once. It's all there again. Every horrible detail."

"Brought what back?" I asked, alert. Something important was happening here.

"Everything," Junior wailed. "I didn't forget because I was drunk. I forgot because I made myself forget. I forgot everything!"

"Everything about what?" I demanded, trying to keep the impatience out of my voice.

"Everything about that homecoming party in 1969. That's when I lost the pin." Lying on the couch, with an arm flung over her eyes, she continued, "I'd asked to wear the pin to school, and Mother said no. She and Daddy went out that Friday night, and I knew they wouldn't be back until late, so I snuck it out under my windbreaker and took it over to Gina's house. I was so worried about getting caught that I didn't even tell Gina that I had it. I wore it attached to a bra strap. I felt glamorous just having it with me."

I had a sudden vision of thirteen-year-old Junior clutching drunkenly at her shirt in the dark, behind the bushes at the river. At least I had thought she was clutching at her shirt. In reality, she had been holding on to a valuable pin that had been smuggled out of my aunt's jewelry box.

"Then we made Lila take us to that stupid party," Junior continued shakily. "We sat behind that clump of trees and he got us drunk."

"He who?" I asked. "Butchie Pendergast?"

"No, Doug Fischbach," Junior said.

I am not a strong believer in the recovered memory

syndrome, but I was witnessing the phenomenon now. Awful memories had popped, whole, into Junior's head, and her words came out in a rush. "He heard us in the bushes, came around and laughed. Then he poured out most of Gina's Coke and filled the bottle back up with rum or something. And like idiots, we drank it."

"That must have been before the fight," I said, thinking back. "Because you were already drunk by the time he punched Stu."

"I have no idea when it was, or what was going on with the rest of the party. You were mad, really angry. You told us to stay put. But then Butchie came, and he asked if we wanted to go swimming. And it sounded like fun, so we trailed after him. We didn't even hesitate when he suggested we skinny-dip. And then he started touching us." She shuddered, her face a portrait of horrified shame. "And we were so drunk, we didn't even tell him to stop."

The sudden onrush of memory was more than she could bear. Tears snaked from the corners of Junior's eyes. She sat up, then lay back down and stared bleakly at the ceiling.

"At least Del and I found you before anything worse happened," I said, which was scant comfort for the miserable Junior. "We stuffed you back into your clothes and took you to my house." Where she and Gina had spent the entire night throwing up.

"I didn't realize the pin was gone until the next morning." Junior sniffed, ignoring my interruption. "I looked frantically for it everywhere at your house. But it wasn't there. I had a horrible headache, but I could still remember everything that happened. I realized right away that the pin must have fallen off at the river. I was terrified of what Mother would do when she found that it was gone. Losing Mother's pin seemed even worse than what *he'd* done. So as soon as you dropped me off at home, I jumped on my bike and rode back to the river to search. But it wasn't there."

I realized that Doug must have found the pin on the riverbank and picked it up on Friday night, before he and Janelle disappeared together.

"And *that's* why I forgot it all," she said, as if amazed at the treachery of her own mind. "I wiped it out completely, as though none of it ever happened," Junior said, voice trailing off. "A complete blank. All gone. Like it never happened."

"Well, getting drunk, and then being molested, is excuse enough to forget," I said gently. "Add to that how furious Aunt Juanita must've been when you told her you'd lost her pin. You were just a kid, after all." Aunt Juanita's fury had wilted many a full-grown adult.

"No, you don't understand, Tory. I didn't block those memories because of a guilty conscience. Or because Mother was angry. I never told Mother. I never said anything to Mother about it all. She assumed she'd lost the pin herself.

"I made myself forget, on purpose. Because when I went back to the river to search, I found Butchie Pendergast instead."

She was sobbing. I sat by her on the couch and held her as she cried. "I can see him now, naked. And dead, in the water. I rushed home terrified, and told Mother. She called the sheriff. She never asked why I went to the river in the first place. She just told me to put it out of my mind." She laughed bitterly. "And like a good little girl, I did. I didn't remember any of it until just now. And now it'll never go away again."

As Junior cried herself out, I combined my memories of that night with her newfound revelations and realized that we had all made an error in one of our cherished assumptions.

35

....

Cherished Assumptions

If we repeat something to ourselves, and to one another, often enough, it becomes firmly fixed in our collective consciousness. No matter that if we examined our own memories closely, the theory would evaporate in the light of established facts.

We believe what we want to believe, goddammit.

And we believed that Doug Fischbach and Janelle Ross ran away together on Friday night, after the 1969 homecoming football game, immediately following a nasty confrontation wherein Doug and Janelle were discovered, by their respective steadies, engaged in some sort of carnal congress.

And we stubbornly clung to those assumptions, at the expense of our own recollections.

I myself knew that Janelle was still at the party after the fight between Doug and Stu. It was Janelle who distracted Butchie long enough for Del and me to get Junior and Gina dressed and away from the river.

And if I had sorted through that memory closely

enough, I would have realized that Doug was still on hand too.

When Del and I rounded the clump of trees, looking for Junior and Gina, the first word out of Butchie's mouth had been, "Doug?" Clearly, Butchie expected him. And even more clearly, Doug and Butchie had planned some sort of unpleasant recreation with the drunken little girls.

Those facts fell into place as Junior recounted her harrowing story. And that brought into focus something Ron Adler had said in the cafe, back when the exciting news broke that J. Ross Nelson planned to visit Delphi. The fragment that I'd almost seen earlier, in the Lutheran Hall.

"Miss High and Mighty J. Ross Nelson didn't disappear until later, because I saw her in town the day after," Ron had said, speaking of the fateful party in 1969.

Ron said it. We all heard it. And we discounted it entirely, because it did not fit in with our romantic notion of how the events had transpired.

I left Junior, dozing fitfully, on the couch in the office, and was relieved to find Ron still yakking with Neil in the hall.

"Ron," I said urgently, interrupting them, "I need to ask you something."

He eyed me warily.

"Remember when Gina first announced that Janelle was coming to Delphi? You said something about having seen her in town the next day? Are you sure about that?"

"I said Gina was in town the next day?" Ron blinked, confused.

"No, dipshit. You said that you saw Janelle in town the next day—the day after the homecoming party in 1969. Right?"

He grinned. "I said that all along, but no one would listen. Yes, I saw her walking down the street by the school, the morning after that party. Why—"

I didn't wait for him to finish his question. I wouldn't have answered it anyway. I just grabbed Neil by the arm, headed for the door, and filled him in, on the way to his house.

"Hi guys," Janelle said, looking up from the book she was reading in one of Neil's overstuffed living room chairs. Sade crooned softly from the stereo, a glass of wine stood on an end table nearby, and a cat curled comfortably in her lap. "How'd it go?"

Neil shot a look at me and raised an eyebrow. The floor was mine.

"Remember that pin that Doug had, the one he thought was yours?" I asked, deciding there was no point in beating around the bush. "I found out who it belonged to. And how Doug got it. And when."

"Oh?" Janelle asked, eyes wide, lovely face innocently curious.

I'd seen that expression on the big screen before too.

"Yeah, it belonged to my aunt, the mother of my cousin, Junior Deibert. She was Junior Engebretson back then. You might remember her, even though she was just thirteen at the time. She wore it to that kegger at the river in 1969. She lost it there, after Butchie Pendergast talked her into taking off all her clothes."

"That's interesting," Janelle said. "But it doesn't really concern me."

"Well, actually it does," I said, sitting on the couch. Neil stood in the doorway, leaning against the jamb, arms crossed.

Janelle looked from Neil to me and back to Neil again. She flashed another smile at us.

"You see, we had all labored under the erroneous notion that you and Doug left that river party together, immediately after Doug punched Stu. Granted, you both helped us to form that opinion. On separate occasions, you both stated that fact firmly."

"That's how I remember things," Janelle said carefully.

"Ah, there's the rub," I said. "Because I just lately have remembered that you helped me to shepherd a young, and very drunk, Junior away from Butchie Pendergast, long after that fight was over. And long after you were both supposedly gone."

"Yes, well, the timing of our departure might have become a little fuzzy over the years," Janelle said, shrugging. "But what difference can that possibly make?"

"Actually, it wouldn't matter that you and Doug were still on the riverbank with Butchie Pendergast. Or that Doug obviously picked up Junior's pin, thinking it was yours," I said, shrugging back at her. "What matters is that Doug kept that pin. Why didn't he just hand it over on your little three-day jaunt? Why wait twenty-five years?"

"Well," Janelle said offhandedly, "we were young, and we were rather busy, if you get my drift. I suppose it just slipped Doug's mind."

A few days ago, I would have bought her seamless performance. But Stu had reminded me that Janelle was, and always had been, an actress.

"Bravo," I said, applauding. "Unfortunately, Ron Adler saw you in Delphi on Saturday, the day *after* that party in 1969."

Janelle sipped her wine, wiped her lips, then tried a wan smile.

"Okay, so now you know," she said, sighing, slumping attractively in the chair. "Doug couldn't have given that pin back to me, because we never ran away together. It was all a story. A fabrication.

"The last time I saw Doug was at the river with Butch, in 1969. And the first time I saw him again was last week, here in Delphi."

Neil and I had worked out the timeline on the way back from the funeral. We knew it was the truth. But we were still flabbergasted to hear Janelle admit it so easily.

"So what really happened?" Neil asked.

"I couldn't tell you where Doug went. I have not a single clue. I didn't know that the whole town thought we'd been together until after I arrived last week. I didn't even know that Butchie Pendergast had died. And the timing of his death was a complete shock to me."

She was so sincere, so sorrowful. So irritatingly beautiful. It was all too natural to sympathize with her.

Unfortunately, there were just a few too many coincidences in her story. And lies in her past.

"Then where the hell did you go?" I demanded. "Since you weren't with Doug."

She inhaled deeply. "I hitched a ride west with a semi driver, and I never looked back."

"But that doesn't explain anything," I said. "Why did you go? And more importantly, why did you go then?"

"Because," Janelle said quietly, "I was pregnant."

36

The Magic Nickel

There are a finite number of things I believe in.

I believe that Congress shall make no law respecting an establishment of religion, or prohibiting the free exercise thereof, or abridging the freedom of speech, or of the press, or the right of the people peaceably to assemble, and petition the government for a redress of grievances.

I believe that the Minnesota Vikings will raise our hopes many times, but they will never win a Super Bowl.

I believe that James Taylor and Carly Simon, Kenneth Branagh and Emma Thompson, and Geena Davis and Jeff Goldblum should all get back together.

And I believed that Janelle Ross could *not* have been pregnant in 1969 when she disappeared from Delphi.

Neil and I stared at her. Openmouthed.

"Really," Janelle said softly.

"You couldn't have been," I said flatly. "I was there, remember? You got your period just before the assembly announcing the homecoming royalty. Del was there. All the cheerleaders were there. I loaned you a nickel for the Kotex machine because you didn't have any money or supplies with you. They *all* remember exactly the same thing."

Janelle shrugged and smiled. "Nevertheless, I *was* pregnant. Three months, as a matter of fact."

"But how can that be?" I asked, confused.

"Tory, it was an *act.* I didn't get my period for another six months. But I wanted a cover for when I had to go away, so I deliberately staged that scene knowing the story would be spread. And believed. The cheerleaders would tell the school mainstream, and Delphine would tell the wild crowd. Everyone knew she hung out in the girls' can."

"Why put me in the middle?" I asked.

"It was just your luck to be there at showtime," Janelle said, smiling softly. "But I realized immediately that you'd be an unimpeachable asset when it came to defending my honor. Since you didn't actually belong to any crowd, you'd be an independent witness. One that everyone would believe."

I was instantly embarrassed that my former self had been so easily duped. And angry that Janelle had read me so correctly—that I *had* defended her honor for more than a quarter of a century.

Neil stood behind me and placed a warm hand on my shoulder. "But why bother?" he asked. "By the time you delivered, your senior year would have been over. Or nearly so. What difference would it have made if everyone had known about the baby?"

"Ah Neil," Janelle said. "You're too young to remember what it was like in those days. Girls in my situation were immediately expelled from school. They were outcasts, regarded as used and dirty." She looked to me for confirmation.

"Things are more enlightened now," I said to Neil. "There weren't any 'single mothers' back then. Just good girls and bad girls."

"And I wanted to stay a good girl. I figured people would think that I had cancer. Or mono." She shrugged. "Or something without any stigma attached, anyway. Even though I didn't plan to come back, I wanted to be remembered well. It's sort of a personality failing of mine."

Among others, I wanted to add. Like the ability to lie so convincingly that I was not sure she was telling the truth, even now.

"So you disappeared completely. But why then? And why leave it such a mystery?" Neil asked, pouring himself a glass of wine. He sat on the couch next to me.

"I thought it would be a hoot to pull a big one on the whole town," Janelle said, reaching for the wine bottle. "And that Friday seemed as good a time as any to make a grand exit. Homecoming was over, I went out in a blaze of glory. Besides, I would have to have left soon, I was starting to show."

"But didn't your parents go crazy worrying?" I asked.

"They knew I was in a home for unwed mothers in California," Janelle said, looking down. "I didn't tell them where, and they were so horrified by the truth that they were content not to know any of the particulars."

"And what were the particulars?" Neil asked quietly.

"That I gave birth to a healthy girl. That I gave her up for adoption immediately, and then went on with my life. No one in Delphi ever knew about the child. And I rarely thought about her myself, until a few months ago."

"What happened then?" I asked, finally pouring myself some wine, before it was all gone.

"My daughter grew up, and found me," Janelle said simply.

"How?"

"I can thank Benny for that," she said bitterly. "Even though he is no longer representing me, his name is on all the old press clippings and bios. The private investigator my daughter hired tracked Benny down and he was more than happy to capitalize on the situation. They corresponded for quite a while before I was told.

"And of course, she wasn't content just to *find* me. She wanted to establish a relationship. And she wanted me to help find her father." Janelle got up and walked to the window and said, with her back to us, "I refused."

"Why?"

"A discovery like that can be wrenching for anyone," she said, still looking out the window. "But for someone even as marginally famous as I am, this sort of revelation becomes tabloid fodder immediately. I decided that her right to discover the identity of her father did not outweigh my right to protect him, and his identity." Janelle turned to us. "Unfortunately, I forgot about Benny.

"He stole my senior Delphi annual and sent it to the girl. Late last summer, she wrote to the school, asking to be put in contact with someone from our class, figuring to trace her father down that way. And the school just happened to have the 1969 homecoming king on staff."

"Oh jeez," I breathed. "Doug."

Doug, who Lisa Franklin Hauck-Robertson had been sure was getting, and keeping hidden, mail from somewhere. Doug, who'd had Janelle on the brain. Doug, who claimed to be responsible for bringing Janelle back to Delphi.

Janelle emptied the last of the wine into her glass and sat the bottle on the end table. "Yes, Doug. He was elated by contact with the girl, more than happy to assure her that he was indeed her father. And while he was writing to her, and while Debbie and Gina Adler were writing polite letters inviting me to make an appearance in this year's homecoming parade, Doug found me too. Through Benny, of course."

"Is that why you decided to come back to Delphi?" Neil asked. He'd quietly gone into the kitchen and returned with another open bottle of wine.

"By then I didn't have any choice. I was doing my best to forestall the happy reunion. It took everything I had to persuade my daughter to let me come to Delphi first, to scout out the territory, so to speak. Doug was already threatening to sell the story to the tabloids himself, though he hinted that he might keep quiet. For a price," she said, disgusted.

"He was blackmailing you about *his* own daughter?" I asked, horrified.

"That's what he thought, anyway," Janelle said, with a

small smile. "I agreed to an appearance here, but my real reason for returning was to make a damage control assessment. That was when Doug informed me that all of Delphi thought we'd run away together in 1969. And to appease him, I went along with his ridiculous story.

"In the meantime, 'our' daughter insisted that Doug take a blood test to prove paternity, which he did happily."

"So now Debbie has to deal with this, on top of Doug's death," I said. Enlightened times or not, surprise illegitimate children are still something of a shock.

"No, actually, she doesn't." Janelle grinned. "Because the test proved conclusively that Doug was *not* the father."

Neither of us said a word, waiting for Janelle to continue. The wine bottle sat sweating and ignored.

"He was enraged at first, of course. But being Doug, he figured he could turn it to his advantage. Without, as he said, having to worry about back child support payments."

Instinctively, we knew that Janelle would refuse to name her child's father for us. But by then, she didn't have to.

I knew who the father was.

37

Many Hats

I'd have gotten there eventually. I mean, there were several threads leading to one particular Delphi door—Janelle said she'd talked to him, he said he hadn't yet had the pleasure; Debbie'd voiced suspicions about who the "other man" had been.

But it was the annual that did it. The senior annual that Benny had stolen to give to Janelle's daughter. The annual that had been published, as they all were around here, *after* the senior class graduation ceremony, and long after Janelle disappeared. She swore she'd had no contact with Delphi in the intervening years, and yet she possessed her own senior annual.

In small-town South Dakota, teachers wear many hats. The football coach is also likely to be the typing teacher, the study hall monitor, and back-up bus driver.

And the chorus director, junior high geography teacher, and senior class adviser can also advise the yearbook staff. For more than twenty-five years running.

"You lied," I said, angrily. "You knew where she went.

You knew why she left. And you sent her a copy of the annual."

I'd realized that Janelle had been more than reasonably reticent about the identity of the father of her child. Though the revelation of an out-of-wedlock baby could make life uncomfortable for both parents, especially if it hit the nightly news, grownups could, presumably, deal with the evidence of their adolescent mistakes.

There had to have been a very good reason for keeping the secret. Perhaps the information would put the individual's career and civic standing in some sort of jeopardy. Even many years after the fact.

"Oh, Hugh, how could you?" I asked him, heartsick, in the impeccably neat kitchen of the house he'd owned since he first started teaching in Delphi. The one right across the street from the school.

"I don't have many rules in my life, Tory," he said sadly. "But those I have, I take seriously. I try not to lie, and I keep the secrets that are entrusted to me. In this case, I had to break one rule to follow the other. It was not a particularly difficult decision."

"I imagine self-interest had a little to do with it," I said harshly. It was probably easy to keep a secret that would have gotten him fired and ruined his teaching career.

"Keeping a confidence hardly qualifies as self-interest," he said gently.

"It does when the secret you kept also saved your ass. Not that there weren't suspicions all along. I just ignored them. We all did."

In high school, the guys mistrusted, and felt uncomfortable around, Mr. Kincaid. The girls loved him.

Evidently literally.

Del's affair with Hugh made me curious, if slightly queasy. But the notion of his having sex with students, *while* they were students, made me physically ill.

"How would knowing Janelle Ross's predicament in 1969 'save my ass,' as you so succinctly put it?" Hugh asked, brows knit.

"*Keeping* Janelle's pregnancy a secret is what saved

your ass," I said vehemently. "Especially since you were the father! How many girls have you seduced over the years? How many lives have you ruined?"

I was near tears.

Hugh felt for a chair behind him, pulled it out, and sat at the table, pale and shaky.

"You think that I fathered Janelle's baby?" he asked, incredulous. "That I slept with students? Who told you this?"

"No one," I said. "It all adds up. Who else would still need protection after this many years? Whose life would be devastated? Who did Janelle, and all the rest of the girls, trust implicitly?

Hugh rubbed his face and ran his hands through his hair. "It was bad enough when Mr. Nelson showed up, demanding to know where Janelle was. I was completely flabbergasted when he informed me that *my* daughter would be contacting me shortly."

"I can imagine that would be flabbergasting," I said, cold and aloof, leaning back against the kitchen sink as Hugh blew all his air out in a whoosh.

"It was. Completely," he said quietly, and then looked at me directly. "Tory, I would never betray my students' trust. I am not the father of Janelle's child. I could not have fathered anyone's child."

I eyed him stonily. He was sleeping with Del, and her minimum requirement was that all male organs be in proper working condition. A claim of impotence would not wash.

"Are you trying to tell me that you're sterile?" I asked.

"No," Hugh said, sighing. "I'm trying to tell you that I'm gay."

The wheels turning in my brain ground to a screeching halt. I had to remind myself to keep breathing.

"But, but . . ." I said, weakly, sitting down.

But what?

The fact that he was so good-looking, that all the girls had crushes on him, that our minds were stuck in a conventional rut and no other option had even occurred to us?

". . . you were married," I finished lamely.

"Not for long, if you remember. I put that sweet woman through hell," Hugh said sadly, "with a doomed attempt to rehabilitate myself. It was a miserable failure."

"What about Del?" I asked. "Is an affair with her another shot at rehabilitation?"

"I'm not having an affair with Delphine," Hugh said, mildly surprised. "though we do see each other socially and enjoy each other's company, Del and I are just friends. She understands that I'm not interested in a sexual relationship with her."

Del never understands when a man is not interested in a sexual relationship with her. "So did you spend all of Friday night together, talking about your mutual noninterest?"

"I didn't spend Friday night with Del," Hugh protested.

"Yes you did. Del didn't come home until morning," I said, annoyed with his protests.

"Well, Delphine may not have come home that night. But I did. Alone." He scratched his head. "If I remember correctly, Del left the river almost immediately following the scene between Cameron and his father."

And when Hugh told me who Del had left with, I nearly fell over.

38

Requited Love's a Bore, Too

In life, there will be occurrences that will catch you off-guard, small revelations that can leave you mildly perplexed. Minor quakes in an otherwise stable topography.

And then there are surprises that will blow you right out of the water.

Between Janelle's baby and Hugh's admission, I'd already exceeded my daily, if not yearly, quota of the latter. Though if the truth be known, I should not have been so completely surprised by the newest anomaly. The clues were there, the changes in attitude and behavior were, in retrospect, obvious.

"What the hell got into you?" I demanded of a startled and slightly defensive Del, who was sitting on our vinyl couch, pretending to watch television.

"Since when do you pass judgment on *my* life, Miss Married Boyfriend?" she demanded back.

"Since when do you spend the night with Ron Adler?"

"Keep your voice down, Presley's not alone." She shot a worried look down the hallway.

"Okay, I'll whisper," I said, more quietly. "But I still want to know why."

"You've had sex—which part needs explaining?"

"It's not the act," I said forcefully, if quietly. "It's your choice of partner that has me confused." I was angry at Del. Her steadfast refusals of Ron's many propositions over the years had seemed slightly noble. I'd chalked it up to a rarely used streak of kindness, toward both Ron and his long-suffering wife.

Silly me. Evidently, it was only lack of opportunity.

"I don't know how it happened. I didn't plan it, believe me." She waved her hands in confusion. "I was all set to go to it with Hugh Kincaid, right there at the river, when he gave me some dumb-ass excuse about it being morally wrong to be intimate with former students. Especially former students whose children are present students. I told him that didn't matter to me. I told him there'd be no strings attached. I told him it would be an entirely guilt-free encounter . . ." Her voice trailed off.

"What'd he say?" I asked. I already figured out what he didn't say. He didn't tell Del the real reason that he turned her down. Though perhaps what he told her *was* the real reason. One of them, anyway.

"He thanked me kindly for the honor of my proposal, but regretfully could not further the acquaintance on those terms. He sounded just like the characters in those Jane Austen books you're always trying to get me to read."

"So Ron was a Hugh substitute?"

"Ridiculous, right?" She laughed without humor. "I was embarrassed. Hell, I was pissed. Then Ron cornered me and said the same thing he's said every time we've been alone since high school—'Hey babe, is tonight the night?' "

"And you shocked the shit out of him by saying yes."

"Something like that." She crossed her arms over her breasts, rubbing her shoulders. "I don't think he even made a flimsy excuse to Gina. He just loaded me into his pickup and took off before I could change my mind."

"So," I said, disgusted with myself for not being able to resist asking, "how was it?"

"A fiasco," she said miserably.

"That bad, huh?"

"No." Del was near tears, something I'd never seen before. "That good."

"So, what's the problem?"

Del never minded that most of her boyfriends were married. If the sex was good, she was content to let the moral issues fall where they may. Sometimes even if the sex was bad.

"*He's* the problem. No one was more surprised than me when it turned out to be great. I mean, look at the guy, for crying out loud. It should have been awful.

"Instead it was fantastic. And I was perfectly willing to continue from there. I told him that. I damn near told him that I loved him. And you know what he did?"

Since he obviously didn't jump for joy, I had no clue.

"He started crying," she said bitterly. Incredulously. "The little fucker blubbered over me about how much he loved Gina, and how sorry he was, and how he never meant to hurt her. And this never shoulda happened, and how it was never gonna happen again. And how it was all my fault. How I made him do it." She blinked in furious imitation throughout the entire recital.

"You gotta be kidding me," I said. "After half a lifetime of propositions, after an entire night of sex, he blames *you?*"

"You know how he's been acting lately," Del said helplessly. "He can hardly look at me anymore. He won't talk to me. I let everyone think I'd spent the night with Hugh, as a cover-up, and he still won't give me another chance. I don't think we can even be friends anymore."

Poor Del, she'd always wielded the power in her sexual skirmishes. This was her first taste of sex as a line drawn in the sand between warring parties.

"A wise woman once told me that the first rule of sex is that you can't un-fuck 'em," I said, reminding Del of her own words. She was so miserable that I considered giving her a hug. But even in that state, Del was too prickly for the sisterhood-bonding stuff. I settled for patting her shoulder.

"I shoulda listened," Del said with a weak grin. She shook her hair back and composed herself. "What the hell are we doing, playing mother confessor when the kid is right down the hall? He's liable to pop out any minute."

As if on cue, Presley barreled from his room, through the living room, past us, and into the kitchen.

"Got any Coke?" he asked, head stuffed inside the refrigerator.

"On the bottom shelf," I said, "where it always is. Are we feeding an army?"

"Just a couple of guys," Pres said, standing up, arms loaded with cans, bags of chips, and dip cartons. "You know, Cameron Fischbach and John Adler."

Del actually blanched.

"How's Cameron doing?" I asked, partly to deflect Presley's attention. But also because I really wanted to know. Cameron had been so distraught at the funeral that he'd been escorted from the service.

Presley shrugged. "He's okay. I mean, he feels awful, of course. Like it's his fault that his dad died. But that's normal, isn't it?"

"As a rule," I said.

"That's what Cameron's mom said too. She told him not to feel bad, clear back on the night of the fight. I mean when he rushed out from behind those trees to tackle his dad by the fire. Even the grown guys could barely hold Coach down. Cameron said that him and his mom sat up all night talking about it and stuff. Even before"—he shrugged and waved his full arms—"well, before anyone knew that Coach was dead. 'Cause Cameron went home right after the fight, and all. I mean . . ." Presley's voice trailed off.

Del had snapped out of her self-pitying mode and was eyeing her son narrowly.

"What fight?" she asked lightly.

"The one between Cameron and his dad. At the . . ." His voice trailed off.

Del frowned.

Pres tried to shrug innocently. "You wanna help me out here, Tory?" he asked hopefully.

"Sorry, kiddo," I said. "You're on your own. I told you it was going to have to come out sooner or later."

"Well, Mom, you see, Mom, old pal, um . . ." Presley floundered. "I, um . . . sorta, was there."

Del arched an eyebrow my direction.

"We sorta were there that night, at the river when you guys were there. We sorta got a little drunk."

"Who's we?"

"Well . . ." He actually shuffled his feet, and then said sheepishly, "Me and Cameron."

"Cameron Fischbach took you to the river and got you drunk?" Del was astounded. She turned to me. "And you knew?"

Presley didn't give me time to answer her. "It wasn't like that at all, Mom. I asked Cameron to take me. He lets me hang out with him, that's all, and I had this stupid idea about spying on you guys. And I got *myself* drunk. I'm the one who took the beer from John's dad's cooler."

The mention of John Adler's father froze Del for a second.

Presley, taking the silence for deepening anger, rushed in. "And all that condom stuff was my idea too. We thought it'd be funny, and we talked Cameron into driving."

Del wasn't tracking her son very well, but I was. From the time I'd seen the words "Be Preparred" circled in Presley's notebook, I'd known he was one of the Safety Car condom tossers. I'd hoped he was the slogan painter too. It would have been too depressing if members of Delphi's senior class could not spell *prepared* or *committee* correctly.

"You're right, Ms. Bauer." Cameron Fischbach stepped into the living room. He must have been listening from the hallway. He was pale but determined. "It was my fault. I should have known better than to take anyone to a party where my old man was. Especially a kid. If you want to report me, go ahead. I deserve it. But I'm not sorry for being there. I'm glad I got the opportunity to throw that damn shirt back in his face. Just to see his expression."

Though he was pale and soft-spoken, the vehemence in Cameron's voice heightened the resemblance between him and the man whose funeral we'd attended this afternoon.

"Yes, you certainly should have known better," Del said, staring at Cameron as if she'd seen a ghost. And considering how much he looked like Doug, maybe she had. "But Presley is a big boy now."

"Boy!" Pres interjected.

Del continued, ignoring her son. "And he needs to take responsibility for his own stupid decisions. However, considering the kind of week it's been, I think we can forget about reporting anyone to the authorities." She forced a small smile. "Young people don't have a monopoly on making mistakes. Just don't let it happen again."

Cameron nodded, subdued. "Yes ma'am."

"Thanks, Mom." Pres grinned.

"Don't get too excited," she said to him. "Your authorities have already been notified, if you know what I mean."

"Jeez," he said dejectedly, ushering Cameron back into his room.

"That was nice of you," I said, impressed with Del's compassionate handling of Cameron. It would have been easy to mistake the boy's bitterness for something other than bereavement.

"I wasn't being nice," Del said, still watching the empty hallway. She turned to me and asked, "Do you suppose he meant it literally?"

39

A Little Knowledge

Friday

They say that knowledge is power. I say that knowledge is frustrating. Never in my life have I known so many secrets, and yet had so little fun with them. There was not a single person to whom I could unburden myself completely.

Neil knew about Janelle. Neil knew about Janelle's baby. Neil even knew that I had suspected Hugh Kincaid of being that baby's father. But he didn't know about Hugh's big secret. And he didn't know about Del and Ron. And, as things stood, I couldn't tell him either of those things.

Terse and gloweringly crabby, Del already regretted letting me in on her secret. She had no desire to share anything else. Not even the meaning of her cryptic question last night.

If Ron and Stu harbored secrets, we sure didn't know about them. Ron was spending more and more time at his own garage, and Stu had been "too busy" to stop in the cafe for ages.

Rhonda had no secrets, just surmises. And an inability to stay in class when she wanted to discuss them.

"There's more to this than we can see on the surface," she said earnestly, staring into her coffee cup. "My professor says that there are no accidents. That our subconscious directs our conscious selves. That the illusion of coincidence is just the way we humans have of rationalizing predetermined events to suit our own purposes."

"Which particular coincidence are we rationalizing today, Madam Freud?" Del snapped. "The fact that the men in this town are all too chickenshit to face their own lives? Or the fact that every one of 'em is dumb as a box of rocks?"

"The genetic and cultural norms set the tone for intergender relationships in any given area," Rhonda said seriously.

"Well, our male genetic norm default switch is obviously set on 'asshole,'" Del said, furiously wiping already clean tables.

"Looks to me like the male default switch is set on 'absent,'" Rhonda said, dropping a slow wink at me. She was goading Del, not a wise decision when Del was in this kind of mood. Rhonda surveyed the empty cafe. "This place looks like Chick Town. What'd you do, piss off all the guys?"

"No, that was just a coincidence," Del said, lighting a cigarette. "Besides, you're wrong. Here comes a walking penis now."

Since hell hath no fury like a Delphine scorned, I figured it was Ron. Or maybe Hugh, taking a free-period break in the cafe, as he sometimes did.

We were surprised to be joined by a morose and subdued Benny Nelson.

"Can I get you anything?" I asked, since Del pointedly ignored him.

"A cuppa coffee and some information," he said.

"I can manage one. But I can't guarantee the other," I said, wary. Though Janelle was still hiding at Neil's house, I was not at liberty to disclose that information. And if I *had* been at liberty, there were a dozen people I would tell before Benny.

"No shit," he said tiredly. "This is the most close-mouthed town I ever run across. Every one of you hicks knows more than you're telling. And hardly any of you will talk."

"Maybe it's your bedside manner, sweetie," Del said from behind the counter, smoking.

He slicked back his oily, thinning hair and fixed Del with an eagle eye. "You know, I usta think that Janelle invented that smart-ass smug attitude all by herself. But I can see now that she got it here. It's in the genes."

"The female cultural default norm in these parts is 'bitch,'" Del said, saluting Rhonda.

The conversation was dangerously close to boiling into real anger. I jumped in. "What did you want to know, Mr. Nelson? Maybe I *can* help."

"First and foremost, I need to find Janelle. No one will tell me anything. Not even that teacher, the one she always said was her only real friend." He looked up at us and then continued, "I wouldn't be surprised if every one of you knew where she was right now . . ." He paused. We all shrugged innocently. At least Del and Rhonda did. "But I would greatly appreciate it if that someone would tell Her Majesty to contact me immediately. Some important shit is going to hit the fan, and it's going to hit real soon now."

"Oh yeah?" Del asked. "Like what?"

"Not as much fun when the shoe's on the other foot, is it?" Benny smirked. "Just make sure she understands that it's the *old* shit, not the new shit. She'll know what I mean."

He stood up and threw a twenty on the table, and then stopped and stared at Rhonda. Placing a finger under her chin, he tilted her head this way and that. Nodding, he dug in his pocket to give her a business card. "You're ever in California, kid, give me a call. You got potential."

He stalked out of the cafe.

"What'd I say? A walking penis, right?" Del asked the air.

"Oh, I don't know." Rhonda was excited. "It all made perfect sense."

"You don't really think that someone's subconscious directed everything that happened over the past couple of weeks, just so Benny Nelson could come into the cafe and discover you?" I asked.

"Don't be silly," she said. "I think everything that happened over the last twenty-some years directed Benny Nelson to come into the cafe this morning."

"So he could proposition you?" Del asked, disgusted. "Isn't that just a little self-centered?"

Rhonda shook her head. "No, no, no. You never listen. I've been saying all along that what happened in 1969 is connected to what happened last week. And now I know I'm right!"

"How so?"

"Tory knows what I mean, I can see it in her face."

Del looked to me for an explanation. I thought I knew what Rhonda was driving at. "He said that some 'old shit' was going to hit the fan, right?" I asked her. She nodded excitedly. "And what 'old shit' is there to haunt Janelle, except that river party?"

"You're basing your whole theory on two words," Del said sourly. "Not sound scientific principle."

I grinned. "Actually, I think the whole theory is based on gut instinct. But that doesn't mean it's wrong."

"Janelle was gone for a long time," Del said. "There could be tons of 'old shit' that doesn't have anything to do with Delphi."

"Yeah, but you don't really believe that, do you?" Rhonda asked me.

For any number of reasons, none I could explain at the moment, I thought she was right. I sighed.

"For my part," she said, tucking her hair behind an ear, "I absolutely believe that every single thing that happened back then has a parallel now."

Rhonda had no idea how close she was to being right.

From hungover adolescents discovering drowning victims, to fights, to timeline discrepancies, to unexplained absences. Not to mention ill-planned infidelities with disastrous consequences.

"And it's not so much like history repeating itself," Rhonda continued, speaking my own reluctant thoughts aloud. "It's more like history cleaning up some unfinished business."

40

Old Shit

No matter what Rhonda says, no matter that I am slowly coming to see that she was right, I still believe in coincidence. I don't think some all-powerful fate gathered us together again at the river, just to point out that there is no such thing as free will.

However intriguing the theory, it didn't take much scrutiny to see the error in the notion that every single thing that happened in 1969 had an exact counterpart in the present. Rhonda didn't seem to realize that her own attendance at last Friday's gathering undermined that theory.

Besides, it wasn't parallels that brought me to Neil's house to confront Janelle again. It was Benny's message. And Rhonda's confidence, which I shared, that the "old shit" did indeed relate to 1969.

By the time I sat at Neil's kitchen table, amid the remains of a Scrabble game Janelle and Neil had been playing before he'd been called downstairs on library business, I had already worked out that Benny's "new shit" concerned the baby.

Janelle's own statements confirmed that Doug had only recently been in contact with Benny about his supposed paternity. The notion was still so new that Janelle's reticence about the child's father led Benny to Hugh Kincaid's door, just before I came to the same erroneous conclusion.

I was determined, now, to find out what the "old shit" was.

"Benny's crazy, you know that," Janelle said, twirling a finger at her own forehead. "Nuttier than a fruitcake. I wouldn't listen to a single thing he says."

"I wouldn't either," I said, "if I wasn't certain you'd been lying to me, and to us, all along."

She folded her arms on the table, leaned forward, tilted her head, and waited for me to continue.

"You said you'd had no contact with Delphi in the intervening years. That you knew nothing about Butchie Pendergast's death until last week. And yet Benny stole *your* copy of *your* senior annual, to give to *your* daughter. That particular edition is dedicated to Butchie's memory—and to you, the twin mysteries of 1969. I know, I dug out my copy and checked.

"There is no way you could have even glanced at that book without absorbing the information. You knew Butchie was dead. You've known all along.

"But you didn't read about it. You didn't have to. You were there."

Tongue snaking out to wet a lower lip, Janelle's face sagged. For the first time, she looked her age.

"I would have figured it out yesterday," I said, tapping a Scrabble letter against the table. "But you distracted me with the baby chase, and I lost track of the thread."

I ticked points off on my fingers. "Junior dropped her mother's circle pin at the river when Butchie talked her into skinny-dipping. You intervened, so Del and I could get the girls away from him. Doug found the pin, and thought it was yours, and turned it into some kind of grisly keepsake, which he tried to return to you, on Friday.

"It finally occurred to me to wonder why Doug had

ever thought that the pin belonged to you. The only answer I could come up with is that he found it on the ground. Under *your* clothes. You were in the same spot where Butch had taken Junior and Gina. And after everyone left, you undressed there too, right?" I asked.

Janelle looked away, rubbing her temples. She exhaled and nodded.

"Doug had already punched Stu," she said, throaty voice ragged. "Debbie and that bitch Lisa blamed me for everything, like they had a lock on fidelity. Both of them had already had a go at Stu, who had no complaints about being in the middle of a revenge-fest, believe me."

"So you and Stu *were* an item," I said sadly.

"For months," Janelle said. "And it was really good for a while. He was so sweet at first. But then everything fell apart."

"What happened?" I asked, trying not to find one of Rhonda's parallels in my own relationship with Stu.

"I don't know. He thought I was screwing around. I thought he was screwing around. I did it because I thought he was. He did it because he thought I was." She shrugged. "By the night of the homecoming game, he was ready to break up. It pissed me off, so I decided to go out with a bang—and give Debbie something to smirk about."

"You knew you'd get caught? And you did it anyway?" The teenage Janelle's cold calculations put even the adult Del to shame.

"I *wanted* to get caught," Janelle said sharply. "I wanted to leave that bunch with something they'd never forget."

"Well, you certainly succeeded."

"Good," she said grimly. She stood and paced the length of Neil's kitchen.

"So how did Butchie fit into all of this?" I asked. But I realized how he fit in as soon as the words left my lips. Butchie was another of Janelle's revenge conquests.

"Well, he let me use his car to stage my little scene, so I figured I'd stick around after everyone left and show him my appreciation." Janelle's voice changed. She no longer sounded like the gracious beauty queen. She sounded harsh, and bitter. And tired. "Ol' Butch was a little short on mental acuity, but he was long everywhere else. I was doing myself a favor too."

"After you purposely got caught doing . . ."—I waved my hands, searching for the right word—"*whatever* with Doug, you then proceeded to screw Butchie Pendergast? Even though you'd interrupted him in the process of molesting a pair of drunken junior high girls?"

I was flabbergasted. I was shocked. I was disgusted. I remembered Stu's bitter assessment of Janelle—that she'd never had a real, human emotion.

"Technically, I was giving Butch a blow job," Janelle said offhandedly, sitting down again. "And vice versa. We liked that best. But you get the point. Anyway, we thought that everyone was gone, then Doug came crashing through the bushes."

Janelle was caught up in her reverie, I'm not sure she even realized I was still in the room. Out of the corner of my eye, I saw that Neil had come in and was standing silently by the sink, grim and just as shocked as I was.

Janelle continued, gesturing for emphasis. "Now, *I* would have figured he already got enough for one night. Not Doug. He was furious. He thought a couple of backseat quickies gave him some sort of Neanderthal property rights to my body." She pointed at me and said, "You know what Doug was like when he was mad. He fumed and thundered and threatened to kill us. Butchie laughed at him, which was definitely a mistake, and invited him to join us. Said everyone could use a little sixty-nine.

"That was all Doug could take. He screamed and grabbed Butchie by the shoulders and tossed him into the river." Her voice rose. "And then he lunged for me. We both ended up in the water."

She was out of breath, eyes unfocused. I have no idea if the memories were that overwhelming, or if the performance was exhausting. Either way, she had us mesmerized.

"The river was cold, so cold, and deep. The current was

horrendous. I was terrified. Over the sound of the water, I could hear Butchie hollering, but it was dark. I don't swim well. There were tree branches and stuff everywhere. The bottom was all mud and gunk; I was afraid I'd sink if I tried to stand up. I thought I was going to drown. It took me forever to struggle up the bank by myself. And longer yet before I caught my breath and saw that Doug had made it out too. Then I realized that I couldn't hear Butch anymore.

"Doug was wet and muddy and out of breath, but he was still furious. Even though he was too exhausted to get up, he shouted at me: 'Butch is dead! He drowned and it's your fault. You killed him!'

"I knew that wasn't true. I knew it wasn't my fault. At least not completely. But I was just a kid. I was pregnant and desperately wanted to leave Delphi. I was scared I'd never be free if I stuck around for the aftermath."

She straightened her shoulders and stared at me defiantly. "I knew it was too late to help Butchie. So I put my clothes on and left right then, while Doug was still lying on the bank. He must have found the pin afterward and thought it was mine.

"I hiked to the highway and hitched a ride west. Benny discovered me not too long after I delivered. He took me under his wing, and like an idiot, I married him. I felt guilty, and dirty, like I deserved his abuse. It took me years, and thousands of dollars in therapists' bills, to get the courage to leave Benny, and all the rest of this, behind. But I did it," she said defiantly. "And it *was* behind me, until a couple of months ago.

"But I never saw Doug until last week, I swear. I suppose he kept that damn pin because he thought he could eventually use it for his own advantage, the creep."

She shook her head with disgust. The pot calling the kettle a creep.

"But I see Butchie *all* the time," she said, nodding confidentially. "In my dreams. I'm wearing my Delphi homecoming robe, and I'm standing by the Mighty Jim River, and he climbs up the bank, wet and rotted and smiling, and asks me if I want some more. He laughs and tells me that I owe him some sixty-nine, it's the least I can do, he says. 'Come on Janelle, you know you love it.' Then I wake up screaming . . ."

She paused, ashen and trembling. "So now you know the whole story." She shot a wavering smile at me, and over at Neil, and then swallowed. "I've never told anyone. It's been bottled inside me all this time."

But of course, she was lying.

41

Baby Love

Though I'd uncovered a couple of insignificant lies during the course of the week, the only consistent liar, so far, had been J. Ross Nelson herself. From her golden adolescence, to her mysterious disappearances, to her bashfully triumphant return, to the astounding revelations of the past two days, she had fooled us all with a bravura lifelong performance that probably contained as many untruths as otherwise.

I'm convinced, now, of the reality of her teenage pregnancy. I also believe that Doug Fischbach was not the biological father of that child, though I think he just as sincerely believed that he was. I believe Janelle was desperate to see Delphi in the rearview mirror, and I believe she would have let Butchie Pendergast drown, if that had served her purpose.

As to the truth of the rest of her enthralling performance, I have no idea. But I had a glimmer as to who could shed a little light on my confusion.

Benny Nelson, while he was bemoaning our closed-mouth small town, probably did not realize how much he'd given away. He would have to have heard the truth about Butchie Pendergast's drowning long ago, for that to have been "old shit." For it to supplant the "new shit" about Janelle's daughter, he must have been reminded. Recently. And that told me who, of all the Delphi rubes, *had* talked to him.

It wasn't me. Ditto Rhonda and Del. Aphrodite wouldn't talk to anyone. Neil would not have let Benny through the library door, and not just because he had Janelle safely ensconced on the second floor. Hugh let him in, but his news gave Benny no satisfaction. I'll admit to a little hesitation when it came to Ron, but a quick phone call eliminated him. A more painfully awkward phone call to Stu provided me with the same answer.

There was only one other person, one that Benny would surely have contacted. One who knew a lot more than she had told so far.

"What were you trying to do, get that poor man all upset?" I asked Debbie Fischbach in her immaculate living room. "He's used to Hollywood-style chicanery. He wouldn't recognize South Dakota passive-aggressive manipulation if it bit him on the nose."

Debbie shrugged, a tiny smirk playing at the edges of her mouth. "I was trying to smoke Janelle out. I imagine she thought that all the old secrets died with Doug."

"Surprise," Lisa sing-songed from an armchair. "No matter what her doofus ex-husband thinks, or the press, or the police, she's still around. I can smell her."

Debbie, drinking some sort of clear liquid in a tall glass, seconded that notion. "She's holed up somewhere. Got some man to take care of her. Poor man."

"He's in for a surprise," Lisa agreed. "Better watch his back."

"He'd better watch his front." Debbie chuckled.

They were sure a jolly pair of girls, those two.

"What would forcing Janelle out into the open have accomplished?" I asked. Butchie's death happened too long ago to open up an investigation now. Besides, with two of the principals dead, who would dispute Janelle's version? And who, besides the good folk of Delphi, would even be interested?

"It would have made her squirm," Lisa said, "and watching Janelle Ross squirm has been a passion of mine."

Debbie nodded.

"You hate her, don't you?" I asked, realization dawning.

"Yup, always have. Always will," they said.

"But why?"

"I should think you'd have a clue. She stayed with *your* boyfriend."

I didn't want to get into a discussion about Stu and Janelle, either now or in the past.

"That's an awful long time to hold a grudge," I said. Besides, I thought, not a single person in this room can afford to throw stones.

"I know exactly how long it's been," Debbie hissed. "I've had to live with her ghost every minute of every single day since she left. And when Doug suggested that we invite her back for that goddamn reunion, I knew fate was calling me, that I could finally expose her."

Lisa had been watching me closely. "You *know* what she's talking about, don't you?"

"About Doug and Debbie not running away together in 1969? About all of them being together when Butchie Pendergast drowned?" I said. "Yes, I know."

"Damn," Lisa said. "I was so looking forward to knocking the shit out of you with our revelations."

Debbie and Lisa were both disappointed. Delphi natives to the core, they knew a tantalizing secret and couldn't wait to tell everyone. But they didn't know everything.

Debbie had worn Aunt Juanita's pin to his funeral, flaunting it. I realized that she must have known how it came into Doug's possession. By then, she also knew that it wasn't Janelle's, or she would not have made a special point of letting everyone at the service get a good look at it. At her own husband's funeral, she went fishing.

"Who told you?" Lisa asked me accusingly.

"Everything pointed in that direction. It took a while for me to see it all, but I figured it out by myself." Which almost wasn't a lie. As I'd told Janelle, I'd have gotten there eventually.

"I'm not as fast at figuring things out as you, I guess," Debbie said, then handed her glass to Lisa for a refill. As she did, the loose sleeve of her blouse slid up to reveal a string of old bruises running up her arm. "It took me years to figure it all out."

It was a safe bet that Janelle had not told Debbie, or Lisa, the details of that awful night in 1969. "You got it from Doug?" I asked.

"Not in so many words." Debbie laughed. "Our Doug was a man with a big mouth and a drinking habit. When he was drunk, he talked. A lot. Not that he ever gave me a definitive statement, or a neatly typed chronology. But here and there, over time, I was able to piece together a reasonable facsimile of that evening."

"Can I get you anything, Tory?" Lisa called from the kitchen.

I would have loved a beer. But this pair would probably have laced it with strychnine. "No thanks," I said.

"At first, like everyone else, I thought Doug and Janelle had run away together, just to humiliate Stuart McKee and me," Debbie said, picking lint from her pants. "Doug called from some motel in North Dakota, three days after he'd disappeared, frantic and wanting to come home. He needed bus fare—he was broke and lonely. And sorry. He told me he'd been with Janelle, and that she'd abandoned him. I forgave him, and, for a time, I believed him. I would have believed anything about that bitch."

She took the glass from Lisa and sipped. "But it didn't take long to figure out that his story didn't jibe. The details came out differently with every repeat. He was at the river with Butch. He never saw Butch at all. He didn't know Butch had died until after coming back home. He and Janelle discussed Butch's drowning at their motel. He kicked Janelle out. She left him in the middle of the night, taking all of his money with her. On and on. The only thing I ever knew for sure is that he'd been drunk and ended up in North Dakota."

"You never confronted him with the discrepancies?" I asked.

"I didn't confront Doug about anything," Debbie said, seriously. "He may have been stupid. But he was a stupid man with a temper. Why do you think we moved back to Delphi in the first place? Doug lost every teaching job he ever had—it was either his drinking, or his temper, or both. And he took it out on us each time. He had to beg the school board to give him a chance here. We all hoped against hope that it would work."

Lisa, the family facilitator, snorted into her glass.

"You'd seen that pin before Doug died," I said, prodding.

"Of course," Debbie said, disgusted. "It was the only piece of jewelry that Doug had. It didn't take long for me to figure out that he thought it belonged to his precious Janelle."

"Then he really loved her?" I asked.

Debbie shrugged. "Whatever love meant to Doug. I think he thought love was possession and obedience and instant gratification."

"Not a textbook definition," Lisa added.

"And you realized that it hadn't belonged to Janelle, since it was still with the rest of his stuff at the river the next day, right?"

"I knew Doug had it with him on Friday night. I assumed he would give it back to her sometime that night. That's why he was so insistent on going to the river to begin with—he wanted to stage some kind of *romantic* scene with Janelle. I knew that my opportunity for exposing her had come finally. That's why I stopped fighting the idea.

"I thought the pin was Janelle's too. And I fully expected to see it pinned to her breast at the reunion." She chuckled weakly. "But nothing about that next day came out the way I expected."

"Ain't that the truth," Lisa, the ever-faithful second banana, echoed.

"Doug had plenty of time to return the pin to Janelle Friday night at the river. And for most of Saturday, I almost hoped they had run off together—just Dougie, Janelle, and a piece of cheap jewelry. For a short time, I actually thought I was free. That I'd never again be confronted with old mysteries and heartbreaks."

I ventured into uncharted territory. "Did you know about Janelle's baby?"

Debbie exchanged glances with Lisa. They nodded, agreeing silently on something. "Now that was a surprise, a secret that Doug managed to keep entirely to himself. He'd been smirking a lot lately, but he never even dropped a hint about what had him so pumped up, except to say that everyone was going to be surprised."

"I can't believe he kept something that juicy bottled up all those years," marveled Debbie.

"Well, if it's any consolation, I think he only found out about her recently," I said.

"I knew something big was brewing," Lisa said. "Those beady little eyes of his lit up just like a kid who can't wait to tell everyone that there is no Santa Claus."

"You heard about her from Benny, right?" I asked.

"The oily little creep stopped here on Saturday afternoon, looking for Doug. He said he had something important to discuss, and left. And then today he came by again and dropped his little bombshell on us. He wanted to buy information—anything we could do to help him trace down the girl's father." Debbie blinked a couple of times and inhaled. "When we heard the rest of his story, it took our breath away—"

"Not the news that Doug was blackmailing him, mind you," Lisa interrupted, with a significant glance at Debbie. "That wouldn't have surprised anyone. Doug *liked* to play games. And he loved to have the advantage. But the fact that the child even existed, that for a short time Doug thought he was her father—that he was planning to use that information to hurt everyone around him . . ."

Debbie laughed. "Old Benny thought that we'd be shocked beyond rational thought. But we took the wind out of his sails by knowing about Janelle and Doug and Butchie."

"And he was horrified when we said we were going public with what could turn out to be a very nasty scandal that could severely affect the career of our glorious Ms. Nelson," Lisa added.

"But Benny wasn't her manager anymore. Or her husband," I said, confused. "If Janelle was publicly disgraced, what difference could it make to him?"

"That's the hold she has on men," Debbie said bitterly. "No one involved with her ever came away unscathed. Not Doug, not Benny. Not even Stu McKee. They loved her, they hated her, they used her. She betrayed them, and they betrayed her. And after all that, and a divorce, *and* a protection order, Benny still wanted to own her."

"That's when he showed *us* the picture," Debbie finished. "He thought that finding the girl's father would give him some sort of hold over Janelle."

"He showed you a picture of the girl? Of Janelle's daughter?" I was surprised.

"Yup." Debbie grinned. "And we both knew immediately that Doug couldn't have been the father."

"How?"

They looked at each other and grinned.

"This girl is tall, slim, fair, and beautiful. You've seen my boys, each one of them is short and dark and powerful. The result of those dominant Fischbach genes."

"Is the resemblance between Doug and his sons just physical?" I asked. That was the real question that had brought me to Debbie's living room. Revealing as it was, the Benny discussion was just a diversion, an excuse for broaching the really important subject.

"My boys may look like their father, but the similarity ends there," Debbie said sharply. "You saw how Cameron defended me at the river on Friday night. He was, and has always been, horrified by the way his father treated me. But interference usually meant an even worse pounding for himself.

"Maybe it was because Cameron had been drinking, and was not totally in control. But on Friday night, he simply could not watch his father hit me again without reacting. He snapped and charged his father. But immediately after, he was filled with remorse. I am so glad that Cameron and I had the whole of Friday night to talk through his feelings of anger and frustration and inadequacy, or Doug's death would have been even *more* devastating for him." Debbie lifted her chin in defiance.

I remembered Cameron's small speech in the trailer. He hadn't seemed very remorseful. Or devastated.

"And I'm glad that I was here to help them work through that crisis," the family facilitator said. "They were so lucky to have had that whole night to begin the healing process."

"So Cameron was here when you got home from the river?" I asked, carefully specific. "And he was here that whole night?"

That had been their story. In fact, they all told it with exactly the same words. Debbie had repeated it to me after Doug's funeral. Cameron had repeated it to Presley at the trailer. Lisa had just parroted it again.

"Of course he was here," Debbie said, indignant. "That's what I just said."

"That's what all of you have said. There's a problem, though. Almost everyone agrees that Cameron left the river early, still wearing Doug's old jersey. But the jersey was on the ground, at the river, when Doug's body was found."

Debbie and Lisa sat silent. The color drained from Debbie's face.

"And Cameron himself told me that he'd taken great pleasure in throwing that shirt back in his father's face."

That had been the subject of Del's cryptic question—whether Cameron had flung the jersey literally or figuratively.

I favored the literal interpretation, since it was still at ground zero the next evening, when Presley and John Adler discovered the body.

"That's nonsense. Cameron wore that ridiculous jersey home!" Debbie stood shakily for emphasis. "I took it back to the river myself. That night."

"You what?" Lisa and I asked together, shocked.

Debbie looked from Lisa to me and back, raised her chin, and announced, "I took that shirt back to throw in Doug's face. I went to confront him, to defend myself and my child. To stand up to Doug, for once in my life.

"But instead, I killed him."

42

Sic Semper Tyrannis

I had a preconceived notion of how the interview at the Fischbach house would go. And for the most part, the answers and revelations were exactly what I'd expected—a couple of lies, a little new information, and the confirmation of a bunch of stuff I already knew.

But nothing, nothing in the preceding weeks and months, nothing in the recent hours I'd spent in her living room, pumping for the aforementioned sound bites, prepared me for Debbie Fischbach's confession.

"What?" Lisa and I shouted together.

Debbie's legs seemed to give out from under her. She wilted into her chair, looking miserably down at the carpet. Her voice barely above a whisper, she said, "I killed him. I deliberately pushed Doug into the water and I watched him drown." She raised her eyes, defiant. "And I'm glad I did. I'm glad he's dead."

"No, Mom," a voice from behind us said. "No, I can't let you do this."

"Go to your room!" Debbie shouted shrilly. "You have no business listening in on our conversation."

Lisa and I exchanged bewildered glances.

Cameron walked over to his mother and knelt down beside her chair. He put an arm around her shoulder and crooned softly, comfortingly. She began to weep silently.

He looked at me, young and scared and determined, and said, over his mother's protests, "It's a cover. She's protecting me. They both are."

Lisa hung her head, not watching mother and son.

"I did it," Cameron said. "*I* killed my father."

"No," Debbie wailed. She appealed to me. "It was an accident. You have to know it was an accident. Cameron never meant for his father to die."

Cameron said softly, "Maybe that's true. Maybe not."

We waited in silence for him to continue.

"They pulled me off him at the river. Mr. McKee and Mr. Kincaid. They tried to calm me down. I was angry. Furious. I couldn't sit there and watch him hit my mother again. But they told me to go home and cool off. That they'd keep Dad for a while. That my mom'd be home soon."

Mother and son sat, united against a single enemy. An enemy that death had not rendered harmless.

"I went behind the trees next to the edge of the water and hid. I didn't *want* to go home. I wanted to have it out with him." Cameron's voice took on a hard edge. He sounded like Doug.

"I waited until everyone left. Dad was still there at the river, throwing things in. Shouting at the sky. Mad at me for losing the football game. Mad at that actress for something. He was still drinking. He started taking his clothes off and throwing them on the ground. I think he was going to go swimming.

"I stepped out of the bushes and called to him. He didn't know where I was at first. It was dark, and I think I startled him because he said something really strange."

"What?" I asked softly.

Cameron's brows knit in concentration. "He said, 'Butch, is that you? Come to get me finally?' That didn't make any sense. I figured it was because he was drunk."

Debbie, no longer crying, straightened up and ran a gentle finger along her son's cheek.

He smiled at his mother briefly and continued. "So I said, 'Yeah, I've come to get you, asshole.' Dad stepped closer and saw it was me, and that made him even madder.

"He started calling me a bunch of names." Cameron reddened at the memory. "Awful names. Said I wasn't fit to wear number 69. That I'd never be a man. That I'd disgraced him, and if my mother wasn't such a slut and a whore, maybe I'd have been something he could have been proud of."

Debbie gasped. We all sat, barely breathing, while Cameron summoned the strength to continue his narration.

"I took off his fucking number 69 jersey and threw it at him. I was screaming, shouting at him. I told him I hated him.

"He stood there with no clothes on, and he caught the shirt. He sniffed at it and said that I'd ruined the jersey, that it was no good anymore, and he threw it over to the side. He dared me to take a swing at him. He said I was too much of a baby. Then he didn't wait for me to start. He charged at me. I ducked and swung, but missed him. He caught me with a punch in the middle of my chest and it knocked me over. We were right by the edge of the water. I tackled him and it must have caught him off-guard because he fell into the water. I could hear him splashing around."

Cameron stopped, closed his eyes, and pressed his lips together. "I knew the river was high. I knew he was drunk. I called out to him. I asked him if he needed help. He told me to go away, that he never wanted to see me again. That he didn't need *anything* from me."

Cameron was breathing heavily, looking down at the floor. "I heard Dad slip and fall back into the water. He was still shouting for me to go home to my mommy when I turned around and left.

"I left my drunken father in the water to die. It's my fault that he's dead."

43

Butchie's Ghost

Though it had taken me a while to come to the correct conclusion, I'd realized, sadly, that Cameron must have returned to the river on Friday night, *after* the fight with his father. He as much as told me so himself, when he talked about throwing the jersey back into his father's face. No one at the party remembered Cameron saying anything coherent at all, much less a specific insult aimed at his father. And nearly everyone said he had left the river still wearing the jersey.

Debbie, incapacitated by her son's confession, wasn't able to enlighten me on any other questions. Cameron attended to his mother, so Lisa took over.

"We were desperately worried about Cameron," she said quietly, watching the pair. "He wasn't home when we got here on Friday."

I'd known that too—their stories were too pat, and too identical, for truth.

"Cameron is a good deal more fragile than he looks. The loss of the football game and Doug's overreaction were bad enough. The scene at the river could have destroyed what was left of that poor kid's self-image. When he finally arrived home, it was very late. He wouldn't tell us where he'd been or what he'd been doing. He wasn't wearing the jersey—Debbie asked him about it specifically. She knew that Doug would be furious if it came up missing.

"Cameron shrugged and said that he gave it back to his dad. And then he went to bed." Lisa sat back in her chair. "We went to bed too, but no one slept. We kept waiting for Doug to show up and go into one of his all-night rages."

From across the room, Debbie said, "Though I was secretly relieved in the morning when Doug still hadn't come home, the thought that Cameron might know more than he'd said worried me enough to send Lisa around asking questions."

"Then Benny showed up that afternoon, and you attended the reunion that evening," I said, saving her an explanation. "And all hell broke loose."

"Not exactly," Lisa said, subdued.

"After we talked to everyone in town, we realized that Janelle was missing too. So we drove out to the river," Debbie said quietly. "Lisa and I."

Cameron rocked back on his heels, staring at his mother.

"We really hoped that this time, Doug and Janelle might actually have run off together. I kept any other fears tightly bottled. Either way, I thought we might find some sort of clue as to his whereabouts. We found a clue all right." She looked at Cameron sadly. "I'm sorry, darling, but my first, horrible thought was that you might need protection. Lisa and I concocted a story about staying up all night together, right on the spot." She turned to me and said, "Even though he wouldn't say anything more about what happened, we forced Cameron to say the same thing."

"Was the jersey on the ground?" I asked, confused. Why hadn't they removed the most damning evidence?

"Sure," Lisa said sadly. "But, we weren't entirely clearheaded. The guy *was* dead, and we panicked. We left it where it was. We decided later that we could say that we saw Janelle with it on Friday night, if necessary—deflect attention, and suspicion, back to her."

"Why didn't you report the death to anyone?" I tried to picture a day spent knowing her husband was dead, floating naked in the river, fearing that her beloved son might have contributed to his death, and at the same time, having to ignore the publicly held assumption that Doug and Janelle were off somewhere together, embarking on another torrid affair.

"We didn't want to be part of any investigation. And we were terrified that Cameron might be implicated. Even if the body washed downstream, we figured someone would find him sooner or later, though the waiting nearly killed us," Lisa said, with a halfhearted laugh.

"That's why we stacked the deck," Debbie said.

I must have looked puzzled.

"When Benny Nelson asked us if we had any idea where Doug might have gone, we said that he liked to sit by the river."

"And then you went to the reunion, and quietly waited for the bomb to drop," I marveled.

"It didn't unfold the way we had expected. But when Mr. Nelson finally showed up at the reunion, and headed for the podium, we knew what he was going to say. We thought we were prepared," Lisa said. "But you looked straight at us, even before Benny opened his weasely mouth. And right then, I realized that you and Stu McKee already knew that Doug was dead."

"And that's why you fainted," I said.

"I thought you were going to rise up and point a finger and start accusing." Lisa shrugged, embarrassed.

I wouldn't have known whom to accuse, then or now—Doug himself, or Janelle, or Cameron, or Debbie. Or Butchie Pendergast's ghost. Everyone seemed equally responsible. Equally innocent. Equally guilty.

The three in front of me were telling me the truth. Their truth, anyway.

But it wasn't the whole truth.

44

Sixty-nine

The Whole Truth is an interesting concept. Like liquid mercury, it moves and rolls, and looks shiny and pretty. But handled incorrectly, it can be a deadly poison.

Debbie's truth involved protecting her son, no matter the cost. Lisa's was good old Delphi snoopiness, cloaked in friendly concern and a malicious antagonism for an old enemy.

Janelle's truth was built on shifting sand. She'd told so many stories, over so many years, to so many people, that the bedrock was hidden under layer upon layer. Janelle's profession itself was lying, and her talent was inborn.

Young Cameron, the one least able to understand the variable nature of truth, believed that he was wholly responsible for his father's death.

That was why I made a few phone calls and asked a single question of each person. Each answered the way I expected. Not with a version of the truth. But with the actual and unassailable truth. A simple yes or no.

Which is why, tired, sad, and feeling a whole lot older, I

said, "Too bad you only lie to protect others. If you were equipped with a little self-preservation instinct, I never would have figured it out."

"It's too late in the game to change the rules now," he said with a shrug.

"All you would have to have done was say that the jersey wasn't on the ground when you left the river. The same as everyone else."

"But they were telling the truth," Hugh Kincaid said sadly.

"And so were you," I said. "The only way you could have seen the jersey on the ground Friday night was to have been at the river *after* Cameron left the second time."

"I didn't think anyone would pick up on the discrepancy—stories about that night were jumbled, and mutating rapidly. By the time I'd realized the hole I'd dug for myself, it was too late to alter my version." He smiled softly. "You'd have picked up on *that* even more quickly."

"Janelle helped," I said. "She protected you so carefully, it was like holding up a sign pointing directly at your house. She repeatedly emphasized that she left Delphi the *night* of the 1969 homecoming party. And even though Ron Adler said he'd seen her walking down the street by the school, which just happens to be across from your house, on the next day, no one listened to him. We were all too enamored of our own romantic notions."

"Janelle knew that it would cost my job if she was seen entering or leaving my house at that time of the morning," Hugh said. "She only came to me in the first place because she was terrified. Her parents had already, in effect, abandoned her. She showed up early that morning, crying hysterically, and certain that the police would be after her. She was sure *she* was responsible for Butchie's drowning."

"I knew she'd told someone," I said. "The story was too horrible, too compelling, to keep secret. At least for a pregnant, scared eighteen-year-old. It just took me a while to figure out that you were her confidant."

"She became convinced that Pendergast was still alive

and that we could help him. The only way to calm her down was to drive out to the river ourselves. Unfortunately, what we found was not a comfort.

"Instead of going into hysterics, she became deadly calm, frozen inside and out. She turned on one heel and walked away. I never saw her again, though we did keep in touch. And I did send her that accursed annual. I thought she would eventually appreciate a reminder of who she was and where she came from."

"All of which proves Rhonda's theory about parallels," I said, though the proof would give her no pleasure. "Almost every awful thing that happened in 1969 had a counterpart in the present."

"Maybe the gods set wheels in motion that no one can stop. Because I didn't go to the river in 1969, Lawrence Pendergast died. He was not an exemplary human being, but he was young, and there would have been opportunities for him to change and grow. If I had gone to the river that Friday, I could have prevented his death. At least at that place and time." Hugh looked out his kitchen window, chin propped on his hand.

So many patterns were set in stone that night. A different outcome then might have meant a different outcome for us all.

Then again, maybe not.

"Why didn't Doug deserve the same consideration?" I asked.

"I imagine that he did," Hugh said softly. "I just wasn't up to making the effort. I think it was the gods' punishment for believing I could change things. They gave me the opportunity to live by my words, and I couldn't do it."

"What happened?" I asked, though I knew all but the smallest details already.

"I stayed late at the river, thinking I could talk to Doug about Cameron. He's a fine boy, who never deserved even a fraction of the abuse he took at his father's hands. But Doug was still too belligerent for discussion, so I left.

"I got halfway into town, decided to take another crack at it, and turned around."

"And you interrupted Doug and Cameron in their fight?"

"I could hear them in the distance. I heard him call his own son a 'fag.' He said Cameron didn't deserve the fine name of Fischbach. By the time I got to the river's edge, Cameron was furiously running away. Doug was already in the water. I called to Cameron, told him to wait, to let me talk to him."

Hugh shook his head at his own folly. "Cameron didn't hear me. Or if he did, he probably thought I was his father. Either way, he didn't turn around. Doug was making his way to the bank slowly. The current was swift and dangerous. I asked him if he needed any help."

"Which he refused," I said.

"In the most vile terms imaginable, calling me his favorite epithet."

"Did he know, or was it a lucky guess?"

"Tory, *fag* was a blunt instrument that Doug used to bludgeon everyone around him. It worked admirably on his son. It kept his football players in line. It had no effect whatsoever on me.

"In fact, Doug stopped by my house recently, also accusing me of being the father of Janelle's long-ago baby. He demanded cash for his silence. He'd got it in his head, as many of you did, apparently," Hugh said with a small smile, "that I was taking advantage of the crushes that most of the girls had on me."

"You knew how we felt?" I asked, embarrassed.

"Tory, I would have to have been blind and deaf, and dumb, not to have noticed. So did all the rest of the staff. It was the best cover a gay teacher could ask for. Doug's insults were just shots in the dark.

"Doug Fischbach wouldn't know a genuine person of the persuasion if he stumbled over him."

"Even if he lived in his own home?" I asked gently.

Hugh knew where I was leading. "Not that I generally take bets on that sort of thing, but I would not hesitate to assure you that young Cameron is as heterosexual as almost every other boy in Delphi. Just because he wasn't slobbering after the girls, his father assumed the worst."

"But it was enough to worry Cameron, wasn't it?" Cameron had been seeing Hugh for advice and counseling before his father's death.

"It would be enough to worry any young man who wasn't absolutely obsessed with procreation. And I worried about Cameron, but not because of his sexual orientation. Growing up in a house like that can cause permanent emotional scars.

"And after last Friday, I was especially worried about how Cameron was going to deal with the fact that his father had died so soon after their confrontation."

"That's the reason I'm here," I said, finally, sadly. "Cameron confessed to his mother. He thinks he killed Doug by not rescuing him from the river. He feels completely responsible for his father's death. I'm afraid he'll go public with it soon."

"But he's not responsible," Hugh said, distressed. "When Cameron left, Doug was in control. It was only after I arrived that he slipped back into the water and got into trouble.

"I stood there, Tory. Dry and safe on shore, and remembered the names he had called his son. I remembered how he punched his wife, and Stu McKee, and anyone else who got in his way. I remembered his temper and his threats. His attempts at extortion. I remembered my notion that Butchie might have changed and grown, improved over time. But Doug Fischbach seemed to be a perfect example of the immutability of character.

"When Doug realized that he was in trouble, he called for help. I thought of all the damage he'd done to good people. People who did nothing to deserve his abuse. I purposely stood there and listened to him flail, and I watched him drown. And I did not lift a finger to help."

Hugh turned to me, face lined and tired, and asked, "Does that make me a murderer?"

Epilogue

LATE OCTOBER

So what is my truth?

Because I fell in love in 1969, I married a philandering man. A number of years later, I took up with a philandering married man.

Was it fate? Or coincidence? Or just piss-poor decision making?

Though we are still seeing each other, Stu has been withdrawn. Uncertain. Distracted.

I understood a little, after seeing a *People* magazine story about the reunion of J. Ross Nelson and her biological daughter. The world was charmed; Delphi was surprised. Ron Adler crowed. In the picture, Janelle stood, looking proud and maternal, her arm around a truly beautiful young woman who was tall and slim, with sandy-brown hair and astonishing green eyes.

I should have known from the start. Lisa and Debbie did when Benny showed them her picture. Stu knew as soon as Janelle hit Delphi, since she hot-footed it over to the feed store to tell him. And then insinuated herself into his house, and stayed around after Doug's drowning, to try to reconcile him to the situation.

Did it work? I don't know. I do know that Stu is seriously considering meeting the girl. I also know that he misses his son terribly. I know that he wants to be a good father. Whether he wants to be a good husband remains to be seen.

Debbie Fischbach has blossomed in widowhood. She joined numerous boards and charitable organizations, playing Lady Bountiful. She made a brave, public showing of the return of the gold circle pin to a very surprised Aunt Juanita. I imagine that Junior had some explaining to do.

Cameron headed into a spiral at the end of September. His attempted suicide prompted Hugh's public confession of his role in Doug Fischbach's death, to the shock of the entire town. There were no charges pressed; the question of whether one who deliberately does not rescue can be called a murderer has not been answered. In his desperation to clear Cameron publicly, Hugh let slip the explosive news of his own sexual orientation. There was a brief and vehement flurry of demands for Hugh's resignation, ostensibly because of the drowning, but the real reason was small-town homophobia. The vigilante crowd will probably get its way.

Janelle drove back to California in her Corvette. I hear she got that major break-through role she wanted. When the movie comes out, I'll go and see it—or rent the video, since first-run movies rarely make it to our wing of the Hotel South Dakota.

Rhonda, in rumpled chinos, flannel, and all-cotton T-shirts, made the transition from Earth Mother to Eddie Bauer Poster Child. One day, she sat in the cafe, talking endlessly about Neil and how much fun she had with him, how cool his cars were, and what a great all-around guy he was.

"Are you falling in love with Neil?" I asked finally, surprised at my own irritation.

She grinned, almost as though she had maneuvered me

into asking. “The real question,” the newly declared psychology major said, “is, Are *you* falling in love with Neil Pascoe?”

I sat back in the booth and looked out the window at the feed store across the street. Then I got up and busied myself behind the counter, ignoring Rhonda’s question.

And her laughter.